"There's no time to explain in detail," said Silverpoint. "The Sleep Angels have passed a condemnation on you for using a Tiger's Egg. Your life is forfeit, but I may be able to save Little if I can convince the Council that she was only trying to retrieve the tiger's soul for them."

"My life is forfeit?" echoed Miles. He was tempted to laugh. It seemed like a bizarre joke to be condemned to death in his absence for something he had been unaware of until mere weeks before, but still it made his stomach tighten.

"I don't want to be saved," said Little, "not on my own. Miles and I stay together, whatever happens."

Silverpoint threw his arms out in exasperation. "You have no obligation to him," he said. "You have already repaid your debt three times over."

"Miles is my friend," said Little.

"Your friend," repeated Silverpoint, as though he were trying an unfamiliar taste. He looked again at Miles, his eyes like ink spots in his pale, narrow face, before turning back to Little. "You've lived here too long," he said. "I should have tried to bring you back with me."

"You couldn't have," said Little. "I gave up my wings to save Miles."

"If the tiger's soul is surrendered I may be able to persuade them to allow you back," said Silverpoint. "I need the Egg," he said to Miles. He held out his hand. His fingers were long and pale. "You must give it you want Little to live."

THE LIGHTNING KEY

JON BERKELEY

ILLUSTRATED BY BRANDON DORMAN

THE JULIE ANDREWS COLLECTION

HARPER

An Imprint of HarperCollinsPublishers

Library of Congress Cataloging-in-Publication Data

Berkeley, Jon.

The lightning key / Jon Berkeley ; illustrated by Brandon
Dorman. — 1st ed.

p.   cm. — (The Julie Andrews collection) (The
Wednesday tales ; no. 3)

Summary: Orphaned twelve-year-old Miles Wednesday
discovers some surprising things about his past when he sets
out with his angel companion Little and the blind explorer
Baltinglass on a quest to recover the powerful tiger's egg stolen
by the evil Cortado.

ISBN 978-0-06-075515-7

[1. Adventure and adventurers—Fiction. 2. Orphans—
Fiction. 3. Angels—Fiction. 4. Explorers—Fiction.] I. Dorman, Brandon, ill.   II. Title.

PZ7.B45255Lig   2009   2007038755
[Fic]—dc22   CIP
                                                         AC

10   11   12   13   14   LP/CW   10   9   8   7   6   5   4   3   2   1

❖

First Edition

For Sara,
whose words dance to a wilder tune

ALSO BY JON BERKELEY

The Palace of Laughter
The Tiger's Egg

CONTENTS

CHAPTER ONE
SURGERY MOST FOUL

Listen: Rain is falling, and what a rain! A billion beads of cold sky slant down through the night, turning the damp earth to mud, and the mud to pools, and the pools to streams that feed the underground river that flows beneath the cobbled streets of Larde. As lightning fills the sky the raindrops pause for a heartbeat, and are released again into the darkness. They roar on the roof tiles and stream from the gutters; they rattle on the dancing leaves and spatter on the pavements, and the people of Larde burrow deeper into their beds with a grateful shiver.

In the dormitories of Partridge Manor, on the

edge of town, sleepless children count down the storm's approach; one second less for every mile closer. Lightning floods the rooms and they count: one . . . two . . . three. . . . Then thunder crashes and rolls through the night, making the windows rattle and the smaller orphans shriek. It's getting nearer.

Miles Wednesday, floating somewhere between wakefulness and sleep, dreams of a tiger who stands below his window and roars in anger, making small birds burst from the treetops and beetles cower in the grass. The tiger's roar shakes the clouds loose and they begin to tumble earthward like boulders. Miles wakes from his dream with a start. The room is lit by a blinding flash and thunder fills the air. He looks across to see if Little is awake. Her bed is empty, the covers thrown back, and she is nowhere to be seen. Miles slides his feet into his slippers and pulls on his old overcoat, a knot forming in his stomach.

He moves to the window and presses his nose to the cold glass, cupping his hands on either side of his face. He can just make out the tree house perched between the twin trunks of the great beech tree in the garden, a dark jumble in the downpour. Smoke rises from the tree house roof like a pale ghost. As his eyes get used to the darkness he can see torn branches hanging from the tree. He catches sight of a light blur beneath the tree house, and as it starts to climb the rope ladder he realizes with a shock that it is Little.

"What on earth is she *doing?*" he says to Tangerine. The orange-gray stuffed bear doesn't answer. He lies curled up in the pocket of Miles's overcoat, pretending to be asleep. For a moment Miles is tempted to climb back into his bed and do the same, but he can hardly leave Little alone in a smoldering tree house in the middle of a thunderstorm. He shivers as he turns to leave the dormitory. At the door he pauses. It's cold outside and he knows that in a moment he'll be soaked to the skin. He slips back across the room, lifts Tangerine gently from his pocket and tucks him under the bedcovers.

"You stay right there until I get back," he says.

Miles Wednesday, squelch-slippered and rain-frozen, ran through the muddy garden, leaping over the deeper puddles, though he was already as wet as it was possible to be. The rain hammered on the top of his head and ran down his neck, plastering his pajamas to his skin. He reached the shelter of the tree house and stood there panting. From the square hole above him a yellow light flickered, and he could just make out the sound of voices through the roar of the rain. He grasped the ladder, pushed his dripping hair out of his eyes and began to climb.

The inside of the tree house was dimly lit by a couple of candles, if the mounds of knobbly wax that grew on Lady Partridge's shelves could be described as candles. Their ragged flames danced in the drafts, making shadows leap among the jumble of bric-a-brac that spilled from shelves and washed up in every corner of the room. Little was sitting on the hammock that was strung between the twin beech trunks in the center of the tree house. Her arms were crossed and she wore a stubborn frown that Miles knew well. The frown was directed at a tall, slim boy who stood facing her, with his back to Miles. The boy was speaking in low, urgent tones, and though his voice was quiet it cut like glass through the din of the storm.

"That's *his* problem. He's already marked, but there still may be a chance for you. I've told the Council that you lost your wings trying to retrieve—" The boy stopped in midsentence and turned, following Little's gaze, to see Miles's head poking up through the square hole in the floor. His dark eyes narrowed, and Miles recognized him at once. It was Silverpoint, the Storm Angel whom Little had been following when first she fell from the sky, a winged boy one thousand years old who could command lightning with a flick of his wrist and herd thunder like cattle. He seemed to be having a little more trouble controlling the anger on his face, but he managed a thin smile.

"Hello, Miles," he said.

Miles climbed the last few rungs and stood dripping on the rug that covered the creaky floorboards. "Hello, Silverpoint," he said, and turned to Little. "Is everything okay?" he asked her, glancing up at the smoldering roof. Smoke was gathering under the ceiling, and a glowing ember fell as he watched, landing on Silverpoint's shoulder. The Storm Angel brushed it away without seeming to notice.

"Silverpoint has brought some news," said Little. The frown had not left her face.

"It doesn't concern him," said Silverpoint, turning back to Little as though he expected Miles to melt back into the puddle that was forming at his feet.

"If it concerns me, it concerns Miles too," said Little.

"Maybe we should go inside," interrupted Miles. "It's dry in there, and the roof isn't on fire. We should also call the fire brigade before this has a chance to catch properly."

Silverpoint spun back to face him, and the air around him crackled briefly with a blue haze. "Forget the shack!" he barked. "There are urgent matters to be discussed, and time is fast running out. You can stay or go as you please. I don't have the time to argue."

Miles opened his mouth to reply, but caught sight of the anxious look on Little's face and closed it again. "Tell Miles what you told me," she said, pushing a lock of her white-blond hair behind her ear.

"He wouldn't understand," said Silverpoint. "What does he know of the Realm?"

"I know what Little has told me," said Miles.

"There's no time to explain in detail," said Silverpoint. "The Sleep Angels have passed a condemnation on you for using a Tiger's Egg. Your life is forfeit, but I may be able to save Little if I can convince the Council that she was only trying to retrieve the tiger's soul for them."

"My life is forfeit?" echoed Miles. He was tempted to laugh. It seemed like a bizarre joke to be condemned to death in his absence for something he had been unaware of until mere weeks before, but still it made his stomach tighten.

"I don't want to be saved," said Little, "not on my own. Miles and I stay together, whatever happens."

Silverpoint threw his arms out in exasperation. "You have no obligation to him," he said. "You have already repaid your debt three times over."

"Miles is my friend," said Little.

"Your friend," repeated Silverpoint, as though he were trying an unfamiliar taste. He looked again at Miles, his eyes like ink spots in his pale, narrow face, before turning back to Little. "You've lived here too long," he said. "I should have tried to bring you back with me."

"You couldn't have," said Little. "I gave up my wings to save Miles."

"If the tiger's soul is surrendered I may be able to persuade them to allow you back," said Silverpoint. "I need the Egg," he said to Miles. He held out his hand. His fingers were long and pale. "You must give it to me if you want Little to live."

Little jumped down from the hammock. "He doesn't even know what it is," she said before Miles could speak.

Miles shook his head. He knew, of course, what the Tiger's Egg was. The small stone, no bigger than an olive but containing the trapped soul of a tiger, had been stitched into the sawdust-filled head of his stuffed bear, Tangerine, when Miles was only days old, and there it had remained hidden for twelve years. He suddenly felt anxious for Tangerine, whom he had left tucked up in his bed. "I have to go and tell Lady Partridge about the fire," he said, though the rain had gotten the upper hand and the tree house roof was giving off little more than a loud hiss and a lot of steam.

"I'll be right here," said Little.

Miles turned and half climbed, half slithered down the rope ladder. The rain twisted with the wind, and thunder rolled continuously as he ran, bent forward against the storm, toward the house. As he turned the corner he collided with something soft and soggy, and both boy and obstacle fell backward into the sodden grass.

"Oof!" said the obstacle, which was large and round and wrapped in silk. Miles scrambled to his feet, and the obstacle did the same, just as they were both lit by a dazzling flash of lightning.

"Doctor Tau-Tau!" gasped Miles, winded and surprised. "I thought you'd been deported!"

"Deported?" shouted the plump fortune-teller over the hissing rain. "Nonsense, boy. I . . . I resumed my travels. But I had to come back to . . ." He straightened his battered fez and stared wildly over Miles's head. "To report a fire! The tree house . . ."

He pointed at the smoldering tree house roof.

"But that's only just started," shouted Miles. There was something in Doctor Tau-Tau's look that was even shiftier than usual.

"Second sight, my boy," replied the fortune-teller. "I can predict . . ." He hesitated for a moment, and as lightning flashed again he smiled nervously at Miles, fidgeting in the pocket of his silk dressing gown. "We had some adventures, you and I," he said suddenly.

Miles stared at him in puzzlement. It was such an odd thing for Tau-Tau to say in the heart of a thunderstorm, his white hair pasted to his forehead and rainwater streaming from the end of his nose. Doctor Tau-Tau stepped forward suddenly and grabbed Miles's hand, pressing a couple of coins into his palm and closing his fingers over them. "Buy something nice, eh?" he shouted. He took a couple of paces backward, a smile still stretched across his face; then he turned and hurried toward the gravel driveway and was swallowed by the darkness.

Miles made his way quickly to the back door of the mansion. The coins felt gritty in his hand. He frowned as he let himself in, dripping, and as he squelched through the kitchen he thought he heard the sound of a motor starting over the roar of the rain. The feeling of unease was spreading up from his stomach, and he began to shiver uncontrollably as he took the broad stairs two at a time. By the time he reached his room, unease had turned to dread. The door stood open and the covers had been dragged off his bed. Something lifeless huddled in the center of the bedsheet. Miles approached the bed slowly, his teeth chattering like castanets. It was Tangerine, and it was not Tangerine. The bear lay in a small pile of stuffing and sawdust, his head almost completely removed from his limp body.

Miles sat down heavily on the edge of the bed, the blood draining from his face. He knew that he had to think of something quickly. He shook his pillow out of its pillowcase and gathered up the remains of Tangerine gently, trying not to miss any of the stuffing. The bear's head felt lighter than usual, but it did not register with Miles. He felt numb, and for a moment he forgot all about Little and Silverpoint. "I'll fix you back up," he said to Tangerine. He placed the bear carefully into the pillowcase and tied it loosely. His damp fingers felt gritty from the sawdust, like the coins that Doctor Tau-Tau had given him, and all at once the fortune-teller's guilty smile swam before his eyes. He stopped dead for a moment, and his heart pumped freezing air. The Tiger's Egg . . . *Tau-Tau* had taken it! He had torn open the sleeping bear and plucked out the little stone, and Miles had let him go. His stomach lurched and the room seemed to tilt. He took a deep breath to steady himself, and rose from the bed on shaky legs.

As he turned to go he spotted his mother's diary, which he kept under his pillow. He had been studying the diary in the hope that it would be the key to the secrets of the Tiger's Egg. The hope drained from him as he remembered what he had read before falling asleep that night, but he picked up the diary nonetheless and slipped it into his pocket along with the dismembered bear in the knotted pillowcase. He stumbled out through the open door, and in the darkened landing he almost ran into a small girl who was hurrying, wide-eyed, in the direction of Lady Partridge's room.

"Jessica," said Miles, "tell Lady Partridge the tree house is on fire."

Jessica Tuesday's eyes opened even wider, and she nodded mutely.

"And tell her," called Miles as he slid down the

curving banister, "that I've had to go out for a while, but I'm okay." He flew off the end of the banister and ran through the darkened kitchen. Outside, the night flung freezing rain in his face as he rounded the house and headed for the driveway down which the thieving fortune-teller had disappeared. He stopped for a moment and squinted into the darkness, remembering the engine he had heard starting up minutes before. "Think," he said aloud. "How are you going to catch him on foot?"

He thought of the tiger, and how the powerful beast had carried himself and Little on his back through field and forest, never seeming to tire. He reached into his pocket and grasped the limp shape of Tangerine inside his pillowcase ambulance, and he closed his eyes. With a great effort he slowed his breathing and listened for the tiger's rumbling voice in the roar of the surrounding rain. He flared his nostrils to let in the odor of damp earth, willing it to turn into the musty smell that had risen from the tiger's pelt as they ran through the rain-drenched vineyards on the way to the Palace of Laughter. He opened his eyes and saw the tiger's stripes appear through the slanting rain, and despite the cold and the awful sense of dread he felt a wave of relief sweep through him. He would have to leave Little behind in the tree house. He could not risk Silverpoint seeing the tiger; nor could he—

The tiger loomed before him suddenly. He looked somehow larger than ever. He stood with his black lips curled back from his teeth, and his eyes burned with a cold fire. For a moment Miles was struck with the horrible feeling that the wrong tiger had somehow appeared. He waited a moment in silence, but for once the tiger said nothing.

"Hello," said Miles uncertainly. He raised his voice to be heard over the sound of the storm. "I . . . I need your help."

The tiger opened his mouth and roared, and if you have ever stood two paces from a furious tiger in a midnight rainstorm you will appreciate just how terrifying an experience it was. The raindrops scattered before the force of the tiger's roar, which almost knocked Miles off his feet. He shook his head to try to clear the sound from his ears, and the tiger took a step closer. "Who are you to call on me, a king among kings?" demanded the tiger in a deep rumble. "Do you think I'll be at your beck and call like a beaten donkey every time you lose a toy or miss a train? I'd snap your neck and swallow you whole, boy, if I could be bothered to spit out the boots."

Miles stared at the tiger in astonishment. He was shaking as much with fear as with the cold. Somewhere at the back of his mind it occurred to him that he was not wearing boots, but he did not think it was a good time to point this out. "I only . . . ," he began, but he got no further. The tiger reached out almost casually, like a cat playing with a small bird, and dealt Miles a blow with his mighty paw that sent him sprawling sideways into the freezing mud. Before Miles could regain his wind, the tiger pounced forward and planted a forepaw on his chest. The weight made stars swim in front of Miles's eyes, and the tiger's face appeared in the middle of the swirling pattern, his yellow teeth bared in menace.

"If you wanted a pet," said the tiger, his hot breath smelling of blood and meat, "you should have gone for a goldfish."

Miles could not take a breath to speak, even if he could have thought of something to say. His head swam, but he held the tiger's eye in the hope that it would somehow save him from being eaten. Just as he thought he would faint from the crushing weight on his rib cage he saw the tiger's ears swivel and felt the pressure ease. The tiger stood upright, and with another earsplitting roar he wheeled suddenly—as though he had just remembered something more urgent than snapping Miles's neck—and disappeared into the night.

CHAPTER TWO

BORROWED WINGS

Miles Wednesday, storm-soaked and tiger-winded, lay on his back in the pelting rain, gasping for breath. He had the dizzying sensation that he was looking down at himself from somewhere above the treetops, a bedraggled boy sprawled in the mud in an outsize overcoat. In his pocket lay the cruelly plundered Tangerine, the fragile life that Little had breathed into him dispersed like smoke on the breeze. The Tiger's Egg was gone, taking with it the friendship and trust that Miles had built up with the tiger. He was wet and cold, alone, except for . . .

Little's pale face swam into view, and all at once Miles was back inside his own body. His head sang from the tiger's blow, and he could feel something warm and sticky on his neck. He struggled to sit up, his hands slithering in the cold mud.

"What happened?" said Little, a worried frown on her pale features. "Your face is bleeding!" She reached out to wipe his cheek with her sleeve, and Miles flinched. The whole side of his face was burning, and he realized that the sticky feeling on his neck must be his own blood.

"The tiger!" gasped Miles. "The Tiger's Egg . . ." He caught sight of Silverpoint standing over Little's shoulder, and stopped uncertainly.

"It's all right," said Little. "You can speak."

"Doctor Tau-Tau has stolen the Tiger's Egg," said Miles, clambering to his feet. "He took it from . . . from its hiding place."

"Doctor Tau-Tau?" echoed Little. "But I thought—"

"He came back," said Miles. "He must have figured out where the Egg was."

"Did Tau-Tau do that to you?" asked Little, her eyes widening.

Miles shook his head. "It was the tiger," he said

reluctantly. "It probably wasn't a good time to call on him, but I didn't think of that until too late." He fought back the hollow feeling that threatened to overtake him.

"That will teach you to meddle with trapped souls," said Silverpoint.

Little rounded on the Storm Angel, and if she had been capable of producing lightning he would undoubtedly have said good-bye to his eyebrows at that moment.

"Silverpoint," she snapped, "don't be such a pain!"

Silverpoint raised his eyebrows (he still had them to raise) and looked at Miles, and for the first time Miles saw his ice-cool expression seem to melt a little.

"Which way did the thief go?" asked Silverpoint.

Miles pointed along the darkened driveway. "He went that way, but he had a car or a van—I heard it start up. We'll never catch him on foot."

Little and Silverpoint exchanged glances, and he gave a little smile. She turned back to Miles. "Are your trousers tied tightly?" she asked.

Miles gave her a puzzled look. He checked the cord that held up his pajama trousers, and nodded.

"Good," said Little, and at the same moment

Miles felt something grasp his coat between his shoulder blades. There was a loud *Whump!*, and he was twenty feet from the ground in an instant, rising rapidly into the heart of the storm with Little by his side. His overcoat held him by the armpits, and his stomach had been left somewhere far below. He looked down in astonishment and saw that they were already above the treetops, and when he twisted his head he could see Silverpoint above and between them, his eyes fixed on the night sky and his mouth a thin line across his pale face. The Storm Angel gripped them, one in either hand, and with every beat of his powerful wings he lifted them higher. Lightning struck away to their left, and Miles saw Little's face lit with the pure joy of flight, even though on borrowed wings. Her delight was so infectious that he laughed giddily and almost forgot his fear. Almost.

They had stopped rising now and were traveling at speed over stubbled fields, rain flying at them like a silver tunnel. They cut across the loops of the road until far below Miles could see yellow headlights careering through the darkness. Silverpoint swooped a little lower and began to follow their winding path. A car approached in the opposite direction, and in its headlights Miles could see more clearly the outline of the vehicle they were pursuing, a battered circus van decorated with a laughing clown's head and the words THE PALACE OF LAUGHTER.

"I don't think he's alone," shouted Miles. The wind whipped into his open mouth and left him gasping for breath.

Little shook her head. "It's Cortado," she said. "It must be."

Miles nodded. He did not want to risk opening his mouth again. He thought of the malignant little ringmaster of the Palace of Laughter, who had been locked away in Saint Bonifacio's Hospital for the Unhinged after Miles and Little had put an end to his sinister scheme, only to escape the hospital more twisted and dangerous than before. It would not surprise Miles to find that the Great Cortado himself was the driver of the van. As devious as Doctor Tau-Tau could be, Miles could not imagine him having the sheer audacity to enter Partridge Manor and steal the Tiger's Egg from inside the bear's head without orders from someone else. He tried to button his overcoat at the neck with frozen fingers, feeling for the lump in his pocket to reassure himself that Tangerine was still there.

* * *

The driving rain stung Miles's face, but after a while the stinging faded into a kind of hot numbness. The steady beat of Silverpoint's wings gave a reassuring rhythm to their flight. The Storm Angel's grip had not slackened in the slightest, and Miles noticed that he was swooping and jinking as he flew. His face gave nothing away, but Little was laughing and whooping with delight with every curve of their flight. As his fear of falling began to melt away Miles felt the thrill of flying radiating from his stomach like a warm glow. Faint memories of many flying dreams rose in the back of his mind, as though they had all been foretastes of this moment. A grin spread across his face and he turned to look at Little.

At that moment he was blinded by an intense flash that seemed to come straight from Silverpoint's mouth. When his vision cleared he saw a streak of blue lightning arrowing toward the van below them. His hair stood out from his head and crackled with electricity. The lightning bolt sped toward the van, and a tree burst into flames by the side of the road. The van swerved dangerously before righting itself.

"What happens if you hit them?" Miles yelled. The wind filled his mouth again, and he tucked his head down to take a breath before continuing.

"You might destroy the Egg."

"I'm aiming for the tires," said Silverpoint. "The Tiger's Egg must be returned intact, and in any case I can't risk killing the occupants. It's not permitted for a Storm Angel to release a soul to the wind. That's the job of the Sleep Angels."

There was another blinding flash, but this time it did not come from Silverpoint. A twisted rope of pure light split the darkness before them, and Silverpoint swerved suddenly to avoid it. Miles felt a tingle all down one side, and a blast of heat, as though they were flying past a furnace. Another bolt of lightning followed the first and Silverpoint dived steeply to the right, his exuberant dodging becoming a grim maneuver to avoid being burned to a crisp. Thunder blasted through the sky and Miles could feel it vibrating in his chest.

"Who knows you're here?" shouted Little as the rumble subsided.

Silverpoint looked paler than usual, if that were possible. "Nobody except Rumblejack," he said.

"Maybe he told someone," said Little.

Silverpoint shook his head, veering to the left to avoid another streak of lightning. His face was strained with concentration, and for some time he said no more as he swooped and tacked through a buzzing, crackling thicket of lightning. Miles tried to keep sight of the van's headlights below them, as much to distract himself from the prospect of being torched in midair as anything else. Sometimes he lost sight of them for a while, but Silverpoint seemed to have an uncanny ability to navigate their course even while performing acrobatics that would put a swift to shame.

The lightning eased off after a while. Whether Silverpoint had succeeded in outrunning it or the Storm Angel who created it had changed his mind, it was impossible to tell. The air grew colder and they left the rain behind as they rose to cross the mountains. Miles could no longer see the van in the darkness.

"I think we've lost them," he said.

"No, we haven't," said Silverpoint. "Look, the trail is still there." He pointed straight downward with his chin, but Miles could see nothing.

"What am I looking for?" he asked.

"The vehicle uses tiny sparks of trapped lightning," said Silverpoint. "That faint silvery line shows the path it took. It will be hours before it fades completely."

"He can't see it," said Little.

"Can you?" asked Miles.

"I can't see the trail," said Little, "but the pattern it makes in the One Song remains for a while also, and I can hear that."

Miles tried to picture what the world might look like to a native of the Realm. He felt distinctly lacking in skills and abilities, and he wondered if Little's own powers would fade in time, like the subtle whispers that the van left in its wake.

They passed over a jagged mountain ridge and Silverpoint swooped downward as quickly as the slope would allow, in search—Miles hoped—of warmer air. Miles caught a glimpse of a circular lake reflecting the pinkish glow that was spreading from the far horizon, and recognized it at once.

"Look!" he called to Little. "There's the lake where we stopped with . . . with the tiger on the way to the Palace of Laughter."

"Do you think that's where they're headed?" asked Little.

"I hope not, softwing," said Silverpoint. "I could carry you all day and night, but your friend is starting to feel like a sack of rocks. I may need to rest soon."

"I can see the van up ahead," interrupted Miles. His own limbs were aching, even though he was doing none of the flying, and he shared Silverpoint's hope that the van would not be traveling much farther. "Couldn't you get ahead of it and let us down in the road?"

Silverpoint laughed. "I could," he said, "but remember the Great Cortado may be driving. Do you really think he'd hesitate about running you over?"

"Maybe you'd better try hitting the tires again," said Miles.

"I can't risk that," said Silverpoint. "We're no longer in a storm, in case you hadn't noticed, and shooting lightning out of a clear sky would draw a little too much attention. As it is we're going to have to land before it gets light enough for us to be spotted."

"Isn't it more important to retrieve the Tiger's Egg?" asked Miles.

"Of course it's important, but the code of the Realm prohibits me from flying around like a lovesick jaybird for everyone to see."

Little laughed. "You really need to lighten up, Silverpoint!" she said.

Silverpoint did not smile back, and Miles felt an unpleasant tingle run through him where he was encircled by the Storm Angel's wiry arm. "Don't preach to me, softwing," he snapped. "There would only be chaos if we all broke every rule we were taught and abandoned our place in the Realm."

"Maybe the Code of the Realm can't teach us every song that's worth singing," retorted Little.

Silverpoint opened his mouth to speak, but Miles interrupted him.

"That's Cnoc!" he said. "The van is driving into the village. It looks like it's heading for Baltinglass of Araby's place!"

"Are you sure?" said Little. "What would they want with Baltinglass?"

"No idea," said Miles, "but they're stopping outside his house. I can see the orchard at the back."

Silverpoint began to spiral downward in broad circles over the village that clustered on the crown of the hill. Two tiny figures stepped from the van and disappeared into the front porch of Baltinglass's house.

"They're at the front door," said Miles, twisting around to look at Silverpoint. "You need to let us down."

"We're already descending," said Silverpoint calmly.

"Not quickly enough!" said Miles. Anxiety clutched at his stomach.

Silverpoint looked at him with his impenetrable black eyes. "You're right," he said. And he let Miles go.

Miles Wednesday, frozen, frightened and free-falling, plummeted earthward through the spreading dawn. After the heart-stopping moment when Silverpoint released his grip, an unexpected calm came over him, and he found himself thinking, "This the end of me, then. I shouldn't have opened my big mouth." Little's laughter echoed through his head from somewhere near his left shoulder. Baltinglass's orchard was coming up fast, and the fear suddenly rushed back into him like an electric shock. He closed his eyes tight, but just as he expected to hit the ground he heard the now-familiar *whump* of Silverpoint's wings. The Storm

Angel's wiry arm grabbed him about the waist and he felt himself righted as they pulled out of their dive, his stomach left behind once more. With his eyes still tightly shut he was landed as softly as thistledown. His knees buckled under him and he sat down with a bump.

Miles opened his eyes to find Little sitting beside him in the long grass of Baltinglass of Araby's orchard, laughing like wind chimes in a spring breeze. Silverpoint stood over them, his arms folded. "*Now* who are you calling a pain?" He grinned.

"Again!" said Little through tears of laughter. "Let's do that *again*!"

Miles opened his mouth to protest, but he was interrupted by a crash from inside the house. Little's laughter ceased abruptly, and Silverpoint's wings folded themselves away as he glanced sharply in the direction of the sound. He put a finger to his lips. Miles and Little got quickly to their feet, and all three crept up onto the patio and peered into the gloom of Baltinglass's cluttered living room. Baltinglass of Araby was tied to a chair, his mouth gagged and shards of china at his feet. He was struggling to free himself, and the gag did little to dim the sound of his muffled shouts. Doctor Tau-Tau stood over him, his arms folded and his habitual red fez perched on top of his fluffy white hair like a beach hut on a cloud. In the corner of the room with his back to the window stood the Great Cortado himself, rummaging through the drawers of a large plan chest and tossing rolled and folded papers in all directions.

Miles looked about him for something that would serve as a weapon. A rake stood against the wall, and he grasped the handle. The wood was old and bleached and the iron teeth rusty. It would not provide much protection against the frightening array of knives and swords that hung within easy reach of the Great Cortado, but it was all there was at hand. His heart thumped. He took a deep breath and pushed open the French windows. The Great Cortado whipped around in surprise, clutching a roll of yellowed paper. There was a patch over his right eye. Below it his cheek was pulled and puckered like a miniature mountain range where the wound that the tiger had given him had healed badly, unstitched and unattended.

"Tau-Tau," said Cortado in an icy voice, "why is this . . . boy . . . still alive?"

Tau-Tau flinched visibly and shuffled his feet. "I . . . er . . . ," he mumbled.

The Great Cortado fixed his humorless smile on

Miles and took a cigar from his breast pocket. "I'm glad to see you've added Spark Boy to your entourage of freaks," he said. "I seem to have come out without my lighter." He placed the cigar between his lips and giggled.

"I want back what you stole from me," said Miles.

The Great Cortado reached up and grabbed a straight-bladed dagger from its place on the wall. "You're not in a position to make demands," he said. "You know I can pin you like a moth from here."

"Go ahead," said Miles, more boldly than he felt. He held the stare of the Great Cortado's remaining eye, which fixed him like a rivet from his ruined face, making Miles feel as though he would be safer in a snake pit. He forced himself not to blink, and wisely so. The ringmaster made as if to turn away, but a sudden deft flick of his wrist sent Baltinglass's dagger spinning through the air. Miles, whose circus training had prepared him well for just such a situation, deflected the blade with a sweep of the rake, and at the same time a bolt of lightning crackled from behind his left shoulder and hit the Great Cortado in the chest, knocking him back against the map chest. The hilt of the deflected knife struck Doctor Tau-Tau squarely in the eye.

Tau-Tau yelped like a small dog and slapped a pudgy hand to his face. The Great Cortado pulled himself upright, smoke curling from a blackened patch on his shirt. His face turned a dangerous white and he unhooked another blade from the wall. It was no dagger this time, but a Hungarian saber with a long, curved blade. Little squatted behind Baltinglass's chair, working at the knots that bound him with quick fingers, and Silverpoint advanced toward Doctor Tau-Tau, who backed away into the corner, still covering his smarting eye.

"Now, then," the fortune-teller quavered, "there's no need for a fracas, young man. A fracas would be unnecessary. I'm a highly respected clairvoyant and a healer of note. I might even be able to do something for your unfortunate static problem."

"Tau-Tau, you mollusk," said the Great Cortado between clenched teeth, "make yourself useful and call up security." He tested the sword edge with his thumb. "This will do," he said, smiling coldly at Miles. Miles held the rake tightly, as though his grip alone might turn it into a sword.

Doctor Tau-Tau fumbled in his pocket and began to mutter an incantation.

"Um . . . Nature red in tooth and claw . . . er . . . in the forests of the night . . . *regit eeht nommus I . . .*"

There was a moment's silence as all eyes turned to Doctor Tau-Tau. His florid face turned a deeper red. "Um . . . abracadabra?" he said hopefully. There was a mighty crash from the room above, and a disembodied roar shook the house. The Great Cortado flinched visibly, and Miles felt his own heart stop with a mixture of excitement and fear. There was a commotion of smashing glass and toppling furniture above their heads.

"It's upstairs, you idiot," said the Great Cortado without looking at Tau-Tau. "I thought you knew how to use that thing." He tucked the roll of yellowed paper under his arm and stepped suddenly toward Miles, lifting the Hungarian saber high in the air. Miles raised the flimsy rake in response, but at that moment Baltinglass of Araby, freed by Little from his bonds, stuck out a gnarled leg and neatly tripped the Great Cortado. The saber slipped from the ringmaster's hand as he stumbled, and Baltinglass caught it and leaped to his feet with the nimbleness of a far younger man.

"Cockroaches in my house!" roared the blind explorer, pulling the gag from his mouth. "I should have had the exterminators in." The sword whooshed as he flourished it wildly, and had the Great Cortado still been standing he would have been sliced clean in half. Instead he crawled hastily toward the door, only to have his fingers trodden on by Doctor Tau-Tau, who had also decided on a hasty exit.

"Out of my way, fool!" hissed the Great Cortado, scrambling to his feet and dusting off his jacket in an attempt to recover his composure. The sound of splintering wood came from upstairs, and another earsplitting roar boomed through the house. The stairs creaked under a heavy weight. A look of panic flashed across the Great Cortado's face as he elbowed Tau-Tau aside and wrenched open the door. "We've gotten what we came for," he said, and turned to Miles with a sour grin. "I'll leave you to play with your pussycat," he said, and he disappeared into the gloomy hallway, followed quickly by Doctor Tau-Tau.

"Well, that's gotten rid of the vermin, Master Miles," shouted Baltinglass of Araby. "Now we just have to deal with the wildlife. Sounds like a male Bengal tiger, maybe five hundred pounds. Should make a fine rug, but we'll need more than a pistol. I've got a twelve-bore shotgun in the pantry that I keep for shooting rats."

"We're not going to shoot the tiger," said Miles.

"I thought you might say that," said Baltinglass,

his voice tinged with regret. "In which case we'd better batten down the hatches. That tiger's not in a mood to parley."

"I'll speak to him," said Miles. "We can't let Cortado and Tau-Tau escape."

"Miles," said Little, "I don't think that's a good idea."

Miles looked at Silverpoint. "Couldn't you stun him?" he asked. "I mean, without really hurting him?"

The Storm Angel folded his arms. His mouth became a thin slit.

"Silverpoint?" said Little.

"It's not my place to interfere," said Silverpoint haughtily. "The tiger would not be here at all if the Code had not been flouted."

"I thought interfering was your specialty," said Miles angrily. He threw the rake aside and marched through the door as a soft thump from the hallway signaled the tiger's arrival at the bottom of the stairs.

"Take a sword, Master Miles," Baltinglass called after him. "I once bit into a club sandwich with the cocktail stick still in it, and I can tell you I spat it out fast enough!"

The tiger waited in the gloom of the hallway,

crouched low and ready to spring, his tail lashing the dusty air. Behind him the hall door swung slowly open in the morning breeze, letting in a strip of cold sunlight, and with it the sound of van doors slamming.

Miles faced the tiger, trying not to think of the outcome of their last meeting. "It's me," he said. His voice sounded thin.

"It's meat," rumbled the tiger mockingly.

"You know me," said Miles. "I'm Miles—Barty Fumble's son."

"You're a persistent irritation," snarled the tiger. His eyes burned with amber fire, and there was a blackness at their center that Miles had never seen before, a nothingness that reminded him uncomfortably of the eyes of The Null. The tiger inched forward, and his great paws shuffled for position. His fur looked bedraggled and dirty.

"I won't ask you for anything again," said Miles. "Just let me past. I need to go after those two men."

"The novelty has worn off your wild-goose chases, boy," snarled the tiger, his tail flicking in anger.

Miles tested his own purchase on the floor. His only chance would be to leap aside if the tiger sprang. There was a rug under his feet, and it shifted slightly on the tiles. An idea began to take shape in the back of his mind. "This wild goose chase concerns you," he said boldly. "Doctor Tau-Tau is the one who's jerking your strings at the moment, and he's doing it on the orders of the Great Cortado. Why else would you find yourself in an old man's bedroom? Were you trying out his false teeth?"

With a roar the tiger leaped. Time slowed to a crawl. Miles saw his mighty claws outstretched and his eyes burning with rage. He saw the massive jaws open and felt in his chest the thunderous roar that swept like a wave toward him. He almost forgot to move, stepping aside only at the last moment. The tiger's forepaws landed where the boy had stood an instant before, and the rug slipped beneath his weight. He slid along the hallway, scrabbling for purchase, and crashed headfirst into the stone wall, knocking himself out cold. Miles held his breath as a shower of old whitewash descended slowly and dusted the stunned tiger like a tiramisu.

"What the blazes is happening?" yelled Baltinglass, sticking his woolly-hatted head out of the living room door. "Are you still in one piece, Master Miles?"

"I'm fine," said Miles, letting his breath out with a whoosh, "but I'm not sure about the tiger. I hope he's not badly hurt."

"Ha!" barked Baltinglass. "Just be thankful you're not lunch. You've got nerves of tungsten, boy, to take on a tiger without a good rifle, and the wit of a magpie to survive it."

Little stepped into the hall, a look of relief on her face, and bent over the tiger's massive head. "He'll be all right," she said after a moment.

"Of course he will," muttered Silverpoint. "You can't kill a tiger when his soul is trapped in the pocket of some buffoon."

CHAPTER FOUR
A TIGER-SHAPED HOLE

Baltinglass of Araby, ungagged and unshaven, cocked an ear and listened to the deep breathing of the tiger who lay stretched out in his hallway.

"Not exactly a rug in the classic sense," he said, "but I suppose it's the closest I'll get." He straightened up with a loud creaking sound. "No time to lose, then. We've got to get ourselves packed and provisioned before the rug wakes up."

"Packed?" said Miles. "What do you mean?"

Baltinglass broke into a wrinkly grin and a glint appeared in his eyes, though they were as white as milk in a pail. "It's time to saddle up and hit the trail,

Master Miles. There are villains to pursue and valuables to retrieve, and I have one good journey left in me."

"They've got a head start," said Miles doubtfully. "How will we ever catch them?" He could not imagine Silverpoint trying to carry all three of them at once through daylit skies, and it was hardly likely that the blind explorer would have a vehicle stowed away in his garage.

"I have a vehicle stowed away in my garage," said Baltinglass of Araby with a wink. "It'll get us to Fuera in fine style."

The mention of the bustling port made Miles's heart leap with excitement. "How do you know they're going to Fuera?" he asked.

"It was my map they stole, remember? Everyone knows that I have the finest collection of maps in the country, and that fool Tau-Tau came straight out and told me where they were headed before his nasty little associate could stop him. They're going to Kagu in the Starkbone Desert, but they'll have to sail from Fuera to get there. Now, enough of this chin-wagging—it's time to open the quartermaster's store." He turned in Little's direction. "You'll get a pot of coffee bubbling for us, young Little. Miles, you can tidy up my map chest. Silverpoint . . ." He paused for a moment, scratching his chin. "Just don't blow up any more of my trees."

"I will be leaving now," said Silverpoint coolly. "I've been away long enough. The storm has ended, and decisions will have been reached in my absence. I wish you good luck on your journey." He motioned to Little to follow him, muttering, "You'll need it," under his breath, and stepped out into the sunlit orchard.

"I'll be back in a moment," said Miles to Baltinglass. He could see Silverpoint talking urgently to Little, and he did not want to miss what was being said. He followed them outside. "What are you going to do?" he asked Silverpoint.

"There's not a lot I *can* do," said the Storm Angel. "The next time I return it will be with Bluehart. He will be here to release your life, and I will be his second."

"You'll have to try to divert him," said Little.

"Until what?" said Silverpoint sharply. Clouds began to darken the sky. "You clearly don't intend to surrender the Egg. Do you think you can dodge the Sleep Angels forever?"

Little looked at Miles and smiled. "I'm sure Miles has a plan," she said.

"Of course," said Miles, looking Silverpoint in

the eye. "I just need a little more time."

Silverpoint sighed. Suddenly he looked like a twelve-year-old boy, and not a veteran of a thousand years who could call up a thunderstorm with ease. "I'll do what I can," he said. "Just remember I'm only a Storm Angel, and we're dealing with more than a bunch of clowns here. Sleep Angels hate to be thwarted once they're on a call, and if Bluehart ever suspects I'm trying to delay him . . ." His words trailed off, and thunder rolled in the distance like a waking tiger.

"I must go, softwing," said Silverpoint. "Be careful, and whatever you're about, be quick. You're on borrowed time already."

The sky was turning blacker by the moment, and fat raindrops began to fall. Silverpoint walked backward through the orchard, exactly as he had done when he took his leave the previous autumn. Miles was determined to watch his departure this time, but when the lightning struck he was blinded once more, and by the time his eyes cleared nothing remained but another blasted apple tree and a whiff of metal on the morning air.

"Come on, Miles," said Little softly. They entered the living room to an eerie silence. The blind explorer was crouched at the door that led into the hallway, a hand cupped behind his leathery ear. He turned as they approached. "Mighty quiet sleeper for a full-sized Bengal," he whispered loudly.

Miles's stomach knotted. Suppose the tiger had died? He crept to the door and peered over Baltinglass's shoulder. The front door stood wide open and a chilly breeze blew in, slowly erasing the tiger-shaped hole in the layer of white dust that sprinkled the tiles. Of the tiger himself there was not a whisker to be seen.

"He's gone!" said Miles in a whisper.

"Gone?" barked Baltinglass. "You sure he's not just lurking? Magnificent lurker, the Bengal tiger. Had one in my tent in Rangoon once, and I never saw the brute till I'd brushed my teeth and read three chapters of *Moby Dick*."

Miles shook his head. He could feel the tiger's absence like the empty shape on the floor. "He's gone," he repeated.

"Well," said Baltinglass, straightening up with a symphony of creaks and pops from his old joints, "must have heard me mention the twelve-bore. That buys us a little more time, eh? No sense in running out the door half-cocked."

"If they get too far ahead we may never catch them," said Little.

"Don't you worry about that, Little. There'll be many a wrong step ahead of that pair, and I know every rock, river and rabbit hole in their way—things that can't be marked on any map. With my experience, your charm and the boy's wits we'll be more than a match for a psychopath and a charlatan." He stumped off toward the larder, swinging his cane in front of him. "Sort those maps out, boy," he called over his shoulder. "You're looking for one entitled 'Unwise Routes Through the Starkbone Desert.' They didn't take that one."

Baltinglass heaved open a trapdoor in the floor of his larder and disappeared, lampless, into the gloom. A racket of rattling pots and clinking jars rose from under the floor, mixed with a muffled commentary in the old man's voice. "Flints, splints, pisspot and poles. Where's the blasted quinine? Mosquito net. That'll need some stitchin'—a buffalo could get through those holes. Parachutes—think we'll need parachutes, Master Miles?"

"Unlikely," called Miles. He gathered up the scattered maps and books from the floor and began to sort through them on the table. There were maps and charts of every place he'd ever heard of, and many that he had not. Some were obviously very old, stained with oil and coffee and tattered with use. Some were unmistakably the work of Baltinglass of Araby himself, and were scrawled with names and comments in his own handwriting. The map he had been looking for, "Unwise Routes Through the Starkbone Desert," was one of these, and Miles spread it out and weighed down the corners with jars of Baltinglass's Famous Homemade Apple and Thyme Jelly from the stack on the sideboard. The sounds of rummaging continued unabated from the cellar.

"Where's Tangerine?" asked Little, as Miles examined the scrawled notes and doodled camels that littered the desert map. He reached into his pocket and carefully removed the knotted pillowcase. He could feel tears start at the back of his eyes, and he was afraid to see the look on Little's face when she saw the ruined bear. Instead he pretended to be immersed in the map and handed the pillowcase to her without looking up.

In truth it was not difficult to keep his attention on the map. The more he examined it the more spectacular a document it seemed to be. Every town and village, every dune and well and water hole had been carefully drawn and named, annotated with details of Baltinglass's own travels in a fine pen. "Ahmet cures scorpion stings with fire," read one tiny note, and another said, "Eat at the Hammam kebab house if you have stainless-steel bowels." There were tiny drawings of camels, their footprints marking out the desert trails, and even rough pen portraits of some of the characters that the explorer had met along the way. It was unlike any map Miles had ever seen, and he lost himself in it for some time.

He became aware of Little kneeling on the chair beside him, examining the map with equal interest. She smiled and handed Tangerine to him. The bear's head had been stitched back onto its rightful place. He appeared to have as much stuffing as he had had before—which was not a great deal—and his crooked smile was unchanged, but he flopped in Miles's palm without a sign of life.

"Is he . . . I mean, did you . . . ?" began Miles.

Little shook her head. "I didn't try, Miles," she said. "The first time I sang him to life it was easier than I had expected. Now we know why, and I don't think I could do it again while Doctor Tau-Tau has the Tiger's Egg. Besides, with the Sleep Angels looking for us it's better not to try. It might draw attention to us."

Miles nodded. He looked at the bedraggled bear that had been his constant friend for as long as he could remember, and forced a smile. "He's just the same as he was to start with," he said, trying to keep the regret from his voice, and he replaced him carefully in his pocket, where he belonged. "Thank you," he said to Little.

There was a loud thump as Baltinglass of Araby heaved an enormous duffel bag out of the trapdoor and dumped it on the tiles. "That should do us," he panted, mopping his brow with a large handkerchief. He climbed out after the bag and tapped his way to the table, where he deposited a pile of musty clothes. "Put them on you," he said. "You should both find something to fit."

"Where did they come from?" asked Miles.

"They were my own clothes when I was a nipper, and an even smaller nipper. Found 'em in my mother's house when she passed on, and I never throw anything out." He pulled up a chair. "Now," he said, taking out his tobacco pouch and his pipe. "Did someone mention a Tiger's Egg?"

Little glanced at Miles. "That was me," she said. "It's a small stone that—"

"... contains the trapped soul of a tiger," said Baltinglass before she could finish.

"You've heard of a Tiger's Egg?" said Miles as he climbed into a pair of patched trousers.

"Heard of it?" said Baltinglass. "I've heard every fib, fable and yarn that was ever told, and made up a few of my own into the bargain."

"The Tiger's Egg isn't a fable," said Little. "It's what Cortado and Tau-Tau have stolen from Miles."

Baltinglass of Araby dropped his pipe and leaped to his feet. "Well, tan my trousers!" he yelled. "You mean I wasn't just imagining jungle carnivores skating in my hallway? I thought that was just a touch of the old brain shivers coming back at me."

"There really was a tiger," said Miles, "and his soul is in Doctor Tau-Tau's pocket."

"Bells and bilgewater!" shouted Baltinglass. "This is worse than I thought. Have you any idea of the damage that fool could do if he ever learns to tell his head from a haddock?" He stomped across to the old writing desk that stood in the corner and pulled a sheet of paper and a pencil from the drawer. "Write this down," he shouted, thrusting them in Miles's direction. The old man cleared his throat. " 'Dear Gertrude,' " he yelled. " 'Don't worry about a thing. Have taken Miles and Little for geography lesson. Back in six months approx, if we survive. Yours, etc., etc., Baltinglass of Araby.' Now, fold that up, boy, and we'll give it to Louis the postman on the way out."

He paused for a moment, scratching the back of his head. "Think I have something that might come in handy," he said. He marched back into the kitchen and began rummaging in the cupboards, returning a minute later with a battered biscuit tin, which he upended on the table. A pile of odds and ends fell out and rolled across the polished wood. There was a cotton reel bristling with needles, some twisted pipe cleaners, a lock of blond hair tied with fuse wire, coins from every continent, rubber bands, pencil sharpeners, half a stick of dynamite, ball bearings, a wax crayon (there's always one of them), a whistle, a dozen wasted batteries, some string, a magnet, two teeth, a roll of solder, a tiger's egg, a broken penknife, two dust-covered bull's-eyes, a small—

"Just a minute!" said Miles, plucking a small stone from the tide of knicknacks. It was egg-shaped and polished, and shot through with deep amber stripes.

"Find something interesting, Master Miles?" said Baltinglass.

"Is this *really* a Tiger's Egg?" asked Miles in astonishment.

"Nope," barked Baltinglass of Araby. "It's a fake. Bought it at a street stall in Hong Kong many years ago. Best place in the world for picking up fakes, Hong Kong. If they made a copy of your head and set it on your shoulder you wouldn't know which one to shave."

Miles held it up to the window, and it glowed with a honey-colored light.

"It's beautiful!" said Little.

"But what use is a fake tiger's egg?" asked Miles. He suddenly realized that he had never seen the real Egg, though he had carried it with him all his life. He wondered just how good a copy this one was.

"No idea," said Baltinglass, "but it has more chance of being useful in my pocket than lurking behind the semolina." He took the fake egg back from Miles and slipped it into a buttoned pocket inside his jacket. "Best if I put it in here for safekeeping, eh? Now, lock the doors and batten the hatches, the two of you. We'll leave through the garage."

Miles rolled up Baltinglass's map while Little locked the French windows and drew the heavy bolts on the front door; then they followed Baltinglass as he marched to a small wooden door in a corner of the hallway. He threw the door open to the sound of skittering mouse feet and a smell of dust and old grease, and they stepped through into a small garage that was carpeted with dust. Bars of sunlight crept in between the planks of the door and striped a large shape that stood under a tarpaulin in the center of the room, so that for a moment Miles thought the tiger stood there waiting for him.

As his eyes adjusted to the gloom he could make out the shape of a car beneath the cover, and he looked at it with curiosity.

"Pull off the tarp, then," bellowed Baltinglass, "and let the old girl breathe."

Miles and Little each took a corner of the tarpaulin and pulled. A massive car emerged from beneath it like a dark green whale. It had leather bench seats and big chrome headlights, and Miles was struck with the feeling that it had been waiting in expectant silence for him to arrive.

"Ain't she a beauty?" said Baltinglass. "Morrigan, I call her. Bought her for a song off a margarine magnate who was on the skids." He rummaged in the duffel bag and brought out a bottle of clear liquid. He uncorked the bottle and sniffed. "That's the stuff," he said. "Shame to waste it, but there's no time to be looking for gas, and Morrigan was always partial to a drop of hard liquor." He felt for the cap of the gas tank and unscrewed it, emptying the bottle into the tank. The fumes filled the garage, making Miles's eyes water.

"Will she run on that?" asked Miles, wiping his eyes on his sleeve.

"She'll run on anything that burns," said Baltinglass. "What's more, anyone following us will get a noseful of that poteen and wrap themselves around the nearest tree in jig time." He tossed the bottle over his shoulder and wiped his hands on his trousers. "Now," he said, to the sound of shattering glass, "she just needs a slight adjustment, and away we go."

"What's the slight adjustment?" asked Miles.

"A driver, Master Miles," said Baltinglass. "Won't get far without a driver." He rummaged in the trunk until he found a long white scarf, a flat cap and a pair of leather goggles.

"Don't you need to be able to *see* to drive?" asked Little.

"Of course," said Baltinglass of Araby. "Nothing wrong with your eyesight, I hope, Master Miles."

Miles looked at Baltinglass, and back at the enormous car. "I can't drive that!" he said.

"'Course you can, boy," shouted Baltinglass. "She drives the same as any other car."

"But I've never driven a car," protested Miles. "I'm only twelve. Besides, it's against the law."

"Good point," said Baltinglass. "That's why you'll need a disguise." He held out the scarf, hat and goggles. "Put these on, then, and make it snappy. I'll tell you what to do once you're in the driver's seat. It's a piece of cake."

Miles put on the disguise doubtfully and climbed onto the bench seat. He felt very high up, and the car seemed to stretch for miles before and behind him. He put his hands on the enormous steering wheel and peered over the dashboard, trying to make himself feel some of Baltinglass's confidence. He had always dreamed of driving a car, and despite his doubts his skin tingled with excitement. Baltinglass of Araby hauled open the garage door, then tapped his way back to the car, raising little puffs of dust with his cane.

"Right so," shouted the old man as he leaped into the passenger seat. "Put your hands on the wheel and your foot on the gas. Stand on the clutch . . . that's the one on the left . . . and ease it out when I tell you. I'll take care of the gears till you start to get the hang of it." He turned on the ignition and the engine coughed loudly twice, then settled into a steady rhythm that sounded something like *gol-gol-gol-gol-gol-gol-gol.*

Miles stared at the rectangle of November sunlight that led out into the world, feeling small in his oversize coat. He wondered how he had come to this point, sitting in the driver's seat of an enormous car and carrying on his narrow shoulders the confidence of a blind explorer and the trust of a four-hundred-year-old girl.

Morrigan's engine idled patiently, and he knew that once he set her in motion there would be no turning back.

"Well," said Baltinglass, as though reading his thoughts, "the longest journey begins with a turn of the key. When you're ready, Master Miles."

CHAPTER FIVE

THE DEPARTED AND THE LOST

Morrigan in motion, spoke-wheeled and fly-spotted, barreled comfortably along the dusty road, heading for south and sea. In the driver's seat Miles gripped the wheel tightly and peered through his goggles, concentrating on keeping clear of the ditches and hoping that the road would remain empty of other vehicles until he "got the hang of it," as Baltinglass had put it. Behind him Little sang a driving song that harmonized perfectly with the engine, and in their wake small birds fluttered dizzily to the ground.

They made good time along the highway, and after a while Miles began to feel more confident.

His shoulders relaxed and he allowed himself to blink now and then. Under Baltinglass of Araby's shouted tuition he learned to use the gearshift, and to slow down on the corners so that he no longer made the tires squeal and chickens and children dive for cover. The smile on his face grew and grew as Little's song threaded its way through the morning and the car ate up the road like an insatiable beast. By midafternoon he felt like a king on a well-sprung throne.

"Where are we now?" shouted Baltinglass of Araby, jerking out of one of his frequent naps.

"We passed through Nape a little while ago," said Miles.

"Hah!" said Baltinglass, clapping his hands together. "A sterling effort, boy. Pull over when you see a shady spot and we'll break out some vittles. My tongue's as dry as a bushman's ankle and I could eat a small bison on toast."

Miles pulled off the road and they rolled to a halt beneath a large oak tree. Baltinglass of Araby hauled the duffel bag from the trunk and before long they were eating tomato bread and vinegar fish, and washing the dust from their throats with parsnip wine. After so many hours of driving Miles could still see the ground rushing toward him, and he closed his eyes to rest them.

"A Tiger's Egg, eh?" said Baltinglass at length, wiping his wrinkled lips with his sleeve. "You're full of surprises, Master Miles. Did you win it in a raffle?"

"It belonged to my mother," said Miles, sitting up. "At least, she had it on loan from the Fir Bolg. Have you heard of them too?"

"'Course I have. Hairy little fellas. In fact, I made those ones up myself to liven up a quiet watch on board the HMS *Calamity*, if I remember rightly."

"I don't think so," said Miles. "I've met them."

Baltinglass pushed back his woolly hat and scratched his head. "Funny. Did you meet the three-eyed baboons who live underwater in a giant banjo?"

"No," said Miles.

"Must have been those that I made up," said Baltinglass. "So how did your mother persuade the Fir Bolg to part with a Tiger's Egg?"

"She made a deal with them," said Miles.

Little leaned over the back of the bench seat. "Did you find out what it was?" she asked, showering him with bread crumbs.

"I'm not sure if it's meant to be a secret," said Miles hesitantly. He had been reading the diary his mother had kept when she met the Fir Bolg all those years ago, and though she had died when he was born he still felt a little uncomfortable at the idea of sharing its contents.

"You can tell us," said Little. "We won't tell a soul."

"Your secret's safe with me, boy," yelled Baltinglass in a voice that could be heard half a mile away. "I can't even remember what I had for supper last night."

"It's hard to make out," said Miles. "Her writing is strange, and she mixes in a lot of words and symbols that I don't understand." He felt inside his coat pocket, where Tangerine was tucked up with Celeste's worn leather diary. He took it out and thumbed through the closely written pages. "The Fir Bolg can't stand the light," he said. "They've lived underground for as long as they can remember and can only come out on moonless nights. As far as I can tell, they asked my mother to find a way to cure them of their sensitivity to light so that they can live aboveground again."

"So that's what they're up to, the hairy little savages!" guffawed Baltinglass. "That would have the peasants locking their doors and windows, all right."

"Did she find out how to do it?" asked Little.

"I haven't gotten that far," said Miles. "But I don't think we'll ever know for sure. She said there was a key to using the Tiger's Egg."

"A key?" said Little. Her eyes shone. "Then you can learn to use it, Miles. Maybe you *will* be able to bring back your father."

Miles shook his head, a lump forming in his throat. His father had been transformed by the bungling Doctor Tau-Tau into The Null, a monstrous, hollow-eyed beast who lived in perpetual darkness, and at first the discovery of the Tiger's Egg had given Miles hope that someday it might help him restore his father to his former self. "I don't think so," he said. "Celeste says in the diary that she will take the key to her grave."

"But we know where that is!" Little laughed, and way above them a skylark began to sing. "We can go to your mother's grave in Iota and find the key."

"That's not what she means," said Miles. "When a person says that it means they'll never tell their secret to anyone."

"That's not what it says to me," said Little. "If she says she's taken it to her grave, then that's the first place we should look."

"She may have a point there," said Baltinglass of Araby, tossing the remains of their picnic back into the duffel bag. "A small detour can't do any harm. You should see signs for Iota about another hour down the road. Fire the old girl up, there, Master Miles, and let's be on our way."

Miles started Morrigan's engine and made a rather jerky exit onto the road. For a while his concentration was taken up with driving the car. His shoulders ached from holding the wheel and he had pins and needles in his feet. Sunlight flashed between the tall poplar trees that lined the road, and dust had filled his eyes before he remembered to pull down the goggles. Still, the powerful engine at his feet gave him a thrill of excitement, and deep down he realized that he was happiest when he was speeding away from home with his closest friends, though danger snapped at their heels and nightmares might await them on the road ahead.

Morrigan ate up the miles, and Miles drank in the sunlight and the breeze, and though he was sure that Little had misunderstood Celeste's words he felt a seed of hope that he might after all find some clue to the mastery of the Tiger's Egg that was his only chance of rescuing his father from lifelong darkness. The shadows lengthened toward evening, and Miles's blind copilot dozed fitfully at the other end of the bench seat, waking now and then to

shout such indispensable driving tips as "Watch out
for crocodiles," and "Step on it, boy; you're driving
like an old nun."

Just as he felt that his eyes would be glued forever
in their sockets, Miles rounded a small hill that he
thought he recognized. Sure enough, he could see
ahead of him the red-tiled roofs of the town where
he was born, and rising above the trees to their right
was the church spire in whose narrow shadow his
mother was buried. He braked the car gently and
pulled into the picnic spot from which he and the
policemen of Larde had set off through the trees
in search of the escaped Null. He felt somehow bigger as he stepped down from the car, as though he
had finally begun to grow into his oversize overcoat
since starting out that morning. He shook the old
man gently, knowing that waking Baltinglass was
a dangerous task at the best of times, and skipped
nimbly out of range as the old man snapped upright
with a loud yell and swung his cane at the gremlins
that haunted his sleep.

"It's all right," said Little, putting her hand on his
shoulder. "We're here. This is Iota."

Baltinglass of Araby relaxed at once. "Lead the
way, then," he said, "and let's see if the departed
Celeste can shed some light on the lost Egg."

They threaded their way through the trees, the blind explorer, the boy and the Song Angel, until they reached the edge of the silent churchyard. There they stopped, and Miles peered into the gloom beneath the spreading yew tree where he knew his mother's grave lay. The headstones crouched menacingly in the gathering twilight. He felt the hair stand up on the back of his neck, and even Little seemed unusually nervous.

"What if Cortado and Tau-Tau have come here too?" she whispered.

Baltinglass cupped his hand to his ear. "Can't hear you, child," he shouted, his customary bellow muffled by the dead silence of the churchyard. "Have you turned into a gnat?"

"I said, what if Cortado and Tau-Tau are already here?" said Little in a slightly louder voice. "The Great Cortado might have found the same page while he had Celeste's diary."

"I don't think they'd come here," said Miles. "Doctor Tau-Tau said Cortado wouldn't be able to interpret the diary without his help, and to be honest I don't believe Tau-Tau himself was able to make much out of it either."

"Whatever they want with the Tiger's Egg, they've gone south to find it," said Baltinglass.

"My mother came from down south," said Miles. "Across the water, the Bolsillo brothers said."

"Is that so?" said Baltinglass, rubbing his stubbly chin with a rasping sound. "You still got family there, Master Miles?"

"I've never met any of them. She had a twin sister who used to visit her once a year, but after my mother died she never came back," said Miles.

"There's your answer, then," said Baltinglass, stepping out into the churchyard as though it were broad daylight. "They'll be on their way to find Celeste's sister so they can pick her brains about the Tiger's Egg. What was her name?"

"Fabio said her name was Nura, but I don't know if she even knows about the Egg," said Miles. "My mother got it after she left home."

"Celeste will have told Nura about it," said Little.

"Without a doubt," said Baltinglass of Araby. "And you can be sure Cortado has a plan up his sleeve for extracting whatever she knows. It won't be good news for your aunt if he catches up with her."

CHAPTER SIX
A MOURNFUL MONK

Baltinglass of Araby, white-caned and woolly-hatted, tapped the granite headstone gently with the end of his stick. "This is the one, Master Miles?" he asked, in a tone softer than his usual bellow.

"Yes," said Miles.

"Read it out to me," said Baltinglass.

Miles cleared his throat. "'Celeste Mahnoosh Elham,'" he read. "'What time has stolen, Let it be.'"

"That's a short epitaph," said Baltinglass of Araby. He reached out again with his cane and swept it through the weeds that grew up around the headstone. "Watch your ankles," he said. He slid the

swordstick from inside his cane and aimed a deft
swipe at the weeds, cutting them to their roots
and knocking sparks from the granite. The plants
tumbled, and Miles could see more writing that
had been hidden behind them. He knelt down and
peered at the words, tracing them with his finger as
he read them out in the dusk.

> *What time has stolen*
> *Let it be*
> *Power grows*
> *From two to three*
> *Embrace the fear*
> *And set soul free*
> *To drink the sun*
> *In place of me*

A stillness like a stopped clock filled the churchyard, softened only by the rasping of distant crows.

"Not your standard epitaph, is it?" said a doleful
voice. Miles and Little spun around to look for the
speaker, and Baltinglass brandished his swordstick.
"Who said that?" he bellowed.

"I did," said a thin man with a bald crown, emerging from the shadows behind the yew tree. He wore
a brown robe with a rope knotted around his waist,

and he held up his hands, palms outward, obviously unaware that the old man could not see him. "Brother Runco is my name," he said. "I look after the churchyard."

Baltinglass of Araby sheathed his swordstick and snorted. "You certainly keep the weeds in fine condition," he said.

"I do try to keep the place tidy," said Brother Runco, whose voice sounded like it was being played at the wrong speed. "But I was asked by this young lady's cousins to leave her resting place to nature's care, and it's a request I have tried to honor."

"Her cousins?" said Miles.

The monk nodded. "Three little gentlemen," he said. "They brought her in the night and asked for a private funeral. I remember it like it was yesterday. One of them was very ill, poor little fellow, but he had insisted on coming along. Normally the priest does the funerals on weekday mornings, but these men were traveling with a circus and couldn't afford to wait."

"Who made the writing on the stone?" asked Little.

A ghost of a smile lifted Brother Runco's face. "I did the engraving myself," he said. "I've carved over half the headstones in this churchyard. Would you like to see some more?"

"Love to," interrupted Baltinglass of Araby, "but we have an urgent appointment with a villain, a fool and a boat. Where did you get the inscription?"

"The lady's cousins left it for me on a scrap of paper. It's a strange little verse, isn't it?"

"Do you still have the piece of paper?" asked Miles.

Brother Runco shook his head. "It fell apart eventually," he said. His breath smelled of sardines.

Miles hunkered down by the gravestone. "We have to go," he said. He took out Celeste's diary and the pencil with which he had written Baltinglass's reassuring note to Lady Partridge, and began to copy down the inscription in his best hand.

Brother Runco sidled up to him and leaned over his shoulder. "It's some sort of riddle, isn't it?" he said, his words gliding on seagull breath. "I've been trying to work it out for years. What power is she referring to, do you think? And what does she mean by drinking the sun?"

Miles gave no answer. He was concentrating on his handwriting, and on holding his breath.

The monk sighed deeply. "There's nothing else to think about in the long evenings," he intoned. "Most epitaphs leave little to the imagination. Take this one—'Sadly missed by loving husband Frank and son Frank junior,' or this—'He should have switched off the power before fixing the canning machine.'"

Miles closed the diary softly. There was no surface left inside the notebook that was not covered in writing, and nothing left to do now but chase the Great Cortado and his bumbling henchfool across hill and desert in pursuit of the Tiger's Egg. He opened his mouth to speak.

"You have to go," interrupted the mournful monk, nodding slowly. He held out his hand, and Miles took it reluctantly. It felt like a fish that had swallowed a handful of bones. "Good luck," said the monk.

"Thank you," said Miles. He stepped away as quickly as he could and took a lungful of clean night air. Baltinglass raised his cane in salute, almost hooking the monk's nostril in the process, and Little left him with a smile that seemed to glow like a firefly before melting slowly into the night.

"Do you think . . . ," called Brother Runco as they made their way into the trees. "I mean, once you find . . ."

"We'll send the answer on a postcard," said Baltinglass of Araby, and he hacked his way through the undergrowth, following the intoxicating aroma that wafted on the night air from Morrigan's slowly cooling exhaust. The car glinted patiently in the clearing. "You'll be tired, Master Miles," said Baltinglass. "We'll pitch camp here and make an early start in the morning."

"I can drive some more," said Miles. He could picture the morose Brother Runco materializing like a reproach from among the trees and watching over them as they slept, and he felt a little distance would do no harm.

"Onward it is, then!" barked Baltinglass. He paused with his hand on the passenger door. "I can always take a turn at the driving," he said. "Makes no difference to me if it's day or night; I'm blind as a worm."

"I think that's why you made Miles the driver," Little reminded him.

"Ah, yes, so it was," said Baltinglass of Araby.

Miles gave Little a boost into the spacious backseat. Though he had known her more than a year it still surprised him how light she was. He smiled, but something tiny shifted at the back of his mind, releasing a ripple of unease. He shook his head and climbed behind the wheel.

Before long they were speeding southward again. The countryside was iced with the light of a half-moon, and the cold wind bit his ears. Baltinglass had sunk down into his coat until his woolly hat sat on his shoulders like a stranded jellyfish, wispy tentacles of white hair flapping from beneath it. He seemed to have fallen into a gloomy mood, and now and then Miles was sure that he could hear the old man reciting muffled snatches of Celeste's epitaph and sighing deeply.

There was silence from the backseat, and Miles pulled himself upright to check the mirror. The car veered and he sat down again quickly, but not before seeing Little curled up asleep in the corner of the enormous seat. She looked small and lost, as she had when first he found her in a locked wagon at the Circus Oscuro. He realized with a start that she hadn't grown a millimeter or changed a hair in the year since then. The uncomfortable thought at the back of his mind began to creep into the light, and this is the shape it took:

He pictured a small girl holding his hand as he grew older, looking less like his adopted sister and more like his daughter with each passing year. She had surrendered her name and ceded her wings to save his life, yet she seemed suspended between the world of her birth and the one she had chosen to live in. It began to dawn on him now that although he had promised to make her new life magical, he would move on and leave her stranded in perpetual childhood instead.

Clouds loomed in the sky ahead, snuffing out the stars as they came, and still Miles drove relentlessly on. The car's headlights shone like a beacon for the angels who would come to take his soul. He was a small boy at the wheel of a big adventure, gaining hour by hour on the villain who wished him dead, and carrying with him an old man on his last journey and a girl to whom he had made a promise he could never hope to keep.

CHAPTER SEVEN

THE MERMAID'S BOOT

The port of Fuera, white-blind and sea-silent, slept inside a mist that was so dense, it made the world end at arm's length. There was not a soul about, for there was no business that could be carried on in such a fog. Seagulls perched, dripping, on bales and bollards, while silent ships stood at anchor out in the bay, their bored crews playing dice to the muffled *ding* of the buoy bells. Onshore the sailors, tailors, chandlers and fishermen who normally filled the streets and swarmed on the quays fidgeted instead in their narrow houses, waiting for the world to reappear.

Above a tavern by the docks was a small room containing two lumpy beds and a single armchair. The armchair in turn contained the Great Cortado, who chewed irritably on a cheap cigar. Pictures of water mills and sunsets hung on the yellowed walls. He was staring at one of these pictures with one watering eye, trying to ignore the muttering and sighing of his companion, Doctor Tau-Tau, who slouched on one of the beds like a narwhal in a fez.

Someone had arranged that fog, thought the Great Cortado darkly. It had risen from nowhere just as they had booked passage to leave this rank backwater, and there would be no departing until it had dispersed. Could Tau-Tau have done it? Only if he was trying to arrange a clear blue sky and a Girl Scout's picnic, the pop-eyed fool. There he sat, thought Cortado, muttering inanely over his stupid notebook while the walls drew closer minute by minute and the Tiger's Egg burned with untapped power.

The Great Cortado's skin crawled. The scar on his cheek pulled at his empty eye socket, and his mouth seemed filled with hundreds of tiny molars marching back into his skull. His bones were small and brittle, and his head pounded with the pressure of the chaos it contained, a universe of schemes shot through with vengeance and hot with bile. He was a

Great Man trapped in a little joke-shop body. Whose idea of a laugh had that been? He should have been broad and tall, or powerful and lean. The water-wheel in the picture turned insolently, and the fool of a fortune-teller said, "Huh!" as though he had just found a nugget of fascinating information in the scribbled drivel that filled his notebook.

"Stop babbling, man!" said the Great Cortado sharply.

Doctor Tau-Tau jumped, and the springs on the bed squeaked. "Sorry!" he said. "I'm studying the notes I made from Celeste's diaries before they were stolen from me. With luck I'll be able to recon-struct—"

"Luck doesn't enter into it," said Cortado. "I'm going to find Celeste's sister, and she's going to teach you how to use that Egg."

Doctor Tau-Tau gave a nervous smile. "That's if she agrees."

"She'll agree once she has a tiger breathing down her neck," said the Great Cortado. "All you have to do is learn to bring it to heel. I'll take care of the rest."

Doctor Tau-Tau looked confused. "I'm on the verge of acquiring that knowledge," he said. "But when I have mastered the tiger, what exactly will we need Celeste's sister for?"

The Great Cortado snorted. He took out his lighter and lit the cigar he had been maiming. Doctor Tau-Tau stared at him expectantly, but the little ringmaster was concentrating on creating a fog inside the room to match the one that pressed against the window, and he said nothing. A cold, smooth plan had hatched itself in the center of his fractured mind, and had been growing for several weeks now. It was a perfect plan, he told himself; a work of uncanny genius, and he had no intention of revealing it to Tau-Tau until it was absolutely necessary.

Soon he would have no more need of this little body, and he could discard the hated thing like a broken toy. Soon he would be all muscle and teeth, all shaggy power and striped majesty. He would become the one thing that he feared, and then there would be nothing more that could stand in the face of his furious hunger. He pictured the fortune-teller roasted on a silver plate with an apple in his mouth, and gave a tinny snigger. Tau-Tau glanced nervously in his direction. "He'll make a good meal when the time comes," thought Cortado, and somewhere in a lost corner of his mind he wondered if that thought should disgust him more than it did.

Miles Wednesday, steam-goggled, flat-capped and dawn-hungry, slowed the car as the mist began to thicken around them. He had slept for a while, parked at the roadside and curled up under his over-coat, and the chill still sat in his bones. He switched on the headlights to see better, but they just lit up the fog and made it seem twice as dense.

"What's the matter?" said Baltinglass, stretching himself awake. "You're driving like a mollusk on fly-paper."

"It's getting foggy," said Miles.

Baltinglass sniffed the air. "So it is. We're a stone's throw from the sea, if I'm any judge. Can you see anything?"

"Not much," said Miles. He could smell the sea now too and feel the car rumbling over cobbles. The mist hid the whitewashed houses of Fuera, but he could picture them clustering invisibly around. It felt like coming home.

"Keep an eye out for the Mermaid's Boot, Master Miles. There's a big, rusty anchor standing outside the yard, if it's still there."

Now, if you know anything at all about mermaids

you might feel there are better things you could do with your time than to be searching for their boots, but Miles knew that the Mermaid's Boot was a small inn that stood at the end of the road into Fuera, just where it met the quays. He didn't think they had come that far yet, but just at that moment a tilted shape loomed from the mist in front of them. Miles stood on the brakes, but Morrigan was a big car and would not be instantly stopped. Her bumper met the shape with a clang, lending the rusty anchor more of a tilt than it had previously had.

"Sorry!" said Miles.

"Think nothing of it," said Baltinglass of Araby. "It's as good a way of stopping as any other. Now pull into the yard and park by the side wall. Tuck her in nice and close."

Miles reversed the car under Baltinglass's instructions and parked it below a window at the side of the Mermaid's Boot. Little yawned from the backseat.

"Are we stopping for breakfast?" she asked sleepily.

"There are few things more important than a good breakfast," said Baltinglass, "but unfortunately a visit to the harbormaster's office is one of them." The car was parked so close to the wall that he could not open the passenger door. He seemed unaccountably pleased about this, and instead clambered along the bench seat and got out of the driver's door after Miles. Together they tapped their way along the street and onto the quays, the blind explorer leading the boy and the angel through the fog in which he himself spent all his days.

The harbormaster's office was a round tower with small windows set into its thick walls. The inside was entirely papered with sea charts and tide tables, and contained a large desk behind which sat an even larger man in a thick woolen sweater. The desk was strewn with papers, and the harbormaster was making notes on them with a sharp pencil. He looked up in mild surprise. "Well?" he said.

"Well, indeed," said Baltinglass. "We'd like to know the next vessel that's headed for Al Bab."

The harbormaster looked back at his papers. "The *Albatross* is loaded and ready to sail since yesterday, but she won't be going anywhere till the fog lifts. You'd better cut along there quick to have any chance of getting aboard. She's already filled most of her berths, and there're no more ships bound that way for another week."

"We're not going anywhere," said Baltinglass of Araby. "I have a packet for my niece's cook's grandmother's brother in Al Bab. Where's the *Albatross* docked?"

"Right here on the west pier," said the harbormaster, and he resumed his pencil annotations without looking up.

They made their way along the quayside, the worn paving stones appearing before their feet and fading just as quickly behind them. Miles and Little knew the harbor well, but it seemed strange and unfamiliar in the ghostly mist. Baltinglass swiped sideways with his cane, counting the iron bollards as they went.

"Aren't we sailing to Al Bab after all?" asked Little.

"'Course we are," said Baltinglass in a hoarse whisper.

"But you said—"

"Rumor spreads like mold in a seaport," said Baltinglass, "and there's no sense in broadcasting our plans. The first thing we need to do is find out if those two villains have sailed yet. We don't want to find ourselves sharing a cabin with them, do we?"

They turned onto the west pier. Miles could faintly see the shape of a ship looming to their right. As they approached the gangplank the silhouette began to sharpen, and he thought he could see on the deck the outlines of two men in conversation, though he could not make out their features. One of the men passed something to the other, and they shook hands. "That's settled, then," said the first man.

Miles recognized Doctor Tau-Tau's voice straightaway. His stomach tightened and he grabbed Baltinglass's arm. "It's Tau-Tau," he whispered. "Let's go before he spots us."

"About-face, then," hissed Baltinglass of Araby. "Set a course for breakfast at the Mermaid's Boot."

They hurried back along the quays to the inn on the corner. The Mermaid's Boot was a rambling, smoky room with numerous nooks and crannies and a small mahogany bar in one corner. The lumpy plaster walls were festooned with every type of nautical knickknack it was possible to imagine. There were shark's jawbones, ship's compasses, shells, bells, starfish, sea urchins, shackles, bolts, cleats, blocks, lanterns, life belts, harpoons and nets, a brass diver's helmet and lead-soled boots, ropes, rattraps, pipes, pails, charts, darts, ship's wheels, ice chests, billhooks, and a skeleton in a tricorn hat, slumped in the corner like a forgotten date.

Behind the bar a colorless man sat on a stool. He looked as though he had been left out in the rain.

He was clouding glasses with a greasy cloth, and he paused to gaze at the new arrivals with watery eyes.

"Breakfast!" barked Baltinglass, and the handful of sailors and stevedores who populated the bar turned and stared at the sound of his voice.

"We don't serve breakfast here," said the colorless man.

"Is that so?" said Baltinglass, slapping his cane on the bar. "Well, if you won't serve breakfast I'll come back there and cook it myself. Have you ever seen what a blind man can do to a stranger's kitchen?"

The barman thought for a moment. "How do you like your eggs?" he asked.

They sat themselves in a dim alcove, tucked away in the corner of the bar. The barman disappeared through a bead curtain and began to make a great deal of noise with some pots and pans. Miles felt in his pocket for Tangerine, as he did whenever arriving or leaving anywhere. The bear slept on, a crooked smile stitched on his grubby orange face, and Miles sighed quietly to himself.

"What do we do now?" he said. "There won't be another ship for a week, and we can't sail on the *Albatross.*"

"Who says we can't?" said Baltinglass.

Miles looked at him in surprise. "We can't sail

with Doctor Tau-Tau and the Great Cortado. You said so yourself."

"I only said we wouldn't want to be sharing a cabin with them," said Baltinglass of Araby. He leaned foward and dropped again into a hoarse whisper. "There's hardly a ship leaves port that isn't carrying an extra passenger or three that no one knows about except the purser or the ship's cook."

"You mean we could stow away?" whispered Miles.

Baltinglass nodded. "Even the smallest schooner has a dozen hidey-holes," he said. "And there's always a member of the crew who makes a few extra coins from filling those places with passengers who don't wish to be seen waltzing up the gangplank in a panama hat."

"That sounds like fun!" said Little. "How do we know who to ask?"

"Simple." Baltinglass chuckled. "The Mermaid's Boot has been the place to buy a berth in the bilges ever since I was a boy, and for many years before that. Anyone who's running a sideline in stowaways on the *Albatross* will be in here before long, looking for a last few coins in his pocket. All we have to do is sit back and enjoy our breakfast."

As if on cue the barman appeared carrying three

plates of grease in which limp morsels of breakfast swam. A moment later he returned with a pot of tea and some chipped mugs. They had just started eating when the inn door burst open and a man with a graying beard and round spectacles entered like a dapper whirlwind, wearing an immaculate blue uniform and an officer's cap.

"Maurice, Maurice," he piped, clapping his hands cheerfully and addressing the barman as though he were a long-lost friend. "A ball of malt, please, no ice." He surveyed the occupants of the bar with a beaming smile. "Gentlemen, good morning!" he said. "A bit foggy, but it's lifting fast. Just the day for an unimaginable adventure, I'd imagine." His eyes lit on Baltinglass and his two companions, sitting in a dim corner under a suspended fishing net full of crabs, and he gave a gasp of delight. He fairly pirouetted across the worn floorboards toward them, coming to rest by the bench where Miles and Little sat staring at him with curiosity.

"May I?" he asked, indicating the end of the bench with a sweeping gesture. Miles scooted along the bench to make room for the neat man and his enormous enthusiasm. "Well, well!" said the stranger in a loud stage whisper. "Baltinglass of Araby, isn't it? You've become a legend since we last met. This is indeed a pleasure."

Miles looked at Baltinglass in surprise. The old man put down his knife and fork and dabbed his wrinkled lips with a napkin. He frowned, and the other man beamed at him patiently. "Sounds like Barrett," said Baltinglass at last. "The cabin boy on the *Admiral Tench.*"

"Well remembered," said the stranger, clapping his hands again. "First Officer Barrett of the good ship *Sunfish*, as I am now."

"The *Sunfish?*" said Baltinglass. "Never heard of her! She a new ship?"

"New, and not new," said First Officer Barrett with a conspiratorial wink. "She's been recommissioned. Just about to embark on her maiden voyage in the capable hands of Captain Tripoli and my good self. We leave for the port of Al Bab as soon as the fog lifts."

"For Al Bab?" said Miles in surprise. "But we heard the *Albatross* was the only ship sailing there for days."

"And you heard right!" said First Officer Barrett, pinching a rasher from Miles's plate with a chuckle. "The *Sunfish* will not be *sailing* to Al Bab; she will be *flying* there. And there's just one cabin left to fill! Think of it, Baltinglass, setting out to explore the uncharted reaches of the sky." He turned to Miles and Little, his face glowing. "Picture yourself, young man, climbing a hundred times higher than the tallest tree! And you, little girl, flying like a bird among the clouds! Can you even imagine such a thrill?"

CHAPTER EIGHT
A HULLABALOO

First Officer Barrett, sea-starched and breeze-polished, drew from his pocket a dog-eared postcard and placed it carefully on the table. "Isn't she a sight to behold?" he said. Miles and Little leaned in and examined the photograph. It showed a long balloon like a fat cigar, with fins at one end and an enormous propeller mounted on either side. The wooden hull of a small ship was suspended from the underside of the balloon by a web of ropes and cables, and the whole contraption floated above a field, moored to a stake in the ground. A number of figures in black and white gazed up at the airship. Some of them were people in their best evening dress. The rest were cows.

"A ship that flies?" said Baltinglass with a snort. "We'll stick to the deep blue sea, thank you, Mr. Barrett."

"It's a sort of giant balloon," said Miles, looking up from the photograph, "with the ship suspended underneath it."

"I was rather hoping you would join us, Mr. Baltinglass," said Barrett. "To be perfectly frank, Captain Tripoli has entered into a bet with Captain Savage of the *Albatross*. Captain Savage boldly claimed that he could reach Al Bab a full day ahead of us, and there is a large stake riding on the wager, not to mention the pride of both men."

"And what does that have to do with us?" demanded Baltinglass of Araby.

"It's a condition of the bet that both ships can set sail as soon as they have a full complement of paying passengers aboard. Captain Savage sold his last two tickets this morning and can leave as soon as visibility allows, but we are still three passengers short."

"She's beautiful!" said Little, who was still staring at the picture and had heard nothing of wagers and tickets.

Miles looked at her. Her eyes were shining, and

he could almost see the clouds in the photograph billowing beneath her gaze. She looked up at him, and he forgot Baltinglass of Araby's skepticism and his own misgivings at once. "There are three berths left?" he said.

First Officer Barrett laughed with delight. "Not if you have your way, I suspect. Three bunks for the voyage, and three meals a day, all for the knockdown price of twenty-four shillings a head, and half-price for the under-sevens."

Miles's face fell. He had not even thought about how they would pay for their passage, and . . . let me see . . . twenty-four plus twenty-four plus half of . . . forty-eight . . . seventy . . . no, sixty shillings seemed like a lot of money. "We'd love to fly, but it sounds very expensive," he said doubtfully.

"The money's not a problem!" said Baltinglass. "I'm not short of a few sovereigns, but you won't catch me dangling from a bag of air in a wooden box. If we were meant to go sailing through the sky why would nature have bothered filling the seas with perfectly good water?"

"Indeed, you're probably right," said First Officer Barrett with a twinkle in his eye. "The skies can be a daunting challenge, even for a much younger man. Hundred-mile-an-hour winds, lethal ice crystals, storms that make a sea squall look like a bubble bath. A man of your towering reputation has no further need to prove himself, and a gentle sea cruise would probably suit you much better."

Baltinglass of Araby stiffened in his seat, and his bristly chin extended itself in Barrett's direction. "What do you mean by that?" he demanded. "I've been struck twice by lightning, young pup, and I still have all that energy fizzing and popping inside me. I'll still be off gallivanting when you're drooling in your rocking chair. Gentle cruise, my backside! Stop your flimflamming, man, and sign us up!"

Miles looked at Little and grinned. He felt pleased, but strangely tired. Little squeezed his hand, but the smile on her face suddenly froze, and she turned quickly and glanced over her shoulder. The door had swung open again, and two figures stepped into the bar. They wore long duffel coats, and their feet made no sound on the floorboards. Miles could make out the pale features of one of the figures, even in the shadow of his hood. It was Silverpoint. The other figure was indistinct, and Miles felt his eyes grow heavy as he tried to see more clearly. He became aware that Little was gripping his hand tightly and kicking him hard on the shin. "Wake up, Miles. Stay awake," she whispered.

First Officer Barrett looked up from the tickets on which he was carefully inscribing their names. "Too many late nights, young man?" He beamed. "You can sleep as much as you like on board, though it would be a shame to miss—"

Miles interrupted him with enormous effort. He knew that the Sleep Angel had come for them, and he would have to think fast, but the fog that was dispersing outside the window seemed to be regrouping inside his head. "There's a problem with the money," he said, kicking Baltinglass under the table in turn. The explorer raised his eyebrows, but Miles carried on before he could speak. "You see those two men who just came in?" he said to First Officer Barrett.

Barrett looked over his shoulder and stared at Silverpoint and his shadowy companion with friendly puzzlement. "Indeed I do, but . . . ?"

"There's no time to explain," said Miles. "They think that we owe them all the money we have, and they won't take no for an answer."

"But that won't do at all!" said Barrett anxiously. "The captain's wager . . ."

"Exactly," said Miles.

"It's all a big misunderstanding," said Little, who had grasped Miles's plan immediately. "Why don't you go over and distract them for a moment while we slip out quietly?"

"And we'll meet you at the *Sunfish*," completed Miles, fighting back a massive yawn.

The dapper officer's face took on a mischievous look, and he winked at Miles. "Leave it to me," he said, tilting his cap and sliding off the end of the bench. "She's moored in the long field just beyond the windmill."

"What's the hullabaloo?" asked Baltinglass, as First Officer Barrett danced across the room toward Silverpoint and the Sleep Angel.

"This is my expedition, right?" said Miles. He was too tired to explain.

"Certainly," said Baltinglass of Araby.

"Then we leave at once," he said. "Where's the back door?"

"There isn't one," said Baltinglass, tightening his grip on his cane, "but there's a window behind us." He reached up and fumbled the catch open.

"You first," said Miles to Little. He picked her up quickly and posted her through the open window like a parcel of dandelion seeds. The irrepressible First Officer Barrett was dancing a jig around the two angels, waving his arms in the air and delivering a barrage of nonsense on a hurricane of enthusiasm.

"You next," said Miles, turning to give Baltinglass a leg up, but the old man was already disappearing through the window with a flash of bleached shins and a few loudly whispered curses. Miles scrambled out after him without looking back, and found himself landing headfirst on the well-sprung front seat of Baltinglass's vintage car.

"Now you know," panted the old man, handing him the keys from the other end of the seat, "why you should always park underneath a window, Master Miles."

Morrigan started with a roar, and they took off from the yard in a spray of gravel, almost colliding with the house opposite before Miles managed to straighten the wheel.

"That's the spirit, boy," shouted Baltinglass, obviously glad to be done with whispering for the moment.

They drove at speed toward the windmill on the hill. There was a knot in Miles's stomach, a mixture of fear and excitement, and from Little's shouts of "Faster!" from the backseat he could tell she felt the same. The sun had dispersed the fog, leaving shreds of bog-cotton mist snagged on the thornbushes, and ahead of them the airship hung silently in the sky like a fat, unfathomable future.

Miles pulled in by the mill, where a number of other cars were already parked. A gangly teenager appeared from nowhere, wearing a battered cap. "It's sixpence to park," he said, peering hopefully into Miles's goggles.

Baltinglass of Araby leaped from the car. "How old are you, boy?" he shouted.

"I'll be eighteen in February," said the boy.

Baltinglass pulled a gold coin from his pocket. "Ever seen one of these?"

The boy's jaw dropped. "Not often," he said.

"You'll see three more of them if you look after this car until we get back," said Baltinglass. "We may be gone some time, so you'd better take her out for a spin now and then."

"You want me to *drive* the car?" asked the boy, who could hardly believe his ears.

"That's what she needs," said Baltinglass, "and you might find yourself more popular with the ladies in the bargain." He sent the coin spinning toward the teenager with a flick of his thumb, and called to Miles. "Master Miles, let's board that contraption before I change my mind, eh?"

Miles pulled the duffel bag from the back of the car and heaved it over his shoulder. It swung around and nearly capsized him, but he felt that as head of the expedition he should be able to carry the kit. He hefted the bag to balance it better, feeling something sharp poking into his back, and set off across the field. Little took Baltinglass's arm and together they half ran, half stumbled past knots of spectators toward the airship's mooring, where a sturdy rope ladder hung from the hull to the ground.

"I hope First Officer Barrett makes it back all right," said Little.

"He's a wily devil, that one," said Baltinglass. "He'll come back with their pocket watches and their gold teeth, whoever they are."

Above them the *Sunfish* seemed to fill the sky. A muscular airman stood at the bottom of the rope ladder, and he took the duffel bag from Miles as though it weighed no more than a coconut. "Tickets?" he said.

At that moment there was a high-pitched shout from the edge of the field, and First Officer Barrett careered into view on a bicycle, his glasses askew and his legs out straight to avoid the madly spinning pedals. "Weigh anchor, able Airman Calloway!" he shouted gleefully. "Embark those passengers at once. That's an order!"

"Aye-aye," shouted Airman Calloway. He picked

Little up under one arm, and with the duffel bag over his shoulder he fairly ran up the rope ladder and disappeared into a square hatch in the hull.

"Rope ladder," said Miles to Baltinglass, placing the old man's hand on a rung. "After you."

At the top of the ladder Miles felt the ropes jerk as First Officer Barrett leaped from the bicycle and began to climb up behind him. "Away!" the dapper man shouted. "Weigh anchor. All hands on deck. Full steam ahead!"

Strong hands reached from the door in the hull and grabbed Miles by the arms. He looked over his shoulder at the last moment, and a shock of giddiness swept through him. He could see no sign of pursuit, but the ground was falling away at an alarming rate. First Officer Barrett swung from the ladder's end like a trapeze artist, waving and shouting, "Arrivederci!" to the dwindling spectators below. Beyond him tumbled the whitewashed houses of the port of Fuera, and out in the bay the *Albatross* rode the sapphire waters under bellying sails, bound for Al Bab with a brisk crosswind and a good head start.

CHAPTER NINE
THE *SUNFISH*

The airship *Sunfish*, reborn and airborne, moved ponderously through scattered clouds, a helium-fed hippopotamus among inflatable sheep. The setting sun bathed the airship in orange light, and the purple shadows of the small clouds slid along her flanks and fluttered briefly on the blades of her propellers. In addition to a crew of seven there were some forty passengers in her wooden belly. They had spent the day lounging in the stateroom, or marveling at the ever-changing skyscape from the observation deck. The deck was enclosed with large windows to protect the passengers from the hundred-mile-an-hour winds and lethal ice crystals that First Officer Barrett had so enthusiastically described.

In the small cabin Baltinglass of Araby straightened his woolly cap as though it were a top hat, and rummaged in the duffel bag for his tobacco pouch. "I'm off to the stateroom for a smoke of my pipe," he said. "I take it we gave those map-stealing reprobates the slip in that tavern with the help of young Barrett's performance."

Miles glanced at Little. "It wasn't them we were escaping from," he said. "They've sailed on board the *Albatross*."

"So you've got more enemies," said Baltinglass approvingly. "A man can't have too many enemies. Keeps you on your toes." He waved his cane around dangerously. "I'm still a spectacular menace with a swordstick, as you may have noticed."

"I don't think a sword would be much good against this particular pair," said Miles. He did not want to mention that one of them was Silverpoint.

Baltinglass grunted. "I'll be happy to put that to the test if we come across them again, Master Miles. You just let me know when you spot them."

"Did you mean what you said to First Officer

Barrett?" asked Little. "About having all that lightning still popping inside you?"

"Night and day, Little," said Baltinglass. He paused with his hand on the door handle. "To tell you the truth, I sometimes wish I could just let it off in a big blast and get some peace. Can't really do that in polite company, though, eh?" He chuckled and stepped out into the corridor, closing the door behind him.

Miles knelt beside Little on the bench seat of their cabin, and for a while they watched the clouds pass by, their noses pressed to the glass of the twin portholes. "Can you see your people?" asked Miles, concentrating hard on a cloud whose shape reminded him of a nautilus shell.

"It depends on whether I'm looking for them," said Little.

"Are you?"

"I'm just looking at the clouds," said Little, keeping her nose pressed to the window. There was silence except for the creaking of the hull and the distant sound of the big propellers beating a soft rhythm through the winter sky.

"That was Bluehart with Silverpoint, wasn't it?" said Miles after a while. Little nodded.

"Do you think they'll find us here?" asked Miles.

Little turned her back on the porthole and sat down on the bench with a sigh. "We might have lost them for a short while, especially if Silverpoint is helping to slow things down like he promised, but I think they'll catch up with us soon."

"We've managed to keep one step ahead of Bluehart for a long time now," said Miles hopefully.

"You had the Tiger's Egg then," said Little. "The Egg is deliberately made to hide itself from the Sleep Angels, and it extends that protection to those close to it. That's why it can help to prolong your life. Now that you don't have it anymore you'll be easier to find."

Miles felt an echo of the leaden sleep that Bluehart brought, and with it came a flush of anger. "Who does he think he is?" he said sharply.

Little looked at him with a shocked expression. "Bluehart is a Sleep Angel. That's his purpose in the order of things."

"You sound like Silverpoint!" said Miles. He had felt the comment rising up through his anger and was unable to stop it leaving his mouth, and he felt bad about it straightaway. Little looked down at her feet.

"I just meant . . . ," said Miles, searching for the words. "What I mean is, how can they pass judgment on me for owning the Tiger's Egg when it was passed on to me as a baby? I didn't even know it existed until a few months ago."

"The Council has known about it for a long time," said Little, "and they've decided that whoever carries the Tiger's Egg should lose his life."

"You don't have it," said Miles, "but they've condemned you too."

"Some of the angels feel I'm just as guilty because I've been with you while you used it. That's why Silverpoint wants to convince them that I'm just trying to get it back."

"Nobody's asked our opinion!" said Miles. "Any proper court gives the accused the right to speak. Remember when Lady Partridge was charged with being a menace to public health because of all her cats?"

Little's musical laugh chimed through the cabin. "I remember," she said. "After her speech the judge apologized, and that pointy-nosed man, the . . ."

"The prosecutor," said Miles.

"That's right, he was fined a hundred tins of cat food for wasting the court's time." A cloud crossed her face. "The Council of Light doesn't quite work the same way."

"I still think I should have the chance to defend myself," said Miles. He looked out of the porthole at the strange landscape of the air. High above the *Sunfish* the sky was striped with thin lines of salmon pink, while below them a smooth cloud was passing slowly aft. It looked almost within reach, as though he could leap from the porthole and bounce on its soft white surface, and he had to remind himself that he would fall straight through and plummet to his death. He sighed. "It's not like it's possible, is it?"

Little said nothing in reply. She frowned and crossed her arms, and for a long time she seemed to be staring through the closed door of the cabin. Miles was about to suggest going in search of Baltinglass when Little spoke. "There might be a way," she said. "But it would be dangerous."

"More dangerous than being condemned to death?" said Miles.

Little smiled. "I suppose we have nothing to lose. I'm not exactly in their good books either."

"How can we get them to meet us?" asked Miles. He pictured the stateroom of the ship filled with bewigged angels, glowing faintly in the dead of night, while he swayed their cold minds with the clarity of his argument.

"We can't summon the Council!" said Little, looking incredulous. "We'll have to go to them, and we'll have to find a way to make them believe you're someone else. If they realize who you are, it's all over."

"But how can we get there?" asked Miles. "You gave up your wings, and I never had any in the first place. The only way we can fly is inside an airship."

Little pushed her hair behind her ears and took a deep breath. It was the kind of deep breath she always took when she was about to try to explain something that didn't want to be explained, and Miles knew he would need all his concentration for what was coming next.

"The Realm is out there," she began, nodding at the portholes, "but it's not *exactly* out there. It exists between the light."

"And what?" asked Miles.

"And what what?" said Little.

"You said it exists between the light. Between the light and what?"

"Just between the light," said Little. She bit her lip for a moment. "Think of the tiger," she said.

"Is that where he exists?" asked Miles. "Is that

how he comes and goes like he does?"

"I suppose so, but that's not what I meant. Think of the tiger's pelt. He's orange with black stripes. But what happens to the orange *behind* the black stripes?"

"There is no orange behind the black. There's orange in some places, and black in others," said Miles a little uncertainly. At one time he would have said this with patient conviction, but he was beginning to learn that Little's ideas often made as much sense or more than the ones he had learned from Lady Partridge's encyclopedias.

"That's what people think," said Little. "And it's the same with the Realm. No one ever considers that there might be anything *between* the light, and that's why few people ever see it. Except when they're asleep, of course."

"You mean dreaming? Is the Realm like a dream?"

"A dream is like the Realm," said Little.

"But my dreams are usually just weird," said Miles.

Little laughed again. The sun came out from behind a cloud and shone straight through the portholes, beaming twin circles onto the cabin wall.

"So is the Realm," she said. "Did you think it would be all shiny and twinkly?" She leaned forward and fixed Miles with her clear blue eyes. "If I do take you there, you had better be ready for anything," she said.

CHAPTER TEN

TRAINING WINGS

Miles Wednesday, sky-sailing and sleep-sentenced, sat on the bench in his cabin and tried to fit the broad sweep of Little's world into his head. He had always taken the simple view that the Song Angel had come from the sky somewhere, a place that was just not easy for earthbound people like himself to reach. Little's description, however, was a bit more complicated, and he suspected that she was putting it simply for him at that.

"How . . . ," he began, chasing his question around his own mind to try to get a grip on it. "How can you visit the Realm? Aren't you banished for using your real name?"

"I was never banished exactly," said Little. "I became tied to the body I had adopted on Earth."

"But without the wings," said Miles.

"The wings are part of what people expect angels to have," said Little. "Once I chose to bind myself to Earth, I became an ordinary girl, and the wings no longer . . . fit."

"Then how can you bring me to the Realm?" asked Miles. He was beginning to feel a little nervous at the prospect of arguing for his life in front of the mysterious Council. What would they look like? What exactly would he say? Perhaps running and hiding was the better option, though he knew he could not do that forever. He reached into his pocket and gently squeezed Tangerine, but the squeeze was not returned as he had half expected, and he was left with a hollow feeling.

"I can still visit when I'm sleeping," said Little.

"Do you go back often?" asked Miles. It had never occurred to him that she might have any way of returning to the life she had left behind, and he was surprised to feel a twinge of jealousy.

Little shook her head. "Hardly ever," she said, "but I can if I need to. I can meet you there, but first you'll have to find your own way into the Realm."

"How do I do that?"

Little scratched her head. "It's hard to explain," she said. "Once you're asleep you've got to look for the light, and . . . get *between* it."

Miles looked at her blankly.

"Look," said Little, "all you need to do . . ." She sighed and stopped speaking for a moment, tracing spirals on the palm of her hand. Suddenly she smiled and looked up. "Actually, it's not that complicated," she said. "There's a lever that will open your way into the Realm."

"A lever?" said Miles doubtfully.

Little nodded. "A big brass lever," she said. "You just need to look for the lever and pull it, and in you go."

"Why didn't you say that already?" asked Miles.

Little shrugged. "I forgot," she said.

"Where is the lever? Where do I find it?" asked Miles. It seemed a highly unlikely idea to him, and not at all like the solutions Little usually came up with.

"I can't do everything for you, Miles," she said with a grin. "You'll just have to look for it yourself."

There was a tapping at the door, and Baltinglass came in. "Are you the traveling companions of Baltinglass of Araby, by any chance?" he said.

"It's us," said Miles.

"That's a relief," said Baltinglass. "I forgot to count the doors on the way out, and this is the third cabin I've tried. The first one had three ladies in it. They must have been in their nighties, because they were mighty relieved to discover I was blind. The one next door is an odd one. Nobody answered me, but I'd swear there was someone in there. I could smell a cigar burning. And pickled socks of some kind."

He felt his way to the bottom bunk and sat down with a creak. "I'll sleep here belowdecks," he said. "These old bones are not as tough as they used to be, and if I fell out of the top bunk I'd shatter like a chandelier. Good night, Master Miles. Night, Little." He threw his head down on the pillow, and within minutes his quiet snoring was added to the sigh of the wind in the rigging.

Miles climbed into the middle bunk and lay down on the hard mattress. He was eager for sleep to come, but he had never felt so completely awake. The more excited he became about the prospect of visiting another world in his dreams, the more his eyes felt like they were glued open. He forced them to close, and listened to the *wup, wup, wup* of the great propellers, driving onward through the darkening night. He pictured the *Albatross*, sailing far below them with Doctor Tau-Tau on board, the

Tiger's Egg in his pocket, and the Great Cortado scheming and sniggering in a lamplit cabin.

Miles opened his eyes and saw to his surprise that the bunk above him was receding into the far distance, and the space in which he slept was rapidly growing to the size of a cathedral. There seemed to be small animals with beady eyes huddling at the end of the bed, just beyond the reach of his toes. They were whispering together, all sharp ears and pointed noses, and casting furtive glances in his direction. He opened his mouth to say, "Shoo," but his voice would not work. He looked around for a bat or a broom handle with which to chase them away. There was something sticking up at the side of the bed. It was a brass lever of some kind, like Morrigan's long handbrake. He was sure it hadn't been there when he went to bed. He grasped the lever tightly and pulled, and without warning the mattress opened beneath him like a trapdoor and dumped him out into the night sky.

He fell through the cold air toward a domed cumulus cloud, his fluttering bedsheets wrapped around him and the beat of the airship's engines fading rapidly into the night. He landed in the cloud before he had time to think. It was like falling into an invisible web of very stretchy elastic, if you can imagine such a thing. His fall had been broken, but he sank rapidly until only his head was free of the clammy whiteness. With a great effort he paddled and pulled himself upward until he was more or less sitting on top of the cloud, and looked around him. The *Sunfish* had receded to the size of a baked bean. Above him the sky was strewn with stars, and all around him a fleet of towering clouds sailed purposefully, much larger now than they had looked from the porthole of the airship. He looked down and found he had sunk back into the cloud up to his chest. He was still entangled in his bedsheets, and struggling back to the surface was difficult and surprisingly tiring. He was not sure he could keep this up for long. He reached in his pocket for Tangerine before realizing that he had left his overcoat in the cabin of the *Sunfish*. The cloud began to suck him in again. He had never felt so alone.

Something hit him on the shoulder, and disappeared before he could see what it was. He turned around quickly, but there was nobody there. Another small object bounced off his chest, and this time he caught it in his hand. It was a pinecone. It did not seem strange to him that pinecones should be flying about in the night sky. He was sure someone had thrown them at him once before. Who had it been?

Not Lady Partridge. Not Baltinglass, or Tau-Tau, or the Bolsillo brothers. "Little!" he said aloud.

And there she was, sitting beside him, a look of exasperation on her face. "Finally!" she said. "You were supposed to look for me as soon as you got here."

"I forgot," said Miles. He had sunk almost up to his neck again.

"What are you *doing* down there?" said Little, who was sitting on top of the cloud without difficulty.

"I keep sinking," said Miles. "I'm surprised a cloud can hold me up at all. They're just made of . . ."

"They're made of cloud," said Little sharply.

". . . water vapor," finished Miles.

Little opened her mouth to speak, but then she seemed to shoot upward and disappear all at once, and Miles was falling through clammy grayness. He felt dampness rushing up at him, then he was in clear air again and the cloud was above him and shrinking fast. Below him the inky ocean stretched to the horizon, tiny wrinkles marching across it. The wrinkles were getting bigger. He was falling fast, and now that he had left the cloud an icy wind shrieked in his ears. He listened for the *whump* of Silverpoint's wings coming to save him, but he knew that the Storm Angel was otherwise occupied.

"Silverpoint's not here," said Little's voice beside him. She was falling too, her silver-blond hair streaming upward. "And I can't lift you. You need wings, Miles."

"I can't just grow wings!" shouted Miles.

"You can't just sit on clouds either, but you managed that at first. *Think* yourself some wings, Miles, or you will die."

A shot of fear ran through Miles. He had never heard Little speak like this before. He closed his eyes, fighting to control his panic, and tried to imagine wings sprouting from his shoulders. If you have ever found yourself plummeting through icy skies and trying to grow a pair of wings at the same time you will understand how impossible a task that was, even in a dream. He opened his eyes again. The water rushed up toward him, and when he thought of the shock of the cold and the prospect of drowning he stretched his two arms out in desperation. The bedsheets flapped crisply behind him, and his headlong dive turned into a sort of deep swoop. He was falling still, but not as quickly, and instinctively he angled his outstretched hands upward. He pulled into a horizontal glide in the nick of time, close enough to feel the spray that blew off the crests of the waves. A panicky laughter rattled around his chest.

"That's better!" said Little, flying beside him. "Now you need to rise again."

Miles flapped his arms, but it only made him lose height. "They're not really wings," he said nervously. "I'm just gliding."

"Just make yourself lighter for now," said Little. "We'll work on the wings later."

An updraft lifted Miles as she spoke, making him feel suddenly buoyant. Why hadn't he thought of that before? He allowed the weight to drain from his body, just as it had done when he had inadvertently healed Dulac Zipplethorpe after the boy was kicked by a horse, or when he had cured the pain in Baltinglass of Araby's leg. At the time he had been afraid he would be carried off by the breeze, but now that was exactly what he wanted. A gust of wind caught beneath his makeshift wings and he soared upward. Little kept pace, and suddenly Miles noticed her wings. They looked exactly the same as they used to, pearly white and fine-feathered, and breathtakingly beautiful. She was laughing now, and her voice seemed to twist the shrieking of the wind into a wild, headlong music. He could feel the thrill of flight race through his body like an electrical charge, and he laughed too. "Up!" called Little. "Higher, Miles!"

"Where are we going?" called Miles. His billowing bedsheets seemed clumsy by comparison with Little's exquisite wings, and his arms had begun to ache all of a sudden. He felt the weight pour back into his body, and he began to lose altitude fast. A look of alarm came over Little's face, and he thought he glimpsed more figures beyond her, indistinct shadows that were growing closer as they flew alongside. She was no longer laughing.

"Close your eyes!" she said urgently.

"Why?" asked Miles, closing them anyway.

"You're not falling anymore, are you?" came Little's voice.

She was right. The wind seemed to solidify into something soft beneath him, and the plummeting sensation faded away. "Does this mean I'm flying?" said Miles excitedly.

"No," said Little. "It means you're in bed."

Miles opened his eyes. The rhythm of his bedsheet wings had turned into the *wup, wup, wup* of great propellers, and he found himself lying in his bunk aboard the *Sunfish*, entangled in his bedclothes.

Little's head hung over the edge of the bunk above, her skin glowing as faintly as a distant star, her wings no longer anywhere to be seen. "You okay?" she whispered.

"Why did we leave?" asked Miles, struggling to disentangle himself from the sheets. "I thought we were going to see the Council."

Little smiled. "You're not ready for that."

"I learned to fly, sort of," said Miles, who was feeling secretly proud of himself. "Is that not good?"

"You learned to stop falling," said Little. "You'll need a lot more than that to survive in the Realm. We haven't even taken the training wings off yet, Miles."

CHAPTER ELEVEN

CAPTAIN TRIPOLI

Baltinglass of Araby, hot-coffeed, fried-egged and streaky-baconed, sat among the ruins of his breakfast in the stateroom of the *Sunfish*, regaling the other passengers with tales of daring between the puffs of smoke that belched from his pipe. "There I was," he said, "face to face with a black mamba, hiding in a hollow log while the privateers sharpened their cutlasses and argued over whether it would be more fun to flay me or roast me."

The blind explorer had a rapt audience, but Miles was sure he had heard this story before. He seemed to know what Baltinglass was about to say a moment before he said it, which was strange, as the old man's stories contained a liberal dose of fiction and were seldom told the same way twice. Miles had an uneasy feeling that there was something he had forgotten to do, and it made him restless. He suddenly remembered his mother's diary, and the fact that he hadn't had a chance to read any more of it since leaving Partridge Manor.

"I think I'll go back to the cabin," he said.

"I'll come with you," said Little.

They took their leave of Baltinglass, who was just then being smoked out of the log by pugnacious pirates, and made their way along the narrow corridor that ran the length of the hull. The curve of the ship made the corridor wider at the top than at the bottom. Stout ribs of oak stood at intervals along the outer hull, alternating with brass portholes that framed circular cloudscapes of spectacular beauty.

As they approached the door of their cabin Miles's anxious feeling became sharper, and he was not entirely surprised to see the door standing ajar and the wood splintered around the lock. He put his hand out to stop Little, and her blue eyes widened as she saw the broken door. Miles crept forward. With Tau-Tau and the Great Cortado far below them on the *Albatross* he had thought they were relatively safe, at least for the moment. It seemed he was wrong. He pushed the door open slowly.

Whoever had been in their cabin was gone, but the duffel bag had been upended on the lower bunk, and the floor was strewn with clothes. "Who could have done this?" said Little. "Our clothes are all over the place."

"That was us," Miles reminded her, "but someone's been through the duffel bag too. We'd better check whether anything is missing." He reached instinctively for Tangerine, but the bear lay quietly in his trouser pocket, just where he had put him when he got dressed that morning.

Little began to gather up the scattered contents of the duffel bag, and Miles suddenly knew exactly what had been taken. He picked up the overcoat that slouched in a corner and put his hand in the inside pocket. Celeste's diary was gone.

A chill crept through him. "It must be Cortado, or Doctor Tau-Tau."

"But they're on the *Albatross*," said Little.

"My mother's diary is gone," said Miles. "Who else would even know about that? They must have an accomplice on the *Sunfish*—a passenger, or even one of the crew." He thought for a moment. "Either way the diary must still be on board."

"But it could be anywhere," said Little, packing

Baltinglass's eclectic travel kit back into the duffel bag. "How will we find it?"

"First I'm going to find the captain and tell him there's a burglar on his ship. You can go to the stateroom and get Baltinglass. The sight of him waving his swordstick around might be enough in itself to make the thief reconsider."

Miles had no idea where the captain might be found, so he made his way toward the stern of the *Sunfish*, where he knew the crew had their cabins. Turning a corner he almost bumped into First Officer Barrett.

"Mr. Wednesday!" Barrett beamed. "You have the look of a man on a mission. Can I be of assistance?"

"I'm looking for the captain," said Miles.

"A ship's captain is a busy man," said Barrett. Standing still did not come naturally to the first officer, and after almost five seconds in the same spot he was beginning to hop from foot to foot.

"It's very important," said Miles.

"In that case," said Barrett, his feet easily getting the better of his caution, "I'll conduct you without delay to the poop deck. Which," he added with a high-pitched laugh, "is not nearly as rude as it sounds. Follow me."

He turned and sped along the corridor, with Miles trotting behind to keep up.

"Poop, from the Latin *puppis*," called Barrett over his shoulder, "meaning a raised deck in the stern of a ship. The real pooping is done in the heads, which are in the front, otherwise known as the bow. Am I going too fast for you?"

Miles was not sure if Barrett was referring to the speed of his explanation or his progress toward the stern. "I can keep up," he said.

"No further need," said First Officer Barrett. "We've arrived."

He ran up the wooden ladder that led to the poop deck and opened a hatch at the top. Daylight streamed in, bringing a blast of cold air with it. Barrett disappeared through the hatch, and Miles heard himself announced. "A young man to see you, Captain. He says he has urgent business." Miles took a deep breath, and without waiting for an invitation he followed the first officer up the ladder.

The poop deck was as spectacular a vantage point as you are ever likely to see. It was open to the wind, as bright and cold as an iceberg. Above it the huge belly of the helium balloon hung like a gray ceiling, and on all sides a patched snowscape of cloud could be seen, stretching away to the distant horizon.

Captain Tripoli stood in the center of the poop deck, a white clay pipe clamped between his teeth. He was tall and straight, with angular features and skin so blue-black that he might have been mined from a seam of coal. He seemed unaffected by the crisp gale that blew across the deck, and looked Miles up and down with a stern expression. It was as much as Miles could do to avoid being blown to the guardrail, but he was careful to stand his ground.

"Passengers are not allowed on the poop deck," said Captain Tripoli, looking at his first officer disapprovingly. His voice was deep, like a cello, and rather than whipping it away the wind seemed obliged to blow around it.

"It's important," said Miles. "Our cabin has been burgled."

The captain raised one eyebrow. "Then we'd better make an exception," he said.

"This boy is a traveling companion of Baltinglass of Araby," piped up First Officer Barrett.

"Indeed?" said the captain, looking at Miles with renewed interest. "You may go about your duties; thank you, Mr. Barrett."

The first officer disappeared down the ladder, slamming the hatch behind him, and leaving Miles alone on the poop deck with Captain Tripoli and the whistling sky of a fine winter's morning. The captain consulted the instruments that were set into a waist-high wooden column by his side; then he looked up again at Miles. "Let's start with your name," he said.

"I'm Miles Wednesday," said Miles.

"An unusual surname," said Captain Tripoli.

"My father's name was Fumble, and my mother's was Mahnoosh," said Miles, "but I grew up in an orphanage. At least until I escaped."

"Then we have something in common," said the captain. "I also grew up without parents, although my escape was from an uncle in whose charge I had been left."

Miles was surprised. He had always assumed that to have family of any kind would be better than being raised by strangers. "Why did you have to escape your uncle?" he asked.

"I learned that he planned to sell me as a camel jockey," said the captain. "I was only seven years old, but I knew what a harsh fate that would be." He frowned and changed the subject abruptly. "What was stolen from your cabin?" he asked.

"A diary that belonged to my mother," said Miles.

"What else?"

"Nothing else," said Miles. "It's the only thing of hers that I have."

"It's not easy to get away with a shipboard burglary," mused Captain Tripoli. "Why would anyone take such a risk?"

Miles said nothing. He did not want to have to explain what the diary contained, or why it might be of interest to anyone else.

"You're not obliged to give me all the details," said the captain. "A description of the diary will suffice for the moment. I'll have my first officer conduct an investigation."

Miles took his leave of the captain after describing the diary to him. His ears stung from the cold, but he was sorry to leave the spectacular skyscape that the poop deck afforded, and as he walked back along the corridor he made up his mind to find another excuse to visit the captain before their journey ended. He was turning this problem over in his head when a foot suddenly emerged from an open cabin door, and as he tripped over it he felt a jarring blow on the back of his skull that made his teeth knock together and sent him spiraling away into emptiness.

Varippuli the tiger, soul-snagged and shanghaied, stood waiting in a room where frost bristled on the

walls and his breath billowed in clouds of steam.
He seemed unaware of his surroundings, and stared
through the walls of the frozen waiting room at
some half-remembered landscape beyond. Miles
found himself standing to the tiger's left, almost
close enough to reach out and touch him. The tiger
gave no sign of having seen him, and Miles stayed as
still as a mouse. Varippuli was no longer his friend
and ally, and he did not want to draw attention to
himself.

He stared at the tiger's heaving ribs, vaguely aware
that he was dreaming, but not daring to blink nonetheless. The wavy black bars of the animal's stripes
seemed to stand out from the gold of his pelt, and
the harder Miles stared the more the gold seemed
to glow. Soon he was enveloped by glaring sunlight
and could not see the black at all. He turned his eyes
away from the light and found himself gliding alongside the patched gray flanks of the *Sunfish*, almost
weightless and lifted by the same stiff breeze that
had blown across the poop deck minutes before.

Through a gap in the clouds below him he could
see the *Albatross* crawling like a beetle on the cor-
rugated blue of the sea. The soaring sensation was
exhilarating, and he tilted himself, cautiously at
first, to test his control. He spotted a cannon poking

from the hull of the *Sunfish*, and he swooped down past the network of cables and ropes by which the hull was suspended to take a closer look.

It was not a cannon at all, he realized as he got closer, but a head. It looked as if someone were trying to climb out through a porthole. "That's not very wise," said Miles into the wind. There was something disturbingly familiar about the tousled head, and with a shock he realized what it was. "That's *my* head!" he said aloud. The head was lolling and the eyes closed, and he could see shoulders now, and his arms pinned to his sides by the narrow hole. There was no doubt about it: He was being posted out through a porthole, just as he had posted Little through the back window of the Mermaid's Boot, except that the only thing waiting to break his fall was the freezing ocean a thousand feet below.

CHAPTER TWELVE

A PRACTICAL JOKE

Miles Wednesday, soul-soaring and billy-jacked, swooped down closer to his unconscious body. It was vital that he return to himself at once so that he could fight back, but he had no idea how to do it. He tried calling on Little for help, but his voice was lost in the wind and she was nowhere to be seen. "She can't hear me when she's awake," he told himself. He reached his inert body and tried to push himself back through the porthole, but he found himself as nebulous as the cloud he had tried to sit on during his first visit to the Realm. His hands plunged straight through his own shoulders. It was a disturbing feeling, and he pulled them out again in a panic.

If you have ever seen iron filings stampeding toward a strong magnet you will have a picture of what happened next. Not a very accurate one, but a picture nonetheless. A strong magnetism exists between a person's body and his soul, and once Miles had touched his unconscious self he was sucked back in like, well, like iron filings stampeding toward a strong magnet.

He was almost sorry when he found himself back inside his own predicament. He was suspended halfway out of a flying ship, and his frozen head throbbed from the blow that had knocked him out. He could not move his arms, and he was about to fall to his death in a body that definitely would not be able to learn to fly on the way down. He could feel strong hands gripping his legs and pushing him slowly out through the narrow porthole. His own hands were almost free now, but once they were it would be too late to use them.

He kicked out desperately with his feet and felt them connect with something solid. The hands loosened their grip on his legs for a moment, then grabbed him again with renewed strength. He kicked again, but their grip was like iron. The hands now seemed to be pulling him back in, and he stopped kicking while he tried to work out this puzzling development. His arms and shoulders were bruised and aching, but at least he was now moving in the right direction.

His legs gave way the moment he was back inside the ship, and he would have fallen to the deck had it not been for First Officer Barrett, who supported him with one hand while closing the porthole with the other. Miles looked around him, shaking uncontrollably, and tried to make sense of the situation. Captain Tripoli stood like a rod of ebony, grasping a shirt collar in each of his strong hands. The shirts in question were occupied by none other than the Great Cortado and Doctor Tau-Tau, the former white-faced with fury, and the latter plum with embarrassment. The captain released his grip (the Great Cortado's feet dropped several inches to the floor), and dusted his hands slowly.

"Mr. Wednesday," he said, "are you all right?"

"I'm a bit shaky," said Miles.

"I'm not surprised," said Captain Tripoli. "Do you know these men?"

"Yes," said Miles. "That one is called Cortado, and

the other man is Doctor Tau-Tau."

"I am the *Great* Cortado," the ringmaster corrected him. He was struggling to master his anger.

"Explain yourself, Mr. Cortado," said the captain icily.

The Great Cortado forced a smile. His regrouping mustache had reached a stage where it resembled one of those extremely bristly caterpillars, and together with the scar and the eye patch it lent his smile a particularly shifty air.

"It was just a bit of high spirits," he said. "A practical joke, if you will. The boy and I go back a long way."

"A practical joke," said Captain Tripoli, "generally involves an element of humor. Had I not intervened when I did, this boy would have fallen to his death. Perhaps you could explain the amusing aspect."

The Great Cortado scowled. "The boy cheeked me," he said. "I was merely teaching him some manners. Perhaps I was a little overzealous, but I had no intention of letting him go."

The captain's arm shot out like a piston and grabbed the collar of Doctor Tau-Tau, who had turned and begun to inch away down the corridor.

"You are not dismissed," said the captain, turning to the fortune-teller. "What's your explanation?"

Doctor Tau-Tau straightened his fez with shaking fingers. "The boy is a notorious troublemaker," he said, avoiding Miles's eye.

"These are the men who stole my mother's diary," said Miles indignantly. "And now they're trying to kill me."

"You see, Captain," said the Great Cortado smoothly, "the boy is a compulsive liar. That's just another of his wild accusations."

The captain turned abruptly to the Great Cortado and fixed him with a hard stare. "Mr. Cortado, this ship is fitted as a pleasure cruiser, and I regret to say that there is no brig. You and your associate will remain locked in your cabin for the rest of this voyage instead, except at dinnertime, when you will join me at my table. Is that clear?"

The Great Cortado and his quasi-mustache bristled with indignation. "You propose to lock us up on the basis of this worthless whippersnapper's whoppers?" he said.

"Try saying that ten times in a row," said First Officer Barrett in a gleeful whisper.

"You are forgetting, Mr. Cortado, that I caught

you red-handed trying to squeeze this boy through a porthole. On this ship my word is law, and you had better obey it without question. You will bring this boy's property to the table this evening, or I will personally see to it that you are locked up for life when we reach Al Bab."

He let go of Doctor Tau-Tau's collar again. "If, however, your behavior is exemplary for the rest of the voyage, I will leave it to the boy whether he wants to press charges. Mr. Barrett, please escort these men to their cabin and take charge of the key. That is all."

"You come with me and I'll fix you a medicinal drink," said the captain, smiling at Miles. He took the boy's arm in a firm grip and guided him toward his cabin in the stern.

The captain's cabin was fastidiously neat. It had three small windows with leaded panes, which sloped outward and gave a spectacular view of the dappled clouds and the ocean far below. There was a polished writing desk spread with a detailed chart, and brass dividers for calculating headings and distances. On the wall were framed certificates and diplomas from the finest naval academies, all bearing the captain's name in ornate script, and a locked glass case containing a pair of dueling pistols with a powder flask and rods.

"Take a seat, Mr. Wednesday," said Captain Tripoli.

Miles sat in a plush red chair while the captain mixed a drink from a small cabinet in the corner. The drink steamed and fizzed slightly. It burned Miles's throat, but his shaking began to subside at once, and warmth spread to his fingertips.

"What makes those men so interested in your mother's diary, I wonder?" said the captain. His jaw was edged by a neatly trimmed beard, Miles noticed, as though he had been outlined with a heavy pencil.

"The diary contains information that may be the key to something else they stole from me," said Miles.

The captain raised one eyebrow. "I'm curious to know why you would choose to sail with men who obviously mean you no good."

"We thought they were aboard the *Albatross*," said Miles.

"Why did you think that?" asked the captain.

"I saw Doctor Tau-Tau speaking to someone on the deck of the *Albatross* the morning we left."

"Indeed?" said Captain Tripoli. He was silent for

a moment; then he leaned across the desk, his long fingers intertwined. "There was a thick fog that morning," he said.

"I'm sure it was him," said Miles. "I don't know anyone else who wears a hat like that."

The captain gave a deep chuckle. "You won't be able to use the fez as a form of identification once we reach Al Bab," he said.

"Can I ask you a question?" said Miles.

"By all means."

"Why did you invite Cortado and Doctor Tau-Tau to dine at your table? I thought that was considered a privilege."

"You are quite right," said Captain Tripoli. "However, a great Chinese general once said, 'Keep your friends close, and your enemies even closer.' It's a notion I've found useful over the years."

Miles thought about this for a moment. "So you can keep an eye on them?"

"Precisely so," said the captain. He got up and walked around the desk, extending his hand to Miles. His handshake was dry and firm. "It's a pleasure to meet you, Mr. Wednesday. I trust you're feeling a bit steadier now."

"I'm fine, thank you," said Miles.

"Capital," said Captain Tripoli, opening the cabin door. "One other thing. It's my pleasure to invite you and your companions to dine at my table also. And in your case," he said with a smile, "I hope you will consider it a privilege."

CHAPTER THIRTEEN
FEUDS AND MISDEMEANORS

Captain Tripoli, dressed, pressed and chisel-sharp, sat at the head of his table and steepled his fingers as the ship's cook, Airman Tang—who doubled as the ship's waiter—spooned couscous and falafel onto his plate. The captain had taken the Chinese general's maxim seriously, seating Doctor Tau-Tau at his right hand and the Great Cortado at his left. If you think Miles might have felt uncomfortable sitting next to the man who had beheaded Tangerine, and opposite the ringmaster who had attempted to kill him only that afternoon, you would be absolutely right. He fidgeted on his seat and surreptitiously checked on Tangerine about every two minutes, and he watched the hands on the stateroom clock to ensure that they had not actually been glued in place.

Little, on the other hand, was as bright as ever. She was soon teaching a wind song to First Officer Barrett, who sat opposite her at the end of the table and happened to mention that he liked to play the accordion.

"Might I ask what business takes you to Al Bab, Mr. Cortado?" asked Captain Tripoli.

The Great Cortado seemed to have made up his mind to be on his best behavior. "I am in the business of animal performances," he said. "I was for many years the director of the finest circus show on the continent."

"Is that so?" said the captain. "I keep a pair of ocelots at my home, although I have not had a great deal of success in training them."

"You probably don't see them consistently enough," said the Great Cortado with unusual politeness, and he and Captain Tripoli embarked on a conversation about the care and training of felines, frequently interrupted by Baltinglass of Araby, who prided himself on being an expert on anything that bites, stings, maims or dismembers.

With the captain and the ringmaster otherwise

occupied, Doctor Tau-Tau paused between mouth-fuls and leaned a fraction closer to Miles. "I hope you realize that it was I who saved your life this morning, my boy," he said in a low voice.

Miles felt himself flush hot, and it was only with an effort that he managed to keep his voice as low as the fortune-teller's. "It was First Officer Barrett who pulled me back in," he said.

"Naturally," muttered Doctor Tau-Tau. "I could not risk blowing my cover by wrestling with the Great Cortado over your ankles. Instead I used my consid-erable psychic powers to alert the captain and first officer to your predicament, and just in the nick of time, if I may say so. If I may say so," he repeated, "it was a timely move."

"Blowing your cover?" said Miles, ignoring the second part of Doctor Tau-Tau's improbable state-ment.

Doctor Tau-Tau glanced nervously at the Great Cortado, who was recommending to the captain a diet of chopped snake to give luster to his ocelots' coats.

"It's vital that I play along with Cortado until I learn mastery of the you-know-what," he mumbled through a mouthful of food, "so that we can be rid of him once and for all."

"You're forgetting that the you-know-what is mine," said Miles through clenched teeth. "You stole it from me, and you have no right to use it."

A wounded look appeared on Tau-Tau's florid face. "My dear boy," he said, "you know that I am always looking after your best interests."

Miles took a mouthful of food to stop himself from answering straightaway. Strangely enough he believed that Doctor Tau-Tau really meant what he said—at least, as much as he meant anything—but he could not forget the sight of his beloved Tangerine cruelly eviscerated in an empty bed on a stormy November night.

"Since you've been looking after my best interests I've been almost sliced open by the Fir Bolg, nearly sawn in half by Cortado, and come within seconds of being pushed to my death from an airship," said Miles in a loud whisper. "I'd rather you just returned the Tiger's Egg and left my best interests alone, thank you."

Miles saw the Great Cortado glance in his direction at the mention of the Tiger's Egg. A forced smile appeared beneath the ringmaster's mustache. "I almost forgot," he said, producing Celeste's diary and placing it on the table in front of Miles. "My associate here blundered into the wrong cabin this morning and picked up this diary, thinking it was his copy of *A Hundred and One Magic Tricks for Beginners*. I only discovered his foolish mistake as we were dressing for dinner."

Miles took the diary at once and put it in his pocket. Doctor Tau-Tau said nothing and stared at the tablecloth, his face growing darker crimson.

"I'd like you to return the other thing that your foolish associate took from me," said Miles. He remembered what the captain had said at the porthole. "Then I might decide not to press charges."

Captain Tripoli fixed Miles with a stern look. "I have already said that my word is law on the *Sunfish*, Mr. Wednesday. However, I have no jurisdiction over events that happen outside the confines of this vessel. Old feuds and misdemeanors must be settled elsewhere, and there will be no further mention of them at the captain's table."

The Great Cortado smirked at Miles. "That sounds like an excellent opportunity to put our differences aside," he purred. "I don't believe you've told me where you're headed once we reach Al Bab."

"We're on an educational tour," barked Baltinglass of Araby. "A journey into the unknown."

"I always find a good map useful," crowed the Great Cortado. "I picked up an excellent one for nothing in a little place in Cnoc. But, of course, you wouldn't be able to read it, would you, old man?"

"Master Miles is well able to navigate," said Baltinglass of Araby.

"Still," said the Great Cortado, "it's kind of the boy to take on the burden of a blind pensioner on an outing, if perhaps a little fool-hurrrk!"

The Great Cortado did not, of course, intend to say "fool-hurrrk," but before he could finish the word "foolhardy," Baltinglass of Araby's hand shot out with lightning speed and bull's-eye accuracy and grabbed the ringmaster's tongue. Baltinglass pinched hard with his thumb and forefinger, and tears came to Cortado's eye. Little nudged Miles, and he fought to keep the smile from his face.

The captain put down his fork. "Mr. Baltinglass!" he said in a commanding tone. "You are a guest at the captain's table! Release that man's tongue at once."

"My apologies, Captain," shouted Baltinglass, giving Cortado's tongue a tweak before letting it go. "Thought I heard a snake there. The old eyesight's not what it used to be, you know."

The Great Cortado sank back into his seat, shaking with rage, and Miles could not resist returning his smirk. "Baltinglass has taught me a lot," he said, "especially about preparing for the unexpected. He's had a lot of experience in dealing with reptiles."

The Great Cortado leaned forward and fixed his one eye on Miles with a look of watery malevolence. "Perhaps you should remind him that I have a very long memory," he said.

Captain Tripoli cleared his throat loudly, and Airman Tang appeared at his shoulder. "We'll take coffee now, Mr. Tang," said the captain.

Miles and Little thanked the captain for dinner and excused themselves. Miles was impatient to revisit the Realm, and anxious to check that his mother's diary was still intact. They lit the lamp in their cabin, and Miles examined the diary by the flickering yellow light. There appeared to be nothing missing, including the inscription from Celeste's gravestone that he had penciled on the last page.

"Do you think they had a chance to copy this?" he asked Little.

"They didn't have it for long," said Little, "and they spent at least part of that time trying to stuff you out through the window." She looked at him and smiled. "We shouldn't have split up," she said.

"But we didn't know they were on board," said Miles. "I wonder what Tau-Tau was doing on the

Albatross that morning anyway?"

Little shrugged. "Maybe he found it was more expensive to sail than to fly."

Miles climbed into his bunk and lay down. He was too tired to read, and he placed the diary under his pillow and rested Tangerine on his chest. The bear lay still, limp with stuffing deficiency, an unquestioning smile stitched on his face. At one time Miles would have talked to him about the events of the day, but lately he had begun to feel a little sheepish about talking aloud to a stuffed bear, and a bit less sure that Tangerine was really listening. Nonetheless the feel of Tangerine's threadbare fur was as reassuring as it had ever been, and he smiled as he squeezed him tight.

"I was in the Realm again this morning," said Miles, "after I got that knock on the head from Cortado."

Little's face appeared over the edge of the top bunk. "Really?" she said. "You found your own way in?"

"I had to do that the first time too," he reminded her. "But this time there was no lever. I thought you said it was the lever that opened the way in."

Little laughed, her face framed by a curtain of silver-blond hair. "Don't be silly, Miles. You can get into the Realm any way you like, once you know where it is."

"How come it was a lever the first time?"

"Because I suggested it," said Little. "I tried to explain the way I go in, but you understand machines and solid things much better, so in the end I just told you to look for a lever."

"But how could it work if you just made it up on the spot?" said Miles.

"In a dream your thoughts *make* the reality. It's the same in the Realm. It's not like in this world, where reality comes in big heavy lumps and it's harder to think them into shape. That's why you have to be very careful to control your thoughts when you're in the Realm." She lay back on her bunk and added through a yawn, "And whatever you do, don't *ever* think of the tiger."

Miles listened to the steady rhythm of the airship's engines. The sound seemed so familiar now that he wondered how he would get to sleep without it. "I called you when I was in the Realm," he said after a while, "but you didn't come. Is that because you weren't asleep?"

There was no answer but the *wup, wup, wup* of the propellers. "*Now* she's asleep," Miles muttered to

Tangerine, and just for a moment he thought he felt the bear shift himself to a more comfortable position. Miles closed his eyes and smiled, and as the airship *Sunfish* sailed on through the starlit night he drifted gently into sleep.

CHAPTER FOURTEEN
RASCALS

Miles Wednesday, falafel-fed and floating at sleep's edge, wondered idly what would happen if he had no dreams that night. What if he never dreamed again? One thing was for sure: He would not ever get to sleep if he didn't close the porthole. Someone must have left it open, and his ears were as cold as ice. He opened his eyes, but there was no bunk above him and no pillow below his head. He was halfway out through the porthole already, suspended over the ocean in a freezing wind.

"Not again!" he thought. He did not feel particularly worried this time. There were no malicious hands feeding him out into the sky. He seemed rather to be squeezing himself out, like toothpaste from a tube. His feet left the ship, and he began to drop through the air. It felt like he had plenty of time. "Little?" he said aloud.

"Behind you," said Little.

He corkscrewed around as he fell. "Hello," he said, admiring again the shimmering wings that sprouted from her shoulders.

"Enough of the practicing, Miles," said Little, who seemed to be a great deal sterner whenever he met her on this side of sleep. "It's time to pick yourself up."

Miles spread out his arms and pulled slowly out of his dive. He could feel a powerful pull on his shoulders, and gave an experimental flap with muscles that he had never possessed before. It was neither bedsheets nor bare arms that were lifting him now. Miles felt a strong temptation to look over his shoulder, but he knew enough about the Realm to realize that one negative thought would make his new wings vanish like a summer snowflake. It was safer just to enjoy the sensation, and he let out a whoop of joy as he swooped upward. There was no airship to be seen, only the endless sky around him.

"What's this?" said a voice behind him that was

definitely not Little's.

"Not one of us," said another by his left shoulder. He was surrounded in an instant by an odd assortment of figures, spiraling and jinking so wildly that it was a wonder they didn't collide. "Looks like a meatmade," said one.

"A what?" said Miles. It was difficult to get a good look at the figures who dived and soared around him. They all looked like people he knew but couldn't quite identify. Maybe people he had known from Larde, or from the circus, except that he had never known anyone who could fly apart from Silverpoint and Little. These strangers seemed to fly without wings, he noticed, and to give off a sort of roaring noise as they flew.

"It talks," said one.

"And flies," said another.

A long, thin character swooped in close to him and poked him in the ribs. "Usually they just sort of . . . drop," he said.

"What have you done with Little?" said Miles.

"I'm here, Miles," said Little. He almost didn't recognize her. She was still Little, but she had somehow become less like herself and more like flying putty. She seemed to change in some indefinable way each time someone looked at her, and now that all the newcomers turned to look at her at once she became almost featureless.

"*She's* one of us," said a voice.

"You can't hide from us, cousin."

"You is a Song Angel, no?" said another.

"Yes," said Little.

"Sing us your song, then."

Little shook her head.

There was a gale of laughter from the others. "Very quiet for a Song Angel," shouted one. "Can't shut 'em up, usually."

"What you doing with a meatmade, song girl?"

"You teach him to fly?"

Little ducked the question, and the questioner, with a neat maneuver, and popped up at Miles's side.

"Who are they?" asked Miles.

"Chaos Angels," said Little.

"Rascals," said one of the Chaos Angels. "Only the Sleepies call us Chaos Angels."

"What do you do?" asked Miles. "Apart from zooming about like jumbo flies."

"Jumbo flies!" One of the Rascals guffawed. "I like that!" He gave Miles a thump on the back that made him somersault in the air and drop like a brick for several seconds, and every Rascal instantly stalled and dropped with him, screaming and hooting in a terrifying way before bursting into raucous laughter as they pulled out of their dive again. Their laughter reminded Miles of jackdaws, and for a moment the entire flock of Chaos Angels turned into tumbling black-and-gray birds before they shook themselves back into shape.

"Did she teach you that?" said one angrily, jerking his finger at Little.

"I taught myself, I think," said Miles.

"Do that again," said the Rascal, "and I'll turn you into *this*." He transformed suddenly into a thing like a rotting fish with dragonfly wings and a mouthful of odious teeth. "For good, understand?"

"Sorry," said Miles. He tried to hold the Rascal's staring eye, feeling it would be rude to look away while the other was making such an effort to be repulsive.

"Don't apologize," said Little in a loud whisper.

"Sorry," Miles whispered back before he could stop himself. The rules of the Realm were becoming very complicated, if they were rules at all, so he simply repeated his question and hoped for the best. "You didn't tell me what you do."

"We make chaos, of course," said Fish-fly, turning slowly back into a less hideous shape. "Ever had one of those days where you stand on a pin when you get out of bed; then you find the window's open and it's rained on your clothes?"

"So you put them by the oven to dry," said another.

"And there's only two slices of bread left, and they're both stale?"

"So you stick them in the toaster, but meanwhile the oven's set your shirt on fire—"

"So you throw a jug of water over it and realize it's not water at all, but the last of the milk—"

"And you've soaked the toaster and electrocuted the cat?"

"And then . . ."

"I get the idea," said Miles. "You're the ones who do all that?"

"That's us," said Fish-fly. "Rascals, Inc. Sowers of finest-quality chaos to the gentry."

"Is it fun making chaos?"

"It's pretty boring, really," said a Rascal to his left. "You meatmades are so inept you don't need a lot of help to mess things up."

"I think we get by pretty well," said Miles, who felt he should offer some defense of his kind.

"Ha! Name one useful thing you make!"

"Well . . . ," said Miles.

"Apart from motorbikes," observed Fish-fly.

"Motorbikes?" said Miles

"We like them," said the other Rascal. "But they're the exception."

Miles realized now what the roaring sound was. He noticed that several of the Rascals had tangles of chrome tubes and blackened pipes protruding behind them, and that they left trails of smoke as they belted through the sky. The long, thin Rascal had a patch sewn on his back, with the words "Fly to Live, Live to Fly" curling around a skull with a rose between its teeth.

"We used to do the big stuff—fires, storms, floods—but we got taken off that a long time ago. They created special departments for them, and staffed them with responsible types," said Fish-fly.

Miles thought of Silverpoint, and his insistence on sticking to what he called the Code of the Realm. "Why did they do that?" he asked.

"We got a bit carried away," said the Rascal. "Solar flares, meteorites—we were having a ball, but a lot of creatures got hurt. Big guys, some of them. Huge jaws, tiny arms, tombstones all up their backs. We didn't mean to wipe them out, but when the smoke cleared and a lot of them were gone, we got demoted."

"Who demoted you?" asked Miles, fascinated.

"The Sleepies, of course. Who else?"

"You mean the Sleep Angels?"

"That's them. Of course, we get back at them now and then. It really gets up their noses when we play our little tricks on them, but it's worth it just to see them pop."

"What kind of little tricks?" asked Miles. "Do you burn their toast?"

Little caught Miles's eye and shook her head minutely.

"Funny," said Fish-fly.

"But not very," said the long, thin Rascal.

"The kind of tricks we like are the ones that make the Sleepies *really* angry."

Another Rascal laughed. "When they get really angry they go off like volcanoes, and lots of people die."

"Which proves they're no better than us."

"That's why we're taking you in."

"Taking us in where?"

"To the Council, of course. A meatmade in the Council will really put the dragon in the hen-house."

"Especially one who's been brought here by a banished Song Angel!"

The Rascals guffawed and honked. "We saw how shiny and new those wings were," said Fish-fly.

"We can see your old ones too," said the long, thin Rascal.

"They never quite wash out, do they, little cousin?"

Little said nothing. She took Miles's hand as they flew onward through the cloud columns, escorted by chaos made visible, like two canaries into a crocodile's jaws.

CHAPTER FIFTEEN

A QUESTION OF GOATS

Miles and Little, meatmade and fresh-winged, flew toward a cloud that Miles recognized from his encyclopedia education as a cumulonimbus. It was a massive tower of white with a bellyful of gray rain and a towering head. Fear clutched at Miles's stomach, but there was no escaping their gleeful escort. Besides, he thought, this was what they had entered the Realm for. He didn't feel ready to face the Sleep Angels, but then, he doubted that any amount of preparation would be enough.

Inside the cloud was an enormous hall with galleries twisting and spiraling around its sheer walls. There was a solid floor beneath their feet. Miles felt his wings fold against his back, and he looked around him curiously. At first he had thought the hall was almost empty, but wherever he looked he could see swarms of figures, talking and arguing and adopting a bewildering variety of shapes and guises. It was not that they appeared out of nowhere; rather that they seemed to come to his notice only when he looked in their direction. The Chaos Angels, quieter than they had been in flight, prodded him into motion, and he and Little walked toward the center of the room. It was strangely difficult to tell if they were walking on the level or climbing a gentle slope, but after a while Miles noticed that they were much higher up in the cloud than they had been. Most of the angels they passed paid no attention to them, but Miles saw that they parted for the Chaos Angels, who walked with a certain swagger.

They reached a broad gallery with a commanding view of the inside of the cloud. A large crowd of figures swarmed around the gallery. The edges of the crowd seemed to ebb and flow, and some angels hovered and swooped above the melee. Little took Miles's hand and squeezed. "Keep your eyes clear and your claws sharp," she whispered, quoting the tiger's advice. "Be very careful what you say, Miles." Her skin, which always glowed with a pale light, looked pure white now, and the look of fear on her face brought home to Miles the danger in which she had put herself for his sake. He felt a hard knot of determination to save her, at least, and he forced a smile and returned her squeeze.

"Way!" boomed one of the Rascals as they entered the crowd.

"Coming through," called another.

Some of the figures at the edge of the crowd turned to face them. Miles could see that many of them were Sleep Angels. He recognized their indistinct shapes, as though they were made of dense gray smoke. It was impossible for his eyes to get a fix on their features, but he felt none of the crushing sleep that he associated with the presence of a Sleep Angel. "It mustn't work that way up here," he thought to himself.

"What mustn't?" said a voice right in his ear. He was suddenly surrounded by the shifting crowd.

"I didn't say anything," said Miles. He could clearly see the face of the angel beside him. It was a narrow face with skin like polished gray stone. It was neither friendly nor threatening, but strangely familiar, as though it belonged to someone he had never met but would someday know very well.

"You don't need to," said another voice behind

him, and as he spoke the face of the first angel dissolved into smoky vagueness. Miles turned. Another stone-faced angel was staring at him. "I don't recognize you," said the second angel. "How come your caste isn't showing?"

Miles glanced around desperately for Little. He felt out of his depth already, but he was saved from answering by a shout from somewhere in the crowd. "Never mind that, Stillbone. What about those goats?" He recognized the voice as that of the Rascal Fish-fly, and allowed himself a sigh of relief. Maybe they were on his side after all.

All eyes turned to the shouting Rascal. "What goats?" asked one of the Sleep Angels in a voice like flint.

"We were talking about goats last Council I was at," said Fish-fly. "Can we grow demons in all of 'em, or just the ones with yellow eyes?"

The Sleep Angel grew visibly sharper and larger. His features became so clear it was almost hard to look at him. "What does their eye color matter?"

Fish-fly gave a shudder that made his whole body ripple. "The yellow-eyed ones are plain creepy. Scares the kidneys out of the meatma . . . the corporeals. Not so sure about the blue-eyed ones, though. They're almost cute."

A sudden thread of song came to Miles's ear. He had never heard a sound described as "goaty," but there was certainly no other word that could describe this snatch of music. It did not simply echo the sound of a goat; it contained the touch of its coarse wool, the curve of its horns, the smell and the shape and the entire essence of the animal. The singer hovered at the edge of the crowd, and she laughed as she finished her song. She reminded Miles of Little, but seemed somehow thinner and sharper.

"I'll go get some goats," bellowed one of the other Rascals. "Blue-eyed, brown, green and yellow. Help you make up your minds."

"Get some?" hissed Stillbone, coming back into focus. "You can't bring goats to the Council! You can't bring any corporeals to a Council."

A sly grin broke out on the Rascal's face, and he extended a finger in Little's direction. "*She* did," he said.

Little shrank visibly. Her pretty features smoothed out until you would have had the greatest difficulty remembering them for more than a second. The entire crowd turned toward her—shock on the faces of the Song Angels and the Whitefire Angels, and menace in the eyes of the Sleep Angels, who began to converge on Little as though they would swallow her whole and spit out her birdlike bones. Miles was paralyzed with fear. He looked around for someone who could help him, but there was nobody. The thought of the tiger began to surface. He remembered Little's warning and tried to block it out, but blocking a thought that you're not supposed to be having is no easy task, as you will know if you've ever had a sudden vision of someone with two carrots up their nose while they're interrogating you about missing homework.

Miles tried to swallow the thought of the tiger, and for a moment it seemed to be working. The thought sat in his stomach like an indigestible ball, but it did not go away. It began to push up through his chest, and what happened next surprised Miles himself as much as anyone. The thought rose through his gullet in a ball of sound, and the thunderous roar of an angry tiger burst from his mouth, silencing at once the babble of the chaotic Council.

The whole assembly froze for a heartbeat. Little stood in the center, pale and frightened, surrounded by a swirling crowd of pointing, gesticulating figures of every shape and hue. The scene came suddenly back to life, and all attention switched at once to Miles, who stood there feeling like he had released an enormous belch at a genteel dinner party.

Stillbone, the Sleep Angel who had questioned him before, suddenly materialized in front of him. His polished black eyes held Miles in a cold stare as he released a single word into the silence: "Who?" he said.

"It's not her fault," said Miles. "It was my idea to come here."

The Sleep Angel took a step backward. "You're not a goat."

"Not the last time I looked," said Miles. There was no going back now, and the very hopelessness of his situation made him bolder. He took a deep breath. It was time to tell the truth. "I came to talk about the Tiger's Egg."

The silence grew tauter. Even the Rascals had stopped their guffawing, and Miles noted that some of them were visibly shrinking. "I don't know you," said Stillbone. "What is your name?"

"Miles," said Miles.

The Sleep Angel gave a humorless smile. He echoed the name Miles. It turned into a dull stone on his tongue, and fell to the floor at his feet.

"Your real name," he said.

"That's the only one I know," said Miles. He realized now that the name that served him in the normal world was of no use here, but if he had another name he had no idea what it might be.

"You cannot address the Council without a name," said Stillbone.

"I already did," said Miles. "But it seems I've wasted my time. If you don't want to know more about the Tiger's Egg I'll just go back where I came from."

"We should let him speak," said a tall figure dressed in black. He waved his hand at Miles as he did so, and tiny points of intense light spilled from his fingers. He was surrounded by these pinpoints, as were several other angels, and Miles guessed that these were the Whitefire Angels whom Little had told him about in a small room buried deep beneath the Palace of Laughter.

Stillbone turned to the Whitefire Angel, crackling slightly with anger. "That matter is now closed. We decided our course of action already."

"*You* decided," called another figure from the sidelines. Miles was sure that one of the Chaos Angels had stood there a moment before, but it was a tall, black-clad figure who spoke, also shedding miniature stars from his fingertips.

A Storm Angel sent a twisted thread of lightning at the speaker, who ducked quickly out of sight and turned into a small bat, fluttering away before he could be spotted.

At this point the whole Council seemed to erupt in shouting. Fingers were jabbed in the air, wings broke open to give their owners more elevation from which to bellow their point of view, and more than a few lightning bolts were traded. The cloud around them flashed with bursts of lightning, and the argument became rapidly more heated. Just as Miles was wondering if he should try roaring like a tiger for a second time, Little shot from the heaving, gesticulating crowd like a stone from a catapult and grabbed his wrist.

"Let's go, Miles," she said, pulling him toward the white wall of the chamber.

"But I was just getting started," protested Miles.

"Nice try," said Little as they burst out into the dawn sky. "Imagine what would happen if you continued. Anyway, you need to get back at once."

Miles was taken aback by the sharpness of her reply. "*I* need to? What about you?" he said.

"We," said Little. "I said we."

She hadn't said that, and Miles knew it. He wondered if she planned to somehow remain in the Realm without him. The thought of losing her gave him a sinking feeling, and he began to lose height quickly. They were flying at speed into the dawn, and he could see up ahead a dark strip of land and the domes and minarets of a town on the shore. He could just make out the outline of the *Sunfish* too, flying close to her own shadow on the water as she approached the port.

"Hurry!" said Little. She had a firm grip on his wrist and was pulling him insistently toward the airship. They were traveling faster than he had ever done in his life, the waves little more than a blur as they skimmed over them. Miles would have been unable to keep up, but Little seemed able to draw him onward like a magnet without his having to use his wings at all. She glanced over her shoulder, and the look on her face hardened into grim determination. There was a pack of distant figures on their tail, silhouetted against the pale yellow cumulus cloud they had just escaped.

"Are they Sleep Angels?" Miles shouted into the wind.

"Must be," said Little.

Something did not feel right. They flew over the *Albatross*, which was making headway under bellying sails but was still some way behind its airborne rival. The *Sunfish* was descending now toward some kind of arena on the outskirts of Al Bab. She was drifting at an odd angle, and as they got close Miles could see a thick column of smoke rising from the starboard side of the hull.

"The *Sunfish* is on fire!" he said.

"So it is," said Little. She seemed neither surprised nor concerned, and Miles stared at her with a rising sense of panic as they hurtled toward the burning airship, with no sign of slowing.

"But the smoke is coming from the cabins," he shouted. "If we go back to our bodies we'll be trapped. There must be something we can do from outside."

Little shook her head. "You've got an appointment to keep," she said. Her voice did not sound right, and she appeared to be stretching as she spoke. He looked at her again, closer now, but she was becoming gray and indistinct, and with a jolt he realized that this was not Little at all. He struggled to free his wrist, but the angel had an unbreakable grip.

"Let go!" shouted Miles.

"Soon," said Bluehart, his stony features emerging as he spoke. Miles could see now why the Sleep Angel's face was so familiar. It was almost a mirror of his own features, but with something missing, something he could not identify. "You've had a good run," said the angel, "but you're way out of your depth, boy. It's your time."

Miles glanced desperately over his shoulder. They were about to fly straight into the *Sunfish*'s smoldering hull, and even if he could escape Bluehart there was a horde of angels coming after him. He realized that his visit to the Council had been a fatal mistake. His throat tightened and he began to cough. "Let Little go," he spluttered. "The Tiger's Egg was mine. She had nothing to do with it."

Miles knew the ship's planking would not be solid to him, but his eyes told him he was heading for a collision, and ignoring the evidence of your senses is not an easy thing to do. He tensed himself for an impact, and as he closed his eyes he felt Bluehart release his wrist. There was an uncomfortable sucking sensation and he sat up with a jerk, his lungs burning, and tumbled from the end of his bunk. The cabin was filled with acrid smoke. Baltinglass's bottom bunk was empty. He tried to get himself to his feet to climb the ladder to the top bunk where Little lay, but the coughing bent him double. He knew she was still trapped at the Council, and that here in the burning cabin her body would be unconscious. He tried again to straighten up. The cabin was beginning to swim before his eyes.

The silhouette of Bluehart stood by the porthole.

"Not long now," said the Sleep Angel, a surprising kindness in his voice. "You have to be present in yourself to die. It's a formality, but one that must be observed." He gave a deep sigh. "That's bureaucracy for you."

CHAPTER SIXTEEN

A LUCKY GUESS

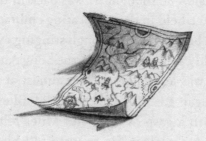

Bluehart the Sleep Angel, smoke-gray and bone-cold, stood in the choking cabin and waited for his moment. The boy was on his hands and knees on the floor now, spit running from his lips, as Bluehart patiently counted down his last gasping breaths. It was a short enough life, he thought—seven . . . six . . . five—but each one had their time—four . . . three—and this boy had already stretched his beyond its limit—two . . . one. . . .

The Sleep Angel stiffened suddenly. There was an unexpected sound from outside the cabin, the echo of a roar entwined with sweet music that had no place here. He stepped toward the boy, but the music tightened around him.

Miles heard it too, slipping from consciousness, and he mistook it for a memory. The blood roared in his ears, and Little's voice cut through it with a song of wild urgency and indescribable beauty. In his confusion he thought he was back in the Palace of Laughter, held in the suffocating embrace of The Null, and he looked up through stinging eyes to see if he could catch a glimpse of the Song Angel.

There was a loud crash, and almost at once the smoke began to thin. The figure of Bluehart dissolved with a gasp of rage, and Miles felt himself lifted from the floor. He tried to tell his rescuers that Little was in the top bunk, but he could only cough.

"We've got you, Master Miles," said Baltinglass of Araby.

"And your little sister too," said another voice.

"Wait." He coughed. He broke free of the airman who had hold of him and grabbed Tangerine from his bunk. He was picked up again and carried at a run along the tilting corridor, past flames that ran up the walls and bubbled across the ceiling. Floating sparks stung his skin, but he held on to the bear for all he was worth. Behind him he heard another crash as the door of the Great Cortado's cabin was broken in, and an excitable shout from First Officer Barrett. "They've escaped through the porthole!"

A moment later there was a grinding impact as the wounded airship plowed into the ground. Miles and Little's rescuers were thrown off their feet, and they fetched up in a tangled heap by the hatch, which had been jarred open in the crash. It was a short drop to the ground, and they jumped from the hull, followed by Baltinglass of Araby. They scrambled out of the way as more passengers, soot-smeared and half-dressed, dropped from the burning vessel, counted out by two airmen who stood on either side of the hatch.

"Are you all right?" said Miles to Little.

She was pale under a dusting of ash, but she nodded. "I'm fine," she said.

They helped Baltinglass to a stone bench at the arena's edge and sat him down. His hair stood out in blackened tufts from under his singed cap, and the duffel bag that he had somehow managed to locate in the burning cabin smoked quietly on the dust beside him. Miles watched as First Officer Barrett dashed to and fro like an ant, helping injured passengers to safety and shouting instructions at the rest of the crew. The fire was spreading rapidly now, devouring the balloon's gray hide and sending a column of black smoke curling into the morning sky. The last two airmen leaped from the hatch as it became a rectangle of yellow flame, and still there was no sign of Captain Tripoli.

"The captain is still on board," said Miles anxiously. "I don't think he got out."

"He's there!" said Little suddenly. "Climbing out of the porthole." She pointed at the burning hull, where the figure of Captain Tripoli was indeed emerging from a circular hole in the planking and sliding down a rope of knotted sheets.

"Why is the brass gone from the porthole?" said Little.

"That must be the one Cortado and Tau-Tau escaped from," said Miles. "They would have had to remove the brass for Tau-Tau to fit through it."

They watched the upright figure of the captain walk slowly away from his decimated ship. He stopped to speak to his first officer, who was waving his arms about like a lunatic, indicating the dazed passengers he had rounded up and the crew he had sent off for help. It looked like he could almost kiss the captain in his delight at finding him alive.

"How did you get away?" Miles asked Little in a low voice. "From the Council, I mean."

"The Rascals got me out," she said. "They were

impressed that you were brave enough to actually bring up the Tiger's Egg at a Council, and once they realized that Bluehart had tricked you they got really annoyed. They grabbed me and we followed you as fast as we could." A smile broke out on her dirty face. "Those Rascals can really fly!"

"But how did you manage to stop Bluehart? You can't sing the One Song anymore."

"The One Song has started to fade from me," said Little, "but I have music of my own, music that I made for the Circus Bolsillo. That's what I sang. I wasn't sure if it would work, but it was all I had."

"Bluehart didn't like it much." Miles grinned.

Little laughed, and dissolved into a fit of coughing. "I don't think so," she said. "It confused him long enough to lose concentration, and when a Sleep Angel loses his focus other things can get in his way."

"Like Baltinglass?" said Miles.

"Baltinglass was there just in time," said Little. "He could not have saved us if Bluehart hadn't been distracted, nor could I have held Bluehart for long if Baltinglass hadn't arrived when he did."

Miles frowned. "So does the Realm control the world, or can the world stand up to the Realm?"

"Which is stronger, wind or waves?" said Little.

"There's no single answer. It depends on which way they are flowing and how they meet. This time we were lucky. The next time we might not be."

Refusing Barrett's offer of a steadying arm, Captain Tripoli walked onward without looking back until he reached the place where Miles and his companions sat. His eyes were red-rimmed, and he carried a singed and battered roll of paper. "My passengers and crew have escaped with their lives," he said in a hoarse voice. "I do not wish to witness the death of my ship, so I will take my leave now and go to the prefecture to make a report."

He looked directly at Miles. "Mr. Wednesday," he said, "Baltinglass informs me that you are the leader of this expedition. I wish you good speed and success in your aims, all the more so if you intend to bring those two villains to justice. I have no doubt that they set this murderous fire, and it is perhaps better if you find them before I do, as I will show them no mercy." He handed Miles the roll of battered paper. "Fortunately I saved your map, which Baltinglass had brought to the stateroom to show me. I took the liberty of updating a few details before . . ." He did not complete the sentence, but shook hands with Miles and Little, and placed a firm hand on Baltinglass's shoulder before walking slowly away toward the town.

The arena was bustling with life now. People were spilling from nearby buildings, bringing bandages and makeshift stretchers. A man in immaculate white robes hurried toward the arena wheeling a cart loaded with water bottles. He stopped his cart and handed them a carafe of water, waving his hands to show that he did not want payment, then hurried on toward the burning airship.

Baltinglass of Araby took a long drink from the water bottle, and wiped his wet lips with the back of his sleeve. "The captain is right," he said. "We've got some villains to catch."

"How will we find which way they've gone?" asked Little.

"They plan to cross the desert," said Baltinglass.

"Which means they'll need camels?" said Miles.

"Correct," said Baltinglass. "Now, put yourself in Cortado's position, Master Miles. What would you ask for as soon as you escaped the airship?"

"I'd ask who has camels for hire that would be ready to leave at once," said Miles.

"Preferably the fastest ones," added Little.

"Exactly," said Baltinglass approvingly. "And how would you prevent yourself from being pursued through the desert for burning an airship?"

Miles thought for a moment. "I'd try to pin the blame on someone else."

"And who would that be?" said Baltinglass.

"Us, I suppose," said Little.

"I hear the sound of boots among the sandals," said Baltinglass. "Would I be right in saying that the gendarmes are heading our way at this moment?"

Miles looked up. Smuts from the burned airship had begun to swirl downward like black snow, and he could see half a dozen men in dark green uniforms marching purposefully through the falling cinders, carefully scrutinizing the crowds from under the peaks of their caps.

"We need a plan, Master Miles," said Baltinglass of Araby.

Miles frowned in concentration. He tried to put himself in the gendarmes' boots, as he had just done with the Great Cortado.

"They'll be looking for two children and a blind man," he said.

"You're right," said Baltinglass. "I'd better take off my dark glasses."

"You don't wear dark glasses," said Miles.

"Then I'd better put some on," said the old man. "That way they'll never recognize me."

"Why don't you just give me your cane?" said Miles.

He looked around him and spotted two elderly ladies who had been aboard the *Sunfish*. They looked lost and disheveled, and one of them was limping badly. "Here," said Miles urgently to Little. "Go and lend this cane to that lady, and tell them you'll find them somewhere to stay. I'll meet you by that tree over there, the tall one, in half an hour." He pointed to a palm tree that stood among the buildings, hundreds of years old and rising above the highest minarets.

Little nodded. "Be careful, Miles," she said, and she took the cane and slipped away.

"Now," said Miles to Baltinglass, "you'll need to walk without your stick. Pull your cap low over your eyes and I'll give you directions."

Baltinglass hauled himself upright with a grunt. "None needed, Master Miles. I have the ears of a bat, though I don't bother with the squeaking part so much."

He hoisted the duffel bag over his shoulder and set off boldly toward the sound of the gendarmes' boots. To Miles's dismay he stopped one of the gendarmes and, with his woolly hat almost covering his eyes, asked him where he could hire some camels.

"None of your hunchbacked donkeys, mind," said Baltinglass in a loud voice. "A blind chap I just met said there was a man around here who breeds good long-range beasts. Ahmed? Wahid? Can't recall the name."

"You spoke to a blind man?" said one of the gendarmes.

"Blind as an alley," said Baltinglass. "Seemed in a hurry. Had two kids with him. They headed off that way." He pointed randomly over his shoulder.

The gendarme frowned. "They went into the sea?" he said.

"The sea?" said Baltinglass. "Yes, the sea. Good swimmers, the blind, so I'm told. Probably wanted to wash off the smell of kerosene."

The gendarme tipped his hat, and hurried his men off in the direction of the beach.

"What did you say the camel dealer's name was?" shouted Baltinglass after them.

"Wahid, like you said," answered the gendarme. "On the Rue Fatima, behind the souk."

"Lucky guess," said Baltinglass to Miles. "Let's head for that tree you mentioned, so we can pick Little up and get ourselves some transport."

"Aren't you tired?" asked Miles.

"I can sleep on a camel. Those two reprobates won't be hanging about in Al Bab to sip tea, and we need to be hot on their heels."

"We know where they're going, though, don't we?"

said Miles as they hurried into the warren of dusty streets.

"Indeed we do," said Baltinglass. "They're going to pay a visit to your aunt, and we need to get there first without them realizing they've been overtaken. We do have a couple of advantages that might help."

"Such as?"

"We've got a map, for a start."

"But they have a map too," said Miles.

"They do," said Baltinglass, "and it's one of my finest. It would be very useful to them if they were in the Gobi Desert."

"But the Gobi Desert is in China, isn't it?"

"Right again, Master Miles. Evidently they missed a few geography lessons, if they were schooled at all."

Miles laughed. "And the other advantage?"

"Me, Master Miles. I'm tough as a walnut and mad as a radish, and they don't call me Baltinglass of Araby for nothing. Now, where did I leave my stick?"

CHAPTER SEVENTEEN

A GEM IN THE PORRIDGE

Miles Wednesday, sunbaked and soot-caked, sat on the stone surround of the palm tree that grew from the center of the square almost to the sky. All around him was the bustle of the market, with stalls selling dates, nuts, salt fish and colored spices piled in perfect cones. There were carpets and jewelry and tall silver coffeepots, saddles, stools, snakeskin bags, baskets, sandals and robes. People crowded the stalls and haggled with their proprietors, and Miles searched among them for any sign of Little. She had been gone for some time, and he wondered if it had been such a good idea to send her off with two elderly strangers as camouflage. The vivid memory of someone he thought was Little turning suddenly into Bluehart did nothing to calm his nerves.

Baltinglass of Araby had waited awhile with Miles, fidgeting like a child, and when a small boy approached offering himself as a guide he had leaped from the stone parapet as though it were red-hot. "No sense in both of us sitting here like a couple of stuffed mongooses," he bellowed. "I'll go and get haggling over some beasts of burden. Meet me at Wahid the camel trader's as soon as Little turns up."

Miles watched a man sitting on his hunkers with a monkey on a long chain. The monkey was performing somersaults as his owner collected coins in an upturned fez. Miles could hear Little's voice as though she were sitting beside him, asking why the man should be earning the money while the monkey did all the work. She was still often puzzled by the way things worked in his world, yet his visits to the Realm had shown him that she no longer fit there either. A cold feeling crept over him, and he felt suddenly sure that she would not be meeting him at the palm tree. He stood up on the stone parapet and scanned the crowd anxiously. There was still no sign of her, but Baltinglass's small guide was dodging through the crowd with the air of someone who had an urgent message and had been promised a big reward to deliver it.

"You must come with me," panted the boy, tugging at the sleeve of Miles's coat. "The white-eyed effendi wants you."

Miles shook his head. He was not sure whether to trust the boy. "I have to wait here for my friend," he said.

"You must come," repeated the boy. He frowned as he tried to remember the exact wording of the message he had been given. "Effendi says the villain and his idiot have stolen the girl."

Miles felt the wind knocked out of him as though he had been punched. He jumped down from the stone wall and took off after the boy, who could skip around people without breaking his stride the way Silverpoint dodged lightning. They ran to the edge of the square and down a narrow alley. The boy turned and ducked through a thick red curtain, and Miles followed.

He found himself in a large dusty yard, open to the sky and shaded with date palms. A long trough of water ran along one wall, and a number of camels drank thirstily from it. Baltinglass was in the center of the yard, shaking the hand of a man in a dazzling white robe and turban. The man had skin the color of roast coffee, with pure white eyebrows and a fat mustache that looked like the hands of a clock showing twenty past eight. His chin was frosted with stubble. He turned and smiled at Miles. "Welcome, young man," he said.

"That you, Miles?" said Baltinglass. "Got some bad news. Wahid here just sold a couple of camels to two men fitting the description of the villain and the fool. Said they had a tight grip on a small girl who wasn't keen to travel with them."

The camel trader spread out his hands and his eyebrows tilted in despair. "They tie her to the camel, so she don't fall off, they say. As soon as they are gone I send my boy to report to the gendarmes, but they have all gone swimming." He shrugged. "What can I do?"

"How long ago was this?" asked Miles.

Wahid shrugged again. "One hour," he said. "Maybe less."

"We have two fine beasts here, Sanaam and Khuff," said Baltinglass to Miles. "Their saddlebags are packed and they've had a long drink. We can get going right away."

"How will we know which way they went," asked Miles, "if they're following a map of the Gobi Desert?"

The camel dealer shook his head in disbelief. "They show me this map," he said. "They ask me where is Kagu, but the map make no sense, so I set them on the road to the oasis. I don't like those men, but my camels must drink."

He went over to the two camels that Baltinglass had bought. They knelt on the ground, one a caramel color and the other almost white. "Sanaam," said Wahid, touching the cheek of the caramel camel, "and Khuff. You will take good care of them, yes?"

"Count on it," said Baltinglass. "I'm no stranger to camels, nor to their spit, for that matter." He rummaged in one of his saddlebags and pulled out two long strips of cloth. "Come here to me," he said to Miles. He wrapped the cloth expertly so that it covered Miles's head and most of his face, and then did the same for himself. "Didn't have time to get properly outfitted," he said, "but these will do for a start."

The camels were fitted with high saddles mounted on woven blankets festooned with colored tassels. Miles mounted Sanaam's saddle with a little help from Wahid, and at a signal from the trader the camel lurched to her feet, almost throwing him off again.

"Hold the pommel," said Wahid. "Talk to Sanaam.

She must learn your voice."

From his perch on the camel it seemed a long way to the ground. Miles was twice as high up as he had been when riding on the tiger, and he found it strange to sit on a saddle instead of directly on the animal's back.

"Hut-hut!" came Baltinglass's voice from behind him, and all at once they were in motion. The camels barged out through the red curtain and into the narrow alley, and Wahid's small boy ran alongside them. "I put you on the road to the Akhdar oasis," the boy shouted cheerfully, and they moved at a fast trot though the crowded streets, their heads brushed by trailing laundry that hung from the windows above. By the time they reached the edge of the town they had acquired a following of a dozen children, a goat and a couple of dogs. A paved road led out into the desert. Low, scrubby bushes dotted the landscape on either side, and between them drifts of sand lay across the road as though the desert were impatient to claim it back.

They stopped in the road, and Baltinglass of Araby tilted his head and took a deep sniff of the desert air. "I've slid through worlds of ice and steamed in the deepest jungles," he said, "but in my dreams I always return to the desert. There's sand in my veins and a hot wind in my soul, Master Miles, make no mistake."

"You ride all day, maybe you reach Akhdar by nightfall," said the boy. He slapped the rumps of both camels and called, *"Bissalma"*; then he turned with his companions and ran back to the shaded streets and alleys of Al Bab.

The sun was rising high now, shortening the shadows and rippling the road ahead. Miles was glad of the turban that Baltinglass had made, which protected his head from the full force of the sun. The camels settled into a rolling lope, and when he looked back the port was already lost in the shimmering distance. They rode in silence for some time, and Miles scanned the horizon ahead for any sign of the Great Cortado, his pompous ally and their captive. From time to time he would spot tiny figures bobbing above the heat haze, but it was impossible to judge how far away they might be, or whether they really were camel riders or just tall rocks or rolling tumbleweeds.

The color slowly seeped from the desert scene until everything looked a faded yellow-blue, and his thoughts began to slide away to other times and places. He found himself in the cool shade of the gazebo, where the hairy bulk of The Null crouched on a bed of straw, reading from the newspaper to the beast that had once been his father. He thought of Lady Partridge, presiding over a hundred orphans and as many cats in her stately home, and of the three diminutive Bolsillo brothers touring the land with their spectacular circus show.

Sanaam's braying grunt brought him back to the scorching desert just in time to stop him from slumping forward onto the camel's neck. The road had faded into a narrow track that curved like a faint scar through the arid landscape. "Good girl," he croaked through cracked lips.

Baltinglass pulled alongside him and handed him a canteen. "Drink," he said. The water was warm and tasted slightly sweet, but it felt like life percolating down through him. "Keep an eye out for some shade," said Baltinglass. "We'll stop and refill."

"Refill?" said Miles.

"Ourselves and the camels," said Baltinglass. "A camel will eat his own harness or the hat off your head, but where there's shade there should be plants to graze them on. I'll rustle up something a bit tastier for us."

They came to a ridge of camel-colored rock that ended in a wind-sculpted arch. Clumps of scrubby plants hid in the shadow beneath. They dismounted stiffly, and Baltinglass of Araby rummaged in his saddlebag for provisions.

"Ever eat toasted scorpion?" he said.

Miles looked at the saddlebag apprehensively. "No," he said.

"Me neither," said Baltinglass. "Sounds horrible, though. Here's a chicken kebab."

They sat in the narrow strip of shade and unwrapped the kebabs that Baltinglass had bought that morning. There were two full canteens of water, and as they expected to reach the oasis at nightfall they were able to quench their thirst and still leave enough for the rest of the day. Miles took the rolled map from his pack and examined the route they had taken. The stone arch under which they sat was drawn in miniature with a fine pen, and beside it was what looked like a scorpion with a cross drawn through it. He memorized the landmarks on the onward route to the Akhdar oasis, then put the map away. "I hope Little's all right," he said.

"Don't you worry about her," said Baltinglass. "She's a gem in the porridge, and those fools will break their teeth on her yet."

Miles stood and shook the sand from his trousers. He would have liked nothing more than to curl up in the relative cool beneath the rocks and give in to sleep, but he felt that every second they spent there was a step farther from Little, and he could not allow himself to rest until he had freed her from the Great Cortado.

"How are we going to get her back, even if we do catch up with them?" he asked, helping Baltinglass to his feet.

"Haven't a bull's notion," said Baltinglass. "I make it a point never to play until I've seen my cards." He mounted Khuff's saddle and the camel got obediently to his feet. "I hope she managed to hold on to my cane, though. There's twenty inches of steel hidden in there that would make a great impression on that flaky ringmaster if the occasion presented itself."

"I can't imagine Little pulling a sword on the Great Cortado," said Miles, sitting astride Sanaam's saddle and wondering what on earth Baltinglass had done to make his camel stand up.

"Nor I," said Baltinglass. "That girl has weapons far subtler and sharper than my old swordstick. Besides," he said, "I'm hoping she leaves the skewering of that particular reptile to me."

CHAPTER EIGHTEEN

THE ELEPHANT OF SURPRISE

Little softwing, cord-bound and camel-carried, sat as low in the saddle as she could manage, hiding herself from the sun in Doctor Tau-Tau's ample shadow. Her wrists were tied tightly behind her, with the other end of the rope securely knotted to the saddle. Doctor Tau-Tau was sweating profusely, and the smell reminded her of an old onion she had once found at the back of a kitchen cupboard in Partridge Manor. She wrinkled up her nose and tried to remember the song of the bees that created the flowers.

It did not help that she had to head-butt the fortune-teller's sodden back now and then to keep him awake. They were some way behind the Great Cortado, who urged his camel on with savage kicks and was probably out of earshot already. If Tau-Tau fell off his camel it would almost certainly be the end of him.

Now, you might think that Little would consider herself better off with Doctor Tau-Tau out of the picture, but she was a thoughtful girl and she had quickly realized that this would not be the case. For one thing she would be tied to a camel's back in the full glare of the sun, without water or shade or the means to free herself. And besides, she would not wish such a death on anyone, even a man as dangerously selfish and vainglorious as Doctor Tau-Tau. Nor, for that matter, did she like to think of a Sleep Angel having any reason to visit that particular stretch of desert. It seemed she was stuck with rotten onions for now.

She wondered where Miles was at that moment. She had no doubt that he and Baltinglass were in full pursuit and making the best possible speed, but there was no way of knowing how long they had waited for her before realizing she had been kidnapped. She had been unlucky enough to run straight into the Great Cortado after she had helped the two elderly ladies to find a hotel, and no one had paid much attention as the ringmaster had dragged her by the arm into the camel yard and threatened her with a beating if she opened her mouth. She had tried to alert the camels, but Cortado seemed to suspect what she was up to, and had squeezed her arm so tightly that she had been forced to stop.

Now she was thirsty and dizzy. The Great Cortado had all the water in his saddlebags, and she thought she herself might soon faint with the heat. She summoned the last of her energy and gave Doctor Tau-Tau's back a head butt that a goat would have been proud of.

"What?" mumbled Tau-Tau, who had been dreaming he was surrounded by electric fires, eating plain crackers in a bath full of toast crumbs. "What are you playing at, child?"

"You were about to fall off," said Little.

"Nonsense!" mumbled Tau-Tau without much conviction. "A man of my experience . . . no journey too short. Soon be at the hostelry."

"I'm sure you'd like a drink," said Little.

"Yes, yes, I'll have masala tea," said Tau-Tau, who had not entirely shaken off the dream of the crackers.

"The Great Cortado has all the water in his saddlebag," said Little, "but he's a long way ahead."

Doctor Tau-Tau straightened up with an effort and squinted into the distance. He wore nothing on his head but his sun-bleached fez, and that afforded him no shade whatsoever. "Is that him?" he croaked indignantly. "He's miles away! This beast's too slow."

"Never mind," said Little. "It's a desert tradition to give the faster camel to the more important person."

Doctor Tau-Tau stiffened with indignation in the saddle. "Outrageous!" he said. "I'm the world's foremost clairvoyant, and he's an unemployed showman on the run from the nuthouse. If anyone deserves a better camel it's plainly me. A better camel," he said, "is no more than I deserve."

Little smiled to herself. A safe distance and a raging thirst had obviously helped Doctor Tau-Tau to forget how afraid he was of the Great Cortado, and she had learned that the angrier adults got, the easier it was to persuade them to do things they would not normally consider wise.

"You're right," she said. "He probably hasn't thought of that, and I'm sure he'll agree when you point it out to him. I think I can make this camel go faster in the meantime. I know a few . . . camel noises." She spoke to the camel for a moment, asking him if he would mind catching up to his friend so that they could get some water. If the beast was surprised to hear her he kept his surprise well hidden, but he grunted and broke into a rolling trot, leaving small puffs of sand in his wake. After a while she could see that they were gradually gaining on the Great Cortado again. Her arms were aching from being tied behind her, and she would have given anything to be able to free them, if only to rub her dust-stung eyes. "One step at a time," she told herself quietly.

Baltinglass of Araby, far away and right at home, pulled the head cloth down from his beaky nose and sniffed the air. "There's water near," he said. "Can you spot the oasis, Master Miles?"

Miles jerked out of his sunbaked doze and scanned the horizon. "I think so," he said, "but I've been seeing trees all afternoon, and every time we get close they disappear."

"That's where a big snout comes in handy," said Baltinglass. "The eyes are easier to fool than the nose."

"I can see lots of palm trees now," said Miles.

"Akhdar is a big oasis," said Baltinglass of Araby. "It's a canvas village. You'd best keep your eyes well peeled as we approach. If Cortado and Tau-Tau are here we want to keep the elephant of surprise on our side."

"You mean the element of surprise?"

"Nope," said Baltinglass. "Ever seen what a surprised elephant can do to a small tent?"

"Someone's coming," said Miles. Two riders were approaching in dark blue robes and head cloths, and as they drew closer Miles could see that they were riding horses instead of camels. They stopped and examined the new arrivals with undisguised curiosity.

"You are foreigners," said one of the men. "State your names and your business."

"Who wants to know?" said Baltinglass. His fingers twitched on the reins, and Miles guessed that he was missing his cane.

"Our master is Kadin al Arfam. He prefers to know with whom he shares the hospitality of the oasis. There are many dishonorable brigands abroad in these troubled times."

Baltinglass stared sightlessly at the man for a moment, then leaned toward Miles and spoke behind his hand in a loud whisper. "Talks like a storybook, this one. Better answer in the same vein, eh?" He straightened up. "We are weary travelers, O vigilant one. We mean no harm, and we will be honored to accept your master's hospitality."

The stranger scratched his head. "That wasn't exactly the meaning of my greeting, weary traveler," he said a little less confidently.

"You mean your master is *not* a great and hospitable one?" said Baltinglass.

The two horsemen held a whispered consultation; then one wheeled his horse and galloped off toward an extensive tent pitched among the palms. The remaining horseman stood facing them in awkward silence while his horse stamped and fidgeted on his behalf. Before long the first man returned. "Our master would be honored if you would sup with him in his tent," he proclaimed.

"Lead on," said Baltinglass.

They followed the horsemen down into the oasis. The air was cooling rapidly as evening fell, and Miles could not remember anything so welcome as the feeling of moisture that touched his skin. A herd of goats drank from a clear pool near Arfam's tent, mirrored on the far side by a group of slender antelope. The tiredness from the day's trek was evaporating in the peace of the evening, but Miles was uneasy at the prospect of losing ground in their hunt for Little. "We don't want to delay for long, do we?" he said to Baltinglass in a low voice.

"We don't," said Baltinglass, "but a straight line is not always the shortest distance from point A to point nine, Master Miles."

They dismounted from their camels, and two small boys appeared, to take the tired beasts to the water while their blue-clad reception committee held open the tent flaps. Baltinglass stepped out of his shoes, and Miles copied him.

"Enter, please," called a rich voice from inside. Miles took Baltinglass's arm lightly and they entered the tent. It was long and low, lit by a number of oil lamps. The walls consisted of intricately woven cloths, and sticks of incense sent thin lines of smoke curling up to the ceiling, which was supported by thick branches of sand-bleached wood.

The voice belonged to an elderly man with a beard but no mustache, who sat on a large rectangular cushion. Miles was taken aback to see that the man's face was a subtle shade of indigo, and he tried not to stare. The man spread his arms hospitably. "Come, come, sit down," he said, waving at another cushion opposite him. Between the cushions a cloth was spread with a variety of dishes, a bowl of fruit and a large water pipe.

Their host watched as Miles helped Baltinglass find himself a seat on the cushion. "You are blind, my friend," he said.

"As a pig's trotter," said Baltinglass.

"Yet you have no cane to guide you," said Kadin al Arfam. "Surely a stick would require less feeding than a boy?" He smiled at Miles. He had one of those faces that could smile and frown at the same time, possibly because his eyebrows were thick and fierce and would continue frowning even if they could be removed and left on the bedside table.

"You've got a point there," said Baltinglass, "but a cane can't shinny up a tree and pick apples."

The blue man picked up a pair of wire-framed glasses and perched them on his nose. He peered closely at Baltinglass. "If it's not a rude question, effendi," he said, "how did you lose your sight?"

"Foolishness, mostly," said Baltinglass of Araby. "I developed a nasty habit of standing in thunderstorms with a copper hat on."

"A domed hat with a tall spike?" said Kadin al Arfam. He gave a great laugh, as though he had just heard the funniest joke ever invented. "I have thought of you often, Baltinglass, my friend, but I'm ashamed to say I cannot remember your given name."

"That makes two of us," said Baltinglass. "Baltinglass of Araby will do fine, and my friend here goes by the name of Miles."

Miles looked at Baltinglass in surprise. "Does he know *everyone*?" he wondered. "I'm pleased to meet you," he said to their host, remembering his manners.

"And I you. Please help yourselves," said Kadin, his smile growing even broader as he waved his hand at the lavish spread in front of them. "You must tell me everything that has befallen you since we parted, Baltinglass." He turned to Miles. "We met when I threatened to decapitate him for killing one of my goats," he explained with a cheerful scowl. "Then he got blasted by lightning, which was a great stroke of good fortune for me."

"Not sure I'd see it that way myself," said Baltinglass, filling his mouth with dates.

"No, indeed," said their host, "but it is a lucky thing that we meet again nonetheless."

"If you're looking for that goat I owe you, your luck is out," said Baltinglass. "I must have left it in my Sunday trousers."

"On the contrary, it is I who owe a great debt to you," said the blue man. He indicated the contents of his tent with a sweeping gesture, forgetting that Baltinglass could not see it. There were bales of colored cloth, ornate saddles, wooden carvings, rich carpets, leather chests with finely tooled decorations in silver and a wealth of other fine merchandise, all presided over by a committee of rainbow-colored parakeets on a tall perch. "After I was given the chance to do you an act of charity, the gods heaped blessings beyond measure upon me. Everything I turned my hand to met with success. My goats multiplied like jerboas, and I soon built up a great herd of fine camels too. All the wealth you see here has grown from that moment like a flower in the desert."

He clapped his hands together, and a servant appeared with a tall silver coffeepot. "And so," said Kadin al Arfam, "you must allow me to return the favor. Just tell me what you would like. I have my finger in so many pies that there are few requests I could not satisfy."

"In that case, a large gin, a new swordstick and a comfortable bed would wrap my day up nicely," said Baltinglass.

"We really need to get back on the road," said Miles. "We're searching for a missing friend."

"Then you must make an early start," said Kadin, "but first you need rest. How did your friend disappear?"

Miles looked at Baltinglass, but he was slurping

thick black coffee from a tiny cup. "She was kidnapped by two men whom we know," said Miles. "We think they may be here in the oasis."

Kadin al Arfam beamed. "This is indeed fortunate!" he said, and Miles wondered if the blue man would consider even being flattened by a palm tree a stroke of good luck. "You will give me a description of your friend, and my men will search high and low. If she is here we will find her and apprehend the culprits."

"They are dangerous men," said Miles, feeling as though he should give their host some warning.

Kadin al Arfam clapped his hands in delight. "And so are my servants!" He beamed. "Don't you worry, young Miles. If your friend is here they will find her, even if they have to search till they are blue in the face."

CHAPTER NINETEEN

A NIGHTMARE BRIDE

Doctor Tau-Tau, chapped, chilled and saddle-chafed, shivered in his thin shirt in the biting wind. He had been ill-dressed to withstand the sun in the daytime, and he was totally unprepared for the night. During their brief stop at the oasis he had replaced the water that his body had lost, but the sweat of their long trek was freezing on his skin. "We need to stop," he said through chattering teeth. "A man of my position should not be expected to travel like a beggar."

"The only position you're in is perched on a camel's hump freezing your backside off," snapped Cortado, making a great effort not to let his own teeth chatter. Still, it was as much as he could do to stay astride his own camel at this point, so he called a halt and tied the beasts to a spiny bush, which they promptly began to eat. He set Tau-Tau to collect some dried vegetation (there didn't seem to be any other kind in this godforsaken place), and to light a fire, then he withdrew the map that he had stolen from Baltinglass of Araby. He frowned at it for a while, muttering to himself and trying to keep his remaining eye focused. They had passed landmarks that appeared to be marked on the map, but they all seemed to be in the wrong places, or facing the wrong way. Others did not look familiar at all. He turned the map upside down, but it didn't help a bit.

He folded the map and checked on the circus freak, who was still tied to the saddle of Tau-Tau's camel and appeared oddly cheerful. "Do you think my wrists could be tied in front instead of behind me?" she asked with an irritatingly uncowed smile. "That way I might be able to sleep."

"You can lie on your face," said the Great Cortado nastily. He did not get the satisfaction he expected from his meanness, which only made him more annoyed as he pulled his sleeping bag from behind the camel's saddle and tried to make himself comfortable on the rocky ground. They were in a bone-dry valley that twisted through the rock following the course of a dead river. The wind whistled and veered along the valley and stole whatever feeble heat the fire produced before he could gain the benefit. It would not be like this for much longer, he told himself. Soon he would be furred, feared and striped, free of all the petty humiliations that he endured on a daily basis.

"It's very generous of you to allow Doctor Tau-Tau to become master of the Tiger's Egg," said the girl, interrupting his thoughts.

The Great Cortado propped himself up on one elbow and glared at Little. "What do you know about that?" he said sharply.

"Oh, not much," said Little. "Only what Doctor Tau-Tau himself told me."

"Which was?" said Cortado, trying not to sound too interested.

Little shrugged. "All that stuff about a Tiger's Egg taking around a week to adopt a new master. I'm sure you know much more about it than me."

"Of course," said the Great Cortado. He did not like the sound of this at all. He needed to winkle more information out of the freak somehow. He got out of his sleeping bag and walked over to where she sat. "Stand up," he said. He untied the rope that bound her wrists, then retied them in front of her. "That should help," he muttered. It was a long time since he had attempted any act of kindness, and it felt strange, like wearing his shoes on the wrong feet. He turned his back abruptly and returned to his sleeping bag.

"Thank you," said Little.

"Tau-Tau is just carrying the Egg for me," said Cortado. "He might as well serve some purpose."

"But the Egg will bind itself to whoever is carrying it," said Little, pretending surprise.

The ringmaster frowned. "It's nothing to do with you," he said. "Get some sleep and forget about it."

"If you say so," said Little. She closed her eyes and began to breathe deeply, but she was still awake when Doctor Tau-Tau returned breathless to the fire and dropped an armload of dust and twigs onto it, promptly smothering the flame.

"You're an idiot, Tau-Tau," she heard the Great Cortado say coldly. His voice lowered, and he said, "Now, give me that thing you have in your pocket."

"What thing?" said Doctor Tau-Tau suspiciously.

"The Tiger's Egg, you fool. Give it to me and get

your sleeping bag. We'll be up before the sun, and I don't want you taking an afternoon nap and falling off your camel."

"The Tiger's Egg should remain in my care," protested Tau-Tau. "I am, after all, the expert in—"

The Great Cortado's voice cut in like a scalpel before the fortune-teller could describe his expertise. It was not a voice that invited argument. "Give it to me, Tau-Tau, or I will personally stake you out at midday and send gilt-edged invitations to the league of vultures."

Miles Wednesday, dry-eyed and sand-jointed, lay awake and listened to the breeze whispering tales of the sea as it riffled through the palm fronds. He and Baltinglass had been given a tent for the night, while the servants who usually occupied it slept with the camels by the water's edge. Although he knew that Kadin al Arfam's men were discreetly searching the oasis for Little, he had slept only fitfully, and as the night drew on without a sign of her he was impatient to resume their pursuit. Baltinglass, on the other hand, had stayed up exchanging stories with Kadin for some time, and now slept like a baby on the other cot, a new ivory-handled swordstick clasped to his chest.

Miles turned restlessly and watched the strip of torchlight that lay across the sandy floor, waiting for a scorpion to cross it. Only when it sidled into view did he wonder how he had known that the scorpion was about to appear. A feeling came over him that was like déjà vu but inside out. It was not that he felt he had seen that same scorpion before; rather that he had known he was about to see it. He knew this was the "far eyes" that the Shriveled Fella of the Fir Bolg had seen in him. He had no idea how it worked, but it happened only when danger loomed, and he held his breath and listened.

As the feeling grew stronger he slid quietly from under his mosquito net and crept to the other side of the tent. The scorpion was not the danger. It scuttled away at the sight of him and vanished under the tent flap. There was something else, but he could not put his finger on it. He crouched by the foot of Baltinglass's cot, trying to remember what was about to happen. There it was! A shadow on the tent wall, and moments later a long sword plunged through the fabric and straight into the bed where he had lain only seconds before.

"Baltinglass!" he hissed, giving the sleeping explorer a sharp poke in the ribs. He knew, of course, that this would have the worst possible effect on the old man, which was exactly what he wanted. Baltinglass leaped from his cot with a hoarse shout, and Miles ducked quickly as the ivory-handled sword shot from its cane and sang through the air. At the same moment a figure with a cloth-wrapped face stepped in through the long slit in the tent wall, and the two swords sparked together as though their owners were electrically charged. Baltinglass, having risen so quickly, had his mosquito net wrapped around his head like some nightmare bride. This was no great hindrance to him, since his fighting technique involved slashing with bewildering speed at any place his opponent could possibly be, but it must have looked quite alarming to the assassin.

Miles had dropped to all fours at once and quickly crawled around behind the stranger. The nightmare bride's veil had given him an idea. As the two fighters circled each other, Baltinglass slicing the air into tiny sections and the other man warily looking for an opening, Miles stealthily unhooked his own mosquito net and crept carefully closer to the fray. He planned to throw it over the stranger and shout a warning to Baltinglass at the same moment. The net was not strong, but with luck the two of them would be able to subdue the assassin long enough for help to come.

The stranger lunged, but Baltinglass's sword met his with the force of a propeller intercepting a bird. The assassin grunted with shock, but before he or Miles could act, Baltinglass did something quite unexpected. He stopped whirling his sword and muttered, "I'm too old for this!" Then he withdrew an ornate pistol from the waistband of his long johns and fired a single shot in the general direction of his opponent.

Miles dropped to the ground again. The assassin stepped backward, clutching the side of his neck, tripped over Miles and fell with a crash onto the vacated cot, which closed around him like an oyster guarding a pearl.

"That did the trick," panted Baltinglass, sitting down heavily on his own bed. "Is he dead?"

"I don't think so," said Miles. The stranger was struggling to free himself, but Baltinglass's shot had brought the sound of running and shouting, and several men came tumbling in through the door of the tent.

"Are *you* dead, Master Miles?" shouted Baltinglass over the uproar.

"No," said Miles, "just lying down." In truth he had no choice. He had been pinned down by two of Kadin al Arfam's men, and others had swarmed over the veiled intruder and over Baltinglass himself, who had fortunately had enough of fighting for one night.

Miles, Baltinglass and the assassin were manhandled to their feet and marched into their host's adjoining tent. The blue man of the desert sat in his habitual seat, but his hair stuck up like a parrot's crest and his robe was misbuttoned. He glowered at his guests and their attacker with his purpose-built eyebrows. "Unwrap those men," he commanded.

The mosquito net and the long black cloth were unwound from their respective heads, and Miles gave a gasp of surprise as the assassin's face was revealed. "Captain Tripoli!" he said.

"I owe you a heartfelt apology, Mr. Wednesday," said the captain. There was a dark welt on the side of his neck where the bullet had grazed him. "And you, Mr. Baltinglass," he added, "though I would have been sorry to miss such an . . . unusual swordfight."

"But . . . *why?*" said Miles. He was beginning to shake with delayed shock.

"A regrettable error," said the captain. "I was convinced that you were the two men who destroyed my ship."

"I thought I was supposed to be the mad one

here," yelled Baltinglass. "How did you manage to mistake us for that pair of hooligans?"

"Do I understand," interrupted Kadin al Arfam, "that you intended to kill both of my guests, but that no one suffered more than a scratch?"

"That was a stroke of good fortune, wasn't it, Mr. Arfam?" said Miles.

"Indeed it was, for both of you," said Kadin, "but it will be less lucky for your attacker, who must now lose his head."

"I don't think that will be necessary," said Miles. "He was really after the same men that we are."

"If that is so," said the blue man, addressing himself to Captain Tripoli, "why did you attempt to murder two of my guests?"

The captain stood ramrod straight, as though addressing a military court. "When I arrived at the oasis I heard that two foreigners were sleeping in your servants' tent," he said, "and that they were in pursuit of three other foreigners—two men and a small girl, who had left after stopping to water their camels. I reasoned that the travelers who had continued on their journey must be my friends here, and therefore the ones who remained at the oasis must be Cortado and Tau-Tau, the arsonists who destroyed my ship."

"That makes sense, in a mildly deranged way," said Baltinglass. "And I must admit I also found our little scrap invigorating. Not a bit sorry I shot you, though. That'll teach you to knock first."

The blue man of the desert steepled his fingers and thought for a while. "For the crime of attacking travelers who are under my protection, you will pay a fine of twelve goats, or six camels, or four white camels, before the next full moon. You will have your sword returned to you only when you leave. If you fail to pay in livestock when the debt is due I will collect your head instead."

"Or you could get struck by lightning," muttered Baltinglass. "It worked for me."

They were interrupted by one of the horsemen who had met them on their arrival at the oasis. "Excuse me, effendi," he said, ducking in through the tent flap. "I have found a boy who gave the two foreigners directions when they stopped for water."

A serious-looking boy stepped into the tent after him. He had ears that stuck out like two coins. "I helped the strangers with their camels," he said. "They had a small girl with them, but she was tied to a camel and could not dismount. They showed me a map, but I did not understand it, and they asked me the way to Kagu."

"Did you tell them to follow the ridge?" asked Kadin al Arfam.

The boy shook his head. "I told them to take the wadi," he said.

"The wadi winds like a snake," said Kadin. "Why did you send them the long way?"

"They did not understand the desert," said the boy, "and they did not have protection from the sun. I told them that way so they would not get lost and they might at least find shade."

"That was wise of you," said Kadin.

"And fortunate for us," remarked Captain Tripoli.

"I was sorry I helped them," said the boy. "They left me with nothing but an insult, and rode away complaining."

"What is your name, boy?" asked Kadin.

"I am Nasir, effendi."

"Go to the end of my tent, Nasir, and choose for yourself the reward you should have received for your kindness. Be sure also that the men who you helped will soon be rewarded for their insult."

The boy nodded his thanks and turned to Miles. "Are you Miles?" he asked.

"Yes," said Miles.

"The girl gave me a message for you while the men were soaking their heads," said Nasir. "She said her eyes were clear and her claws were sharp. I did not see any claws."

"You wouldn't," said Miles, smiling. "They only come out when they're needed."

CHAPTER TWENTY
A CHEAP CONJURER

Captain Tripoli, pencil-black and desert-raised, urged his camel onward through the withering heat with his sword by his side and his captain's epaulettes in his saddlebag. His mind seemed to point like an arrow at his objective, and his brusque entry into the tent during the night showed he was a man who liked to act decisively. Miles worried that things could get swiftly out of hand if Captain Tripoli reached their quarry before him.

Baltinglass rode beside him, nodding slightly now and then, but never looking as if he were in any danger of slipping off his mount. They had been outfitted properly for the desert by Kadin al Arfam, with new indigo head cloths and comfortable robes, and as Miles grew more skilled at riding it was becoming harder to spot that they were foreigners.

"I think we should catch up to Captain Tripoli," said Miles.

"The captain knows where he's going," said Baltinglass.

"That's what I'm worried about," said Miles.

"I see your point," said Baltinglass. "Tell me, Master Miles, who's the leader of this expedition?"

"I thought I was," said Miles, "but now I'm not so sure."

"If you don't hold on to the lead, the dog will run away," said Baltinglass.

Miles thought about this. He remembered something the captain had said aboard the *Sunfish*, and he urged Sanaam on until he caught up with him. "Captain Tripoli," he said.

"Mr. Wednesday?" said the captain, without turning to look at him.

"You said before that only what happened aboard the *Sunfish* was under your jurisdiction."

"That's true," said the captain, "but the *Sunfish* is destroyed, and for that crime I carry my justice with me."

"I have reasons to want the Great Cortado and

Doctor Tau-Tau punished too," said Miles, "but they have Little with them as a hostage, and there are other things complicating the situation."

"Each of us must follow his own path," said the captain. "I will be careful not to harm the girl."

"You've joined my expedition," said Miles, keeping a wary eye on the captain's sword, "and I think we need to be careful about charging in waving our swords about."

"I have joined nothing," said Captain Tripoli. "We are just traveling the same route for the present. Remember that if it weren't for you I would still be sailing the skies in the *Sunfish*."

"If it weren't for me you would be riding the desert with your head under your arm," said Miles. "And as for the *Sunfish*, maybe she should have had a brig after all, instead of cabins with complimentary books of matches in them."

The captain reined in his camel and drew his sword, and you might be interested to know that a swiftly drawn sword really does make the sound *zzingg*. There was an answering *snick* from behind as Baltinglass cocked his pistol. The captain spoke coldly. "You would do well to remember how close you came to finding yourself on the end of this sword."

"I do remember," said Miles, "but I got out of the way, and all you murdered was a mattress."

Captain Tripoli was silent for a moment; then his eyes creased with amusement and he laughed. He sheathed his sword. "You are right, of course," he said. "Restraint was never my strong point, I'm afraid. How do you plan to deal with these men when we catch them?"

"I never play until I've seen the cards," said Miles. He glanced at Baltinglass, who had lowered his pistol with a look of disappointment.

"I suppose I don't get a second shot, then?" said Baltinglass. "Draws a bit to the right, this gun, but I wouldn't make the same mistake twice."

"And I wouldn't stand still for you twice either," said Captain Tripoli. He turned his camel's head to the path. "Perhaps you'd like to lead the way, Mr. Wednesday."

They rode into the gathering heat along a sandy ridge that curved gently through the desert for as far as they could see. Miles had examined the map and knew that the dried riverbed wound more tortuously to the west of them. This was the route that Cortado and Tau-Tau had taken, and Miles and Baltinglass had worked out that they should be able to intercept them at a place where the wadi cut a wide arc around a tall pillar of rock. He could see the pillar even now, dancing on the horizon ahead of them. The harsh sunlight sucked the distance from the landscape, and as the camels padded steadily on he watched their long-legged shadows stretching out to the right, like a stand of violet palm trees stalking along the rippling sands.

In the midafternoon they reached the bend in the wadi, and drew cautiously to the edge. Down below them was a broad river of sand and pebbles that would run with water no more than once a century. In the center of the loop a tall finger of rock stretched to the sky, draping its shadow down into the riverbed and back up the far bank. Two figures could be seen in the shadow, and their angry voices echoed from the sandstone bluffs.

"I have made a deep study of the subject," came Doctor Tau-Tau's voice, "and I am the best qualified to divine—"

"You're nothing but a cheap conjurer, Tau-Tau. The only divining you've done lately is divining where the water skin is kept," said the Great Cortado, his words echoing from every side.

"I'm big-boned. I need a lot of hydrating."

"You even wasted water on the freak!" said Cortado.

"She'll die if she doesn't drink."

"Better her than us. She's of little value anyway. They haven't even come looking for her."

The two men stood cloaked in the rock's shadow, silhouetted against the glaring sand. Cortado reached into his pocket and handed something to the fortune-teller. Miles searched anxiously for Little. He could see the outline of a sitting camel beside the two men, but there was no sign of the Song Angel.

"Here," came an echoing sneer from the Great Cortado, "prove yourself useful with this. If you can divine a fast route to the next oasis you might live. Right now there's only enough water left for me."

Doctor Tau-Tau's voice took on an unexpectedly hard edge. "Now you see it; now you don't," he said, spreading the fingers of his empty hands. "There are some advantages to being a cheap conjurer, Cortado. We share the water, or the Egg is mine."

"You tasseled baboon!" shouted Cortado, his voice rising to a dangerous pitch.

"Sounds like they might finish the job for us," whispered Baltinglass of Araby.

"That would be disappointing," said Captain Tripoli.

"I can't see Little," said Miles.

The captain produced a small spyglass and put it to his eye. He swept the wadi and stopped at the base of the rock pillar. "One of their camels is wandering," he said. "I can't be sure, but it looks like the girl might be on it."

"Let me see," said Miles, almost snatching the spyglass from the captain. The rocks leaped toward him, dancing giddily before he got the hang of steadying the glass. He found the camel and recognized Little's shape perched on the saddle. She seemed to be slumped forward, but he could not tell if she was unconscious or just trying to keep a low profile. If he had not been so worried he would probably have realized that she was leaning down to whisper in the camel's ear without being heard. She was fifty yards or more from her captors, and the camel was moving as quietly as a camel possibly can, pace by pace toward the shelter of the rock column and out of the Great Cortado's reach.

CHAPTER TWENTY-ONE

A CRACK SHOT

Miles Wednesday, sunbaked, dust-caked and thirsty, returned the spyglass to Captain Tripoli. "It's her," he whispered. Down below them the Great Cortado and Doctor Tau-Tau had resorted to a wrestling match, their shouted curses echoing around the wadi. Cortado was trying to search the fortune-teller's pockets, while Tau-Tau attempted to subdue him by sitting on him. Their movements were slow and clumsy, and their skin was red and blistered from the sun.

Captain Tripoli crawled back from the edge and got to his feet. "The girl is safe enough," he said, mounting his camel. "It's time to dispatch them to the world beyond, before they manage to do it for themselves."

"Wait," said Miles. "It's not that simple. You don't know what they took from me."

"We can retrieve your property when I've exercised my right," said Captain Tripoli, no longer bothering to whisper. He spurred his camel over the edge of the wadi and set off at a gallop down the crumbling slope, drawing his sword as he went. Little looked up from her camel in surprise, but the ringmaster and his bulky opponent seemed so caught up in their futile wrestling match that it was several seconds before they noticed the captain bearing down on them at the head of an expanding cloud of dust.

They sprang apart quickly. The Great Cortado scrambled for his saddlebag, but Doctor Tau-Tau merely straightened his fez, confident that it would be clear to the stranger that he was the innocent party and his associate was the real villain. It was as well he thought that, as his saddlebag was halfway up the wadi on an escaping camel and contained no weapon in any case.

As the shrouded figure of Captain Tripoli continued to gallop nearer, his sword held high, Tau-Tau became less sure of this strategy. He reached hastily up his sleeve and retrieved an egg-shaped stone no bigger than an olive. "Catch!" he said in a high-pitched squeak, and tossed it to the surprised Cortado. The ringmaster dropped a slim throwing knife he had just taken from his saddlebag and fumbled to catch the Tiger's Egg, almost dropping it in the sand. "He's got it!" shouted Doctor Tau-Tau, pointing at Cortado. The captain thundered on.

"Don't give it to me, you idiot," shouted the Great Cortado, tossing the Egg back to Doctor Tau-Tau. "*Work* the thing. Call up the tiger!"

Meanwhile Miles had mounted his own camel and taken the plunge over the edge of the bluff. He could feel Sanaam's broad feet sliding on the scree as they descended, and all his attention was focused on not falling off and breaking his neck. He did not know whether to go to Little's assistance or to join the impending battle, only that whatever he should do would not be achieved by sitting safely on the ridge.

"Give me a fix," bellowed Baltinglass after him. "Just give me a fix when you get there. I'm a crack shot when I know where the target is."

Miles reached the riverbed in time to see Tau-Tau and the Great Cortado scrambling to mount their remaining camel, having realized too late that the other one had wandered off. Doctor Tau-Tau was babbling a frightened mix of incantations and pure nonsense as he fought for saddle space, and the Great Cortado was using his crop to thrash both the camel and the fortune-teller with equal vigor. Captain Tripoli was almost upon them now, with only a large boulder of striped sandstone in his path. It looked as though it was all over for the ringmaster and his henchfool, but if the captain had been a patient man he might have learned from Miles that they had one desperate trick up their sleeve.

As the captain reached the striped boulder it reared up suddenly, and his camel shied and stumbled, kicking up a cloud of dust and almost pitching the captain to the ground.

Miles could see now that it was not a boulder that stood in the captain's path, but a Bengal tiger. The tiger lunged at Captain Tripoli's camel, who kicked out wildly before tumbling to the ground. The captain rolled over and sprang to his feet, raising his sword, but the two animals were locked in a savage struggle and he could not see an opening in the dust cloud they created.

The sight of the tiger had spurred Cortado's camel more effectively than any amount of whipping could have done, and he was now bolting away along the riverbed with the two fugitives still scrabbling for position on his back. As they galloped off into the shimmering heat the Great Cortado twisted in the saddle, and with a deft flick he sent a blade spinning back the way he had come. The tiger sprang up with a furious roar, leaving Captain Tripoli's camel lying motionless in the sand, and the captain himself facing his enraged attacker with nothing to protect him but a drawn sword and a coating of beige dust.

Miles dismounted from his camel at a safe distance and warily approached the tiger and the captain, who circled each other in the dry riverbed. The tiger, snarling and bedraggled, had lost the luster and majesty that once had marked him out as a king among beasts. He looked a desperate animal now, savage and hungry, and were it not for his distinctive face markings Miles would hardly have recognized him.

"You don't need to fight each other," said Miles.

"This is a dangerous beast," said Captain Tripoli, without taking his eye off the tiger. "It killed my camel."

"And you can stay out of this," snarled the tiger.

The captain started at the sound of the tiger's voice. He glanced quickly at Miles, as though he suspected the boy might be a skilled ventriloquist.

"Captain Tripoli is not your enemy," said Miles to the tiger. He could not remember his throat ever being so dry.

"And you are not my master," growled the tiger.

"What trickery is this?" said the captain.

"It's not trickery; it's conversation," said Miles. "The tiger was once my friend."

The tiger pricked up his ears suddenly, as though hearing a distant call, and without further warning he opened his mouth in a snarl and leaped at Captain Tripoli. The captain, distracted by the marvel of the talking animal, reacted too late. In a moment he was down, and the tiger was tearing at the cloth wrapped thickly around his head.

Miles could think of nothing better than to run forward shouting, "Shoo!" as though chasing a goat that was chewing the laundry. The captain's sword lay in the sand, but Miles could not bring himself to contemplate using it on the tiger. Captain Tripoli called out in fear as the tiger bared his teeth and prepared to bite, and so Miles did the only thing he could think of to do: He ran around behind the tiger, drew back his foot and delivered the hardest kick he could muster to the striped backside of the king of the beasts.

Now, if you have ever stood in a dried riverbed and kicked an irate tiger in the backside, you are either a very fast runner or blessed with a catering-size portion of luck, assuming you are not reading this from beyond the grave. Miles himself was no stranger to good fortune, but his first instinct was to rely on his sprinting abilities, and he ran toward the pillar of rock as fast as his legs would carry him. He could hear the tiger gaining on him, his paws spitting pebbles and a growl rumbling in his chest like the sound of an empty crate dragging on the ground. Miles ran faster.

He caught sight of a shadow out of the corner of his eye. It was too close to be Little, who should have reached the ridge by now. The tiger's breath was right behind him, and everything seemed to switch into slow motion. He felt as though he were running through molasses, but he was sure the tiger had slowed too. He risked a glance over his shoulder. The tiger had indeed slowed to a walk, and as Miles watched he came to a halt ten paces behind, his hackles rising. The shadowy figure that Miles had glimpsed moments before was seated on a shelf of rock that jutted out from the bluff. Miles could not make out the features, but he knew at once that it was Bluehart.

"Well, well," said Bluehart's voice, which seemed to come from everywhere and nowhere. "Two birds with one stone."

Miles felt the expected wave of tiredness creeping up behind his eyes. There he stood, half-baked in sand, a vengeful captain lying motionless behind him, his father lost in the darkness, his wingless sister weak with thirst, a tiger on his tail and a blind man waiting to fire a crooked pistol on his command. He felt like telling Bluehart to come back later, when he had the time to deal with him, but he did not think the angel would take his busy schedule into account.

The tiger let out a low growl and took a step toward the Sleep Angel.

"You can see him too?" said Miles.

"I'm not blind," the tiger rumbled. His nose twitched. "But I can't smell him. What kind of person has no smell?" He seemed to have forgotten his pursuit of Miles for the moment.

"Don't go any closer," said Miles. "He's come to take our souls."

"Surrender the Egg," said Bluehart to Miles, "and I will make your death a quick one."

A crazy notion came into Miles's mind. He was by no means sure he was right, but a hollow, hungry sleep was washing over him, and it was as much as he could do to come up with plan A. There was no plan B, and no time to think of one. He looked the Sleep Angel in the eye. "Come and get it," he said.

Bluehart came. He did not walk, rather removed himself from the place where he sat and remade himself in front of Miles. It happened in no more than a second, but it was not too fast for the tiger's nimble eye. The tiger sprang at the same moment that Bluehart made his move. He bowled straight into the Sleep Angel, who dispersed sideways like a plume of smoke hit by a cannonball. They rolled over in a cloud of dust, and when it cleared there was nothing to be seen. No tiger, no angel, nothing but an ancient thirsty riverbed, spotted with pebbles and veined with the zigzag tracks of lizard tails.

CHAPTER TWENTY-TWO
TEMZI

Little Song Angel, light-headed, liberated and rehydrated, danced in a circle with her arms stretched out, flapping her hands to get the feeling back into them. She took in a deep breath, savoring the absence of fortune-teller sweat in the subtler aromas of the desert evening. They had set up a makeshift camp by the base of the stone pillar, close in so that they would benefit from its shadow for as long as possible. Baltinglass had rigged up an awning from camel blankets, and now sat beneath it, puffing on his pipe. The injured Captain Tripoli lay stretched beside him, his eyes closed and his breathing shallow.

Little spun over to where Miles sat on a rock, a smile lighting up her face. "What's the matter?" she said.

Miles shrugged. The deadly tiredness that Bluehart brought had settled like an ache in his bones. "I'm worried about Varippuli," he said. "Where did he go? How did he just disappear?"

"The same way he just appears," said Little. "He has always come and gone since you've known him, and we never know where he is in between times."

"Maybe Bluehart has taken him . . . somewhere," said Miles.

Little shook her head. "The Tiger can't die while his soul is in the Egg," she said, "and Tau-Tau still has that."

"That's the problem," said Miles. He scuffed at a pebble with his toe, burying it in soft sand and excavating it again. "We never seem to get any closer to getting the Tiger's Egg back, and without it I can't do anything for my father."

"Of course we're getting closer," said Little. "Cortado and Tau-Tau are bringing the Egg to your aunt Nura because they believe she might know the key to using it, and they're probably right. All we have to do is get there before them."

"And if we don't?" said Miles.

"We have Baltinglass with us," Little reminded him, "and they have bad sunburn and a map of the Gobi Desert."

"We also have Captain Tripoli," said Miles in a low voice, "and he doesn't look well enough to travel."

Little sat down opposite him and looked at him with her sky-blue eyes, as though she were waiting for something.

"What?" said Miles.

Little sighed. "You could help him, Miles," she said.

"Me?" said Miles.

"You've done it before," said Little.

"Yes, but that was just . . ."

"Just what?"

"By accident," said Miles lamely. "I've never tried to do it deliberately."

"You never tried to fly before, but you seem to be getting the hang of that," said Little with a tuneful laugh. She got to her feet and resumed her spinning dance. The ache began to lift from Miles's bones, and over her shoulder he could see a star sparkle as though it had just been switched on.

He got to his feet and went over to the captain. He did not relish the prospect of the dizzy feeling that had come over him when he revived Dulac Zipplethorpe and chased the pain from Baltinglass's leg, but they could not leave with the captain in his current state, and they could certainly not leave without him.

Captain Tripoli lay with his hands crossed on his chest like a knight on a tomb. Miles put his hand on the captain's arm, trying to make it seem as natural a gesture as he could. The captain's face had a bluish tinge, and Miles realized all at once that it came from the indigo headcloth he had worn. "So that's where the blue face comes from!" he said under his breath.

Captain Tripoli's eyes flickered open. "Of course." He smiled. "The dye rubs off on the skin. I'm not dead yet, if that's what was worrying you."

"How are you feeling?" asked Miles. A lightness was coming over him, as though he might lift off like the *Sunfish* into the sky. The desert breeze had dropped, and the whispering sounds of a million desert animals fell silent. He felt hollow, filled with crystal air from some far-off glacier.

"I'll be all right," said the captain. "I'll be up and about in a day or two." He thought about this for a moment, and a surprised look came over him. "Maybe sooner." He sat up gingerly and felt his rib cage. "I was sure I had some broken ribs," he said, "but they may just be bruised."

Miles sat back on the cooling sand, trying not to look like he was about to faint. "Good," he managed to say. "I'd like to set off as soon as possible."

"As would I," said the captain. He got carefully to his feet and winced with the pain. "I don't seem to be as badly hurt as I first thought," he said. "Nonetheless I will go to Wa'il for a while until I get my strength back. You will have to go on without me."

"I think Wa'il is on our route," said Miles. He retrieved Baltinglass's map and unrolled it.

"If you are headed for Kagu it is on your way," said Captain Tripoli. "Wa'il is my home village, and as a child I sold goat's cheese to the camel caravans that passed through on their way to Kagu."

Miles ran his finger along the map. "It's not far from here," he said.

"A couple of hours' ride," said Captain Tripoli, "but I no longer have a camel."

"Little and I will share," said Miles.

"Very well," said the captain with a faint nod.

They struck camp and mounted their camels, taking advantage of the cooler evening air and climbing back up to the ridge to resume their journey. They were getting close to their destination now, their onward path on the map much shorter than the road they had already traveled. As he settled into the rolling rhythm of the camel's stride Miles found his thoughts turning to his lost family, and what it would be like to finally meet them. The prospect made him every bit as anxious as he had felt facing the Great Cortado or the unstable tiger.

They rode on through the darkening night, each in his own separate world, watched over by a slice of moon that emerged faintly at first and strengthened to a crisp silver crescent as the sky darkened behind it. "Who takes care of the moon?" asked Miles.

"What do you mean?" said Little, sitting behind him and holding him loosely around the waist.

"Which angels?" asked Miles.

Little gave a silvery laugh that matched the sparkle of moonlight on the dunes. "The moon is a huge ball of rock orbiting around the Earth!" she said. "Nobody takes care of it."

"But . . . ," said Miles, then fell silent. He would never know what to expect from Little, but he was wise enough to know that that was part of her charm. They rode on until he glimpsed lights in the distance. A small village nestled at the foot of a bluff, surrounded by groves of palm trees whose shaggy heads nodded slowly against the sky.

"Wa'il," said Captain Tripoli, pointing at the cluster of lights. "We will make inquiries to see if your enemies passed this way, but you must rest at my family home, at least for as long as your chase permits."

They rode down a winding path into the village. It was late and there were few people abroad. A girl of about Miles's age stepped out from a rectangle of yellow light and stared curiously at the travelers. She gave a little cry of delight and ran toward them. "Abun!" she said. "You have returned early."

"And you have grown quickly, Temzi," said Captain Tripoli, dismounting carefully from his kneeling camel. He took the girl in his arms and kissed her on the cheek. "My friends will stay the night," he told his daughter quietly, "but we must keep it a secret."

The girl laughed. "I like secrets," she whispered. She gave Miles and Little a dark-eyed smile, though she could not see their faces; then she turned and ran back inside.

Captain Tripoli led his guests into a courtyard, where his family sat at supper. His wife came to greet them in a robe of intense blue, like a piece of the evening sky, and he introduced her as Dassin. "You are welcome in our house," she said, and she led them to a stone bowl that she filled with water from a pitcher. She had strong black eyebrows and a fine henna tattoo across her nose and cheeks, and in the darkness of her face her smile was dazzling.

Once they had washed their hands and faces she found places for them among the captain's numerous children, seated around a low stone table spread with a patterned cloth. Miles tried to count how many children there were, but as none seemed particularly good at staying in one place he soon gave up. The captain sent one of his older boys to see what he could find out about any other strangers who may have passed through; then they sat and ate as though they had never seen food before.

Captain Tripoli's scout returned before they had finished eating. "There are two burned men lodging with the medicine woman," he said. "They will be there until the morning."

Dassin rose from the table and began to issue commands to her children in a soft voice. They cleared the table and returned with a smoking hookah pipe and the inevitable syrupy coffee; then the younger children left, and the captain and the blind explorer settled down to share the pipe. Dassin looked searchingly at the captain's face, but she did not ask him about his injuries, or why he had returned early, and he made no mention of dueling with a tiger or the burning of the *Sunfish*.

Miles took a small glass of coffee from the silver tray on the table. It tasted like bitter sludge, but he felt it would be polite to drink it. He was thinking hard about the Great Cortado and Doctor Tau-Tau. They were nearby, probably asleep. Surely they could be arrested and the Tiger's Egg taken from them.

"Are there police here in Wa'il?" asked Miles.

"We have our own laws," said Captain Tripoli, "but do not fear. Cortado and Tau-Tau will get no farther, and your property will be returned to you."

"Will they be put in prison?" asked Miles.

"They have twice attempted murder," said the captain. "They will certainly face execution."

Miles pictured a terrified Doctor Tau-Tau floundering in a pool of water in the underground caverns of the Fir Bolg, and remembered the start of fear in the Great Cortado's eye at the sound of the tiger in Baltinglass's bedroom. He was aware that the captain's daughter, Temzi, was watching him from her father's side.

"I don't think I would want that to happen," he said.

Captain Tripoli raised his eyebrows and exhaled

a curling plume of smoke. "They tried to push you to your death, or had you forgotten?"

"I hadn't forgotten," said Miles, "but I think Doctor Tau-Tau tried to stop it, and the Great Cortado . . . well, he's not in his right mind."

"They tried to take the lives of my passengers, and for that they deserve to lose their own."

Miles looked at Temzi, leaning on her father's shoulder and regarding him with dark eyes. "I know what it's like to be under a death sentence," said Miles, looking pointedly at the captain, "and so do you. You wouldn't be here now if I hadn't objected to your beheading."

Dassin's eyes widened, and she turned to look at her husband. "Is this true?" she asked.

The captain nodded without meeting her eye. "It was a mistake," he said. "I tried to avenge the loss of my ship, but thankfully nobody was hurt." He turned to Miles. "You are right, Mr. Wednesday. Perhaps these things are not so simple. But we must bring these criminals to justice nonetheless."

"I intend to," said Miles, "but if we have them killed, how do we know we are any better than they are?"

"Miles is right," said Little. "When a bad note gets into the One Song, singing another one does not fix it. It just makes the discord worse."

"Then what are you going to do?" asked Temzi.

Miles smiled at her. "I think I'm coming down with a plan," he said. "Do you have any goats?"

CHAPTER TWENTY-THREE
SUNBURN AND SUBTERFUGE

Temzi Tripoli, long-limbed and dark-eyed, called at the house of Xaali, the medicine woman, where the two sunburned foreigners were passing a very uncomfortable night. They were lying on their stomachs while the old woman lit fragrant barks and recited incantations over them to ease the burning, having first assured herself that they were able to make payment.

"We've heard that you have a famous healer under your roof," said Temzi. "We have a patient who is in need of his help."

The medicine woman, whose lined face looked about to collapse inward like a broken deck chair, frowned at her. "What are you talking about, girl? I will come myself, when I've finished with these two sand lobsters," she said.

Temzi gave her a broad wink over the blistered backs of the strangers. "My father says only a healer of international repute will do." She winked again, in case Xaali had missed the first one.

"If your father says so," said the old woman with a wrinkled smile, "then it must be for the best."

"That would be me he is referring to," said Doctor Tau-Tau in a cushion-muffled voice. "A reputation like mine is a hard thing to escape. To escape a reputation like mine is no easy thing."

The Great Cortado snorted. "Just make sure you charge double what this old crone is squeezing out of us."

"Don't worry," muttered Tau-Tau. "I know just how to milk a situation like this."

Temzi led the hastily dressed fortune-teller across the village to the house of her father. "I am glad to hear you are an expert in milking," she said with a secretive smile.

"What's that?" said Doctor Tau-Tau. Being on the run from sword-wielding desert folk made him nervous about walking around in full view. You never knew when these lunatics were going to fly off the handle. The Great Cortado had warned the medicine woman to keep their presence a secret, yet already the local peasants had come to pester Tau-Tau for his services, and he was concentrating on keeping his protruding eyes peeled for danger.

"The patient is our best goat, Queenie," said Temzi, showing the foreigner into the goat shed. "She has . . . milk constipation."

"Milk constipation?" said Tau-Tau, wrinkling up his nose at the close air of the goat shed. "I'm not a vet, child."

"Of course not," said Temzi. She glanced at a crack in the boards that separated the pens, knowing that Miles was watching through the gap. "But if you are really as good a healer as they say, you will just need to lay your hands on her and she will be able to produce her milk. If she cannot, she will die."

The girl placed a milk pail under the goat's swollen udders and looked expectantly at Doctor Tau-Tau. He knelt down awkwardly. The goat was staring at him with a sinister yellow eye, making him nervous. He placed his hands experimentally on the animal's flanks, and the girl pulled on her teats, producing two streams of milk that rapidly dwindled, leaving the bucket less than a quarter full.

"That's very strange," said the girl.

"What is?" said Tau-Tau. "It's milk, isn't it?"

The girl looked at him as though he were feeble-minded. "That's only a tiny amount. She would normally fill this bucket and have more to spare."

"I told you I'm not a vet," snapped Tau-Tau. He could feel his irritation cranking up a notch or two. "A vet," he reiterated, "is not what I am."

"Xaali uses a talisman," prompted Temzi, "though she's not internationally famous, of course."

Doctor Tau-Tau scowled and rummaged furtively in his pocket. He pulled out the Tiger's Egg, and holding it with his thumb against his palm so the girl couldn't see it, he again held his hands out toward the goat. He was apprehensive about using the Egg, half expecting the savage tiger to materialize on the spot and swallow the goat whole, a thought that gave him a certain grumpy satisfaction. The girl whispered something in the goat's ear, and the animal suddenly gave a twisting leap, as though a demon had gotten into her. The Egg was knocked from his hand and fell into the milk pail with a *plunk*.

"Stupid beast!" said Tau-Tau. He peered into the pail. The milk looked warm and slightly lumpy, and he was very reluctant to dip his hand into it.

"I'll get it," said Temzi. She reached into the milk without hesitation and plucked out the Tiger's Egg.

She wiped the milk off with a rag that hung over the edge of the stall and handed it back to Doctor Tau-Tau. The fortune-teller snatched it from her with a wounded look. If he had been paying attention he would of course have realized, in his capacity as a cheap conjurer, that the girl had made a simple switch. The real Tiger's Egg still lay submerged in fresh goat's milk in the bottom of the pail, and what he replaced in his pocket was the clever fake that had traveled all the way from Cnoc in the pocket of Baltinglass of Araby.

The fortune-teller's mind, however, was on sunburn, subterfuge and the faint hope of supper, and when the goat's milk inexplicably began to flow again he left with relief and scurried back to Xaali's house, forgetting even to ask for payment.

Miles Wednesday, blue-cheeked and smoke-skinned, knelt over Baltinglass's map, which was spread out on the low table, and examined it in the lamplight. Their journey from Al Bab covered a surprisingly small part of the map, and though they were not far now from the town where Celeste had come from, the desert beyond it seemed to stretch to the very edge of the world. Beside him sat Little, carefully stitching the Tiger's Egg back into its home inside a small, grubby orange bear.

"Well, Master Miles," said Baltinglass. "What's the next move?"

"If we leave early enough we can get a good head start on Cortado and Tau-Tau," said Miles. He was watching Little out of the corner of his eye, half hoping that Tangerine would spring to life with the reintroduction of the Egg, and half afraid that he would do so in full view of everyone. Little glanced up and smiled as though she knew exactly what he was thinking, which she almost certainly did.

"They have only one camel between them, so they'll make heavy going," said Baltinglass of Araby.

"Or they'll have to spend time here buying another one," said Little.

"I can help that to go slowly," said Temzi.

Captain Tripoli frowned at his daughter. "In order for them to leave this village I would have to forgo justice for my ship," he said.

Temzi drew herself up and looked the captain squarely in the eye. "Miles has promised they will not escape justice, Abun," she said. "I think he bought his own right to justice with your life."

The captain's glare deepened, and the air almost crackled between father and daughter as they faced each other across the table. The captain opened his mouth to speak, but Dassin's soft voice interrupted him before he could begin. "Temzi is right. She speaks with the clarity that you yourself taught her. You are angry at the loss of your ship, but the boy's justice has been longer maturing, and it should be done his way."

The captain sighed deeply and deflated a little, wincing with the pain in his ribs. "Very well," he said, turning to Miles. "Tell us what you intend and we will help you whatever way we can."

"If they can be tricked into returning to our own country they can be turned in to the police, and they'll spend a long time in prison," said Miles.

"Why did you not do that before they boarded ship in Fuera?" said Captain Tripoli.

Miles glanced around, but with the exception of Temzi the captain's children had left the table. He felt that he was in a place where a secret would be kept safe without his having to ask. "Cortado and Tau-Tau stole the Tiger's Egg from me. It was a gift that my mother left me, and I needed to get that back first. It was the Tiger's Egg that Temzi helped to retrieve tonight."

"Surely that would have been returned to you once you had turned in the thieves?"

Miles hesitated before answering. He had not had to put his reasons into words before, and he had to think for a moment to make them clearer. "Do you remember the tiger in the wadi?" he said.

"How could I forget?" said Captain Tripoli ruefully.

"The tiger is . . . closely connected to the Egg," said Miles. "If he appeared in a police station I might have found myself in more trouble than the Great Cortado was. It's better that the Egg was returned directly to me."

Captain Tripoli contemplated this information. "And how will you trick them into returning to your country?"

"They don't know yet that they've lost the real Tiger's Egg. They're going to visit my aunt, who they believe will be able to teach them the key to the power of the Egg. I think they'll accept anything she tells them, and with her help we can trick them into returning home."

"How do you know she'll want to help us?" said Little.

"I don't," said Miles simply. He had not had much experience of family, and had no idea how his might react to him appearing out of the blue. "We'll have to deal with that part when we get to it."

Little handed Tangerine back to Miles. He took the bear carefully, but though Tangerine had regained his more familiar weight with the replacing of the Tiger's Egg he lay limply across the boy's palm, and Miles placed him carefully in his pocket with a mixture of relief and disappointment.

They settled on cushions that had been laid out around the embers of the fire, and Miles and Little dozed intermittently, waiting for the dawn. Temzi was again dispatched to the house of the medicine woman with a suggestion that the Great Cortado and Doctor Tau-Tau should be given plenty of prune juice for breakfast to keep them—as Baltinglass put it—in the outhouse for some time.

Miles was woken by Little just before the sun rose. They thanked Dassin for her hospitality and went outside to find their camels kneeling patiently, already saddled and equipped with plenty of water and food. Miles had hoped to see Temzi, so that he could thank her for helping him to relieve Doctor Tau-Tau of the real Tiger's Egg, but when the time came to leave she was nowhere to be seen.

CHAPTER TWENTY-FOUR
NURA

Baltinglass, Little and Miles, map-led and morning-lit, crested a rise in the shifting sands and caught their first glimpse of the village of Kagu. A tall rock stood at its heart, with square buildings of mud and stone clustered around it as though they had washed up there on a tide of sand. The houses were squat and low on the outskirts, and grew taller as they got closer to the rock. Many were topped with matching pairs of windows, keeping watch over the surrounding desert. The rock in the center had sprouted its own buildings and grown over the ages into a sort of jumbled castle. Here and there tiny gardens perched among the arched windows, and white birds spiraled slowly around it.

They rode down a gentle slope toward the village. A knot was forming in Miles's stomach, like the feeling that would come over him before his performances at the Circus Bolsillo. He had no idea what his family would be like, or even if they lived here still. Would they welcome him or treat him as a stranger? He wondered if it might be better not to reveal who he was straightaway, but if he kept his identity secret how could he get to speak to his aunt?

As they entered the outskirts a gaggle of small children emerged from the violet shadows and ran to meet them. Their skin was dusty and their hair uncut, and they chattered and laughed excitedly at the travelers.

"Mahnoosh?" said Miles. "Do you know the Mahnoosh family?"

The children turned as one and pointed at the rock castle that loomed over them. *"Qal'at Mahnoosh!"* they said. "Mahnoosh Castle."

Miles looked up at the towering jumble. It was impossible to tell if it consisted of one enormous residence or a cluster of a dozen houses, but there was no shortage of small guides willing to bring them there. They followed the children up through the winding streets until they reached the bottom of a broad staircase that was cut from the rock itself. They dismounted from their camels and tethered them by a well. "That's a tall shadow we've followed," said Baltinglass. "Is there a big climb ahead, by any chance?"

"It's pretty steep," said Little.

"In that case I'll stay here and rest my bones for a while," he said. "I don't think you'll have need of me for the moment, and my little friends here can help me keep watch for those two vagabonds on the road behind."

Miles showed Baltinglass to the well; then he and Little followed some of the smaller children, who cantered up the steps like mountain goats. They reached an ornate door with a curling triple arch above it, and one of the boys hammered on the wood as hard as his little fist would hammer. The door was opened almost immediately by a man in white robes and a wine-red fez. He looked his visitors up and down, taking in their dusty indigo clothes and peering closely at their half-hidden faces. The village children all began speaking at once, but the man said something to them, and they turned and ran back down the stairway, laughing and shrieking.

"You are welcome," said the man politely, with a

flash of gold teeth. "How can I help you?"

"I'd like to have my fortune told," said Miles.

The man raised his eyebrows. "Do you have an appointment?" he asked.

"I didn't know I needed one," said Miles.

"We've traveled a very long way," said Little.

"I can see that," said the man. "You had better come in, but I can't promise to grant your request."

"Thank you," said Miles. They were brought up two flights of stairs and into a small courtyard painted a cool blue and filled with lush plants. A jug of water stood on a round mosaic table, and the man filled two glasses before leaving them alone. There were two wrought-iron chairs, and they sat opposite each other and drank thirstily. Miles put his hand in his pocket to check on Tangerine as he drank. The bear was in his usual place, floppy and familiar and fast asleep as always. Miles suddenly noticed over Little's shoulder a tall, dark woman dressed entirely in black. He was not sure how long she had been standing there, but her sudden appearance reminded him of the Sleep Angels, and he jumped despite himself.

The woman came forward and stood behind Little's chair. She did not smile. Little followed Miles's eye and quickly vacated her seat. The woman sat down and took Miles's hand. Not a word had been spoken.

Miles was glued to his chair by the woman's gaze. He expected her to examine the lines on his hand, but instead she looked deeply into his eyes, and he could not have looked away if his life had depended on it. He felt as though he were being unpacked like a suitcase, and things swam to the surface of his memory that he had not thought of for years. Suddenly the woman's grip tightened; then she gave a little cry and released his hand quickly.

"They told me you had died," she said.

Miles felt his face flush red. His plan to keep his identity hidden seemed idiotic. "Are you Nura?" he said.

"I am Nura," said the woman. "How did you find me?"

"We have a good map," said Miles. It was not just the intensity of Nura's gaze that made him stare at her now. He knew that this was the closest he would ever come to seeing his mother's face, and he was hungry for every detail, as though he could make up for a lifetime's loss. He could see in his aunt's features a strength born of the harsh desert, but her eyes were softened by sorrow. Miles had to fight the sudden urge to sit on her knee and let her fold him in her arms.

Nura looked at him searchingly, and for a moment the ghost of a smile lifted the sadness from her face. She had earrings of silver coins and a cowrie-shell necklace, which looked strangely out of place in the dryness of the desert. "You are like my sister," she said, "and you are not like her. Why have you come?"

Miles felt himself swept on a flood of confused feelings. All at once he wanted to tell his aunt everything about his life: how he had fought against the gray regime of Pinchbucket House, how he had learned to fend for himself, and befriended Little, and brought down the Palace of Laughter. Although he had met her only moments before, he realized that he wanted Nura to be proud of him, as he hoped his mother would have been. He knew, of course, that he could not let all these feelings flood out to someone who had only just learned of his existence, so he swallowed them with difficulty and began with a more practical matter. "We came to warn you about the Great Cortado," he said. "He and Doctor Tau-Tau will arrive here later today."

"I remember Cortado," said Nura. "Celeste was friendly with him, but I never liked him."

"I think you'll find he's gotten much worse since then," said Miles.

"Who is the other man?" asked Nura.

"He calls himself a clairvoyant," said Miles, "but to be honest I don't think he's any good."

"And who is the spirit?" asked Nura.

"The spirit?" said Miles. Nura inclined her head in Little's direction.

"This is my sister, Little," said Miles. Nura looked at Little sharply, and Miles corrected himself. "She's my adopted sister," he said.

"She is not from here," said Nura. Something about the way she said it made the hair stand up on the back of Miles's neck, and he suddenly realized that Little's presence frightened Nura.

"I know that," said Miles. "It's all right. She chose to stay here to save my life."

"We sort of adopted each other," added Little.

Nura turned her dark eyes back to Miles. "The spirits we know make people ill and must be driven out."

"I'm not that kind," said Little, smiling brightly.

"It's true," said Miles. "Though we know a few of those too."

"And what . . . ," began Nura; then she stopped abruptly. An old woman was passing by one of the arches that led off the courtyard. She shot Miles a suspicious look from eagle eyes as she passed. Nura sucked in her breath, but said nothing.

"Who was that scary old woman?" asked Little when she had gone.

"She is my mother," said Nura. "It's better if you don't meet her yet. Are the ringmaster and his friend following you, or coming to see me?"

"A little of both," said Miles, "although they will be hoping to get here before us. Do you know anything about the Tiger's Egg?"

"I know that Celeste had one," said Nura in a low voice, "but it was lost or stolen when she died."

"The Great Cortado and Doctor Tau-Tau think they have it, but the one they have is really a fake," said Miles. "They're coming here to make you tell them how to use it."

"Use it for what?" asked Nura.

"I'm not exactly sure," said Miles, "but it won't be for anything good."

Nura reached out and held Miles's hand again. It was not a harsh grip exactly, but there was more firmness than friendliness in it. She looked into his eyes in that unnerving way.

"*You* have the real Egg!" she said. "It was hidden by the last thing I expected—a surviving child. That is why I could see neither the Egg nor you." She loosened her grip. "It clings to you like it did to Celeste.

Not a color nor a smell, but something in between."
She sat back and looked at him curiously. "Have you
mastered the tiger at such a young age?"

"I wouldn't say that," said Miles. "We were sort of
friends, but we've had a falling-out."

"Friends?" Nura laughed. "You're a strange boy,"
she said, "and I haven't even asked your name."

"It's Miles," said Miles.

"And what do you think we should do about
the ringmaster and the clairvoyant, Miles?" asked
Nura.

"I was hoping to string them along for the
moment," said Miles, "and trick them into returning to where they came from, so they can be handed
back to the police. The Great Cortado is already on
the run from a secure hospital, and he's a dangerous
man."

"Trick them?" said Nura. "I don't remember Cortado as a fool. You must have great confidence in
yourself."

"We were hoping you would help us," said Little.

"They've come all this way to find out from you
how to master the tiger," said Miles. "I think they'll
believe whatever you tell them."

"This is a difficult and dangerous thing you are asking, Miles," said Nura. "And I have only just met you."

She was interrupted by the jangling of bells somewhere deep in the house. "How close behind were they?" asked Nura. She stood and swept out to where a window opened onto a commanding view of the village.

"That depends on how long it took them to buy a camel," said Little.

"And on the strength of the medicine woman's prunes," added Miles.

CHAPTER TWENTY-FIVE

SOMETHING SOMETHING

Nura Mahnoosh Elham, pepper-black and twinless, leaned across the sill and looked down at the doorstep below. "If that is Cortado," she said, "a life of wickedness has not been good to him."

Miles peered cautiously over the sill beside her. She smelled faintly of cinnamon and orange peel. "That's not Cortado," he said. "That's our friend Baltinglass of Araby."

"I have heard that name before," said Nura.

"Everybody's heard of him," said Miles. "He seems to know half the people on this continent."

"That you up there, Master Miles?" called Baltinglass, cupping his hand behind his ear. "The villains are coming down the track. You'd better let me in before I get carried away with my new swordstick."

Miles looked out over the flat roofs and saw two distant figures on camels, one small and the other considerably larger, approaching the village. "That looks like them," he said, stepping back from the window. Nura closed the shutters and a moment later came the sound of the door opening down below, and the *clunk, clunk, clunk* of Baltinglass's cane as he climbed the stone staircase.

The blind explorer marched into the courtyard, following the sound of voices. "Found my own way up," he said. "Hope you don't mind. The ringmaster and his fool are on their way. What's the plan, Master Miles?"

"Nura will talk to them," said Miles, glancing hopefully at his aunt, "while we keep out of sight. We hadn't really gotten any further than that."

"Hmm," said Baltinglass. "A bit half-baked by your standards, boy, but it will have to do. I'm pleased to meet you, ma'am, wherever you are."

"And I you," said Nura. "You had better step into the next room. There is a screen through which you can listen, but you will have to keep silent."

She led them into a small room that was filled with clean laundry, and they sat themselves down on neat piles of sheets and pillows. The wall of the room was an ornate wooden screen that allowed them a broken view of what happened in the courtyard, but kept them hidden in the darkness.

The doorbell jangled again below, and the man with the gold teeth appeared at the top of the stairs. He looked a little flustered.

"We have more unannounced visitors," he said. "It's turning into a strange kind of day."

"You have no idea," said Nura. "You may send them up."

She stepped under the arch where Miles had first noticed her, and almost disappeared into shadow. "That must be one of her favorite tricks," thought Miles, and he hoped it would unnerve the Great Cortado as much as it had unnerved him.

Cortado and Tau-Tau appeared at the top of the stairs and were ushered into the courtyard by the man in the white robes. Both men had tried to smarten themselves up a bit. They were wearing clean clothing, which they must have bought or stolen before leaving Wa'il. Doctor Tau-Tau had replaced his faded fez with a new one, and the Great Cortado wore a large and impressive turban that made him look like a freshly picked mushroom with an eye patch.

"Remember, let me do the talking," said the Great Cortado in a low voice. "If things don't go our way, then is the time to bring out the big cat." He ran his fingers over his scarred cheek and a high-pitched giggle erupted from him, which he rapidly suppressed. "Are you sure you've got the hang of that now?"

Doctor Tau-Tau cleared his throat nervously. "Of course," he said, but he glanced over his shoulder to check his escape route when the ringmaster wasn't looking.

Cortado downed a glass of water and drummed his fingers on the table. "She obviously didn't foresee our arrival time very accurately," he muttered.

"I'm sorry to keep you gentlemen waiting," said Nura at that moment, emerging from under the arch. Miles was pleased to see both men jump. She sat down on the chair opposite the Great Cortado, leaving Doctor Tau-Tau standing.

"It's been a long time, Nura," said the Great Cortado.

"It has passed quickly, Cortado," said Nura.

"This is my associate, Doctor Tau-Tau," said Cortado, waving dismissively in Tau-Tau's direction.

"It's a pleasure to meet you," said Tau-Tau. "I had the good fortune to be apprenticed to your sister,

Celeste." The parts of his face that were not sun-burned were turning redder as he spoke. "It's good to see your face again. Not that I've seen it before, but on Celeste, you understand. That is—"

"Shut up, Tau-Tau," said Cortado. He took out a cigar and offered one to Nura. She refused it and produced a clay pipe instead. Miles stared through the carved screen. He had never seen a woman smoke a pipe before, but his aunt lit it with a prac-ticed hand and was soon trading smoke clouds with the ringmaster.

"I wonder," said the Great Cortado, fixing Nura with his one gray eye, "if you have had a visit recently from a blind trickster and his two young accomplices?"

"I think I would remember such an unusual visit," said Nura.

"Quite," said Cortado. "But if these characters do call on you it might be the last thing you remember. The old man is in fact a ruthless killer, and the two children are his accomplices."

"Nobody has ever managed to bring harm to the occupants of this house," said Nura.

The Great Cortado smiled. "I am sure of it, but these cunning individuals require particular cau-tion. The old man gains sympathy by pretending to be blind, and he uses the two children to charm the unwary. The young boy often poses as a long-lost relative to gain entry to a house. He can be very convincing." He leaned forward and tapped his ash on the tiled floor. "Together they have murdered and thieved their way up and down the country, and just yesterday they tried to rob us as we lodged in a nearby village."

"You did not travel across sea and desert to deliver this warning to me," said Nura.

"Indeed not," said Cortado. He seemed very uncomfortable on his chair, shifting his position continually, and there were violent gurgling sounds from his stomach that even Miles could hear. "I have need of your expertise," said Cortado. He clicked his fingers and held out his hand to Doctor Tau-Tau, who scowled and fumbled the bogus Tiger's Egg from what he imagined was a hidden pocket.

The Great Cortado held up the Egg between his thumb and forefinger. "I think you know what this is," he said to Nura.

"It's a Tiger's Egg," said Nura. "Doubtless the one that belonged to my sister. I often wondered what became of it."

"It was entrusted to me by Celeste," said the Great Cortado. He leaned forward across the table.

"I will get straight to the point, Nura. I have reason to believe that your sister was poisoned by Barty Fumble for this Egg, but that she foresaw her fate and gave it to me for safekeeping."

Nura's face remained expressionless as she listened to this story, but Doctor Tau-Tau's jaw dropped and his eyes bulged in disbelief. "Impossible!" he blurted. "No clairvoyant can predict her doom!"

The Great Cortado turned to him with a look that made it suddenly very easy for Tau-Tau to predict his own doom. "I think I may have left my camel untethered," said Cortado. "You'd better go and check, Tau-Tau."

The fortune-teller made as if to answer; then he changed his mind and hurried sulkily out of the courtyard and down the stairs.

"What do you want from me?" asked Nura.

"The soul of the tiger is contained in this Egg, is that not so?" said the Great Cortado.

Nura nodded.

"Then it should be possible to put another soul in there and combine the two, should it not?" said Cortado.

Nura looked at him in silence for a long time, sending curls of white smoke up into the leafy sky of the courtyard. "It is possible," she said at last, "but

I could not say what the result would be. It would take a strong person to share such a tiny room with a tiger and come out on top."

"I'll worry about that," said the Great Cortado. "Can you do it?"

"Perhaps," said Nura, "but why should I?"

Miles held his breath. It seemed Nura had made up her mind not to cooperate, and he feared that things could get rapidly out of hand.

"For two reasons," said Cortado. "I too have a score to settle with Barty Fumble, and I have recently had reliable information as to where he's been hiding all these years. He is a wily man and hard to get at, but he has a weakness for tigers, as you probably know. In the tiger's body I could avenge your sister's murder and settle my own score at the same time."

"Why become the tiger when you already own him?" said Nura. "Have you not gained power over him in the eleven years you have held the Egg?"

"Of course," lied the Great Cortado smoothly. "But I am no longer content just to pull the strings. A tiger is power in its purest form. I intend to *be* the power." He looked over his shoulder to see if anyone was listening. "Does that seem . . . crazy to you?"

"It's not something that would interest me," said Nura. "You said there were two reasons I should help you. What's the other one?"

"Money," said Cortado. "I don't expect you to provide a valuable service for free."

"You would not be able to afford me." Nura laughed.

The Great Cortado stubbed out his cigar and produced a purse, from which he emptied an avalanche of coins onto the table. "There's plenty more where that came from." He giggled.

Nura eyed the money on the table. "All right," she said. "I'll do what I can."

"Oh, there's one other thing," said Cortado casually. "I fear those robbers I warned you about have some inkling of the value of the Egg, and they will almost certainly trace us here to make another attempt on it."

"You leave that to me," said Nura. "If they come here it will be the end of their careers; you may be sure of that."

"Excellent!" said the Great Cortado. He scooped the money back into his purse. "So, when do we start?"

"I will have to take a look at the key first."

"The key?" said Cortado. He turned the flawless Egg over in his fingers and shrugged. "It didn't come with a key."

"A Tiger's Egg must have a key," said Nura. "That is how it can be opened, and how a soul can be locked inside."

"What would this key look like?" asked Cortado, shaking another cigar from his silver case.

Nura laughed. "I can see why you need my help," she said. "It's not a physical key. It's usually a verse or a riddle of some kind. It was created with the Egg, and the Egg can't be altered without it."

"Tau-Tau?" said the Great Cortado sharply, without turning his head. His voice echoed through the courtyard, and was followed by the huffing and panting sound of the fortune-teller climbing the stairs.

"All's well with the camels," said Tau-Tau in a breezy tone.

"Never mind that," said Cortado. "Did you find in that notebook a verse of any kind? Something that might unlock this Egg?"

"There was one written in pencil," said Tau-Tau, "on the last page of the book."

Miles sucked in his breath, and felt Little's hand on his wrist. He cursed himself for copying the inscription from his mother's grave into her diary. If only he had committed it to memory instead.

"I don't suppose you copied it down," said the Great Cortado.

"Not at all," said Doctor Tau-Tau. "We clairvoyants are expert in memorizing incantations. They are our bread and—"

"Out with it," barked Cortado.

"Yes, of course," said Tau-Tau. He put on his reading glasses in a fluster, as though they would help him with his memory. "What time has stolen, Let it be . . . um . . . Power something, something three . . . er . . ."

Nura laughed. She had a deep chuckle, rich with tobacco smoke. "I don't think 'something something' is going to get us very far," she said.

The Great Cortado put his head in his hands, and his turban slid forward over his fingertips. He pushed it back and spoke with that air of patience that usually means someone is just about to lose theirs in a big way. "Stop . . . right . . . there," he said. He looked up at the fortune-teller with eyes that were red-rimmed from sand and fatigue. "Do you know this, or do you not?"

"I think so," mumbled Tau-Tau, shuffling his feet like an overgrown schoolboy.

Cortado sat back and smiled. "That's good news,"

he said, "because if you don't get it right this time I will tie you to your camel by the ankles for the return journey. Can you foresee the result of *that*, Tau-Tau?"

" 'What time has stolen let it be power grows from two to three embrace the fear and set soul free to drink the sun in place of me' do you think I could use the bathroom?" said Doctor Tau-Tau all in one breath.

The Great Cortado turned to Nura. "Did you get all that?"

"Of course," said Nura. "Out through the arch and first on the right," she said to Doctor Tau-Tau.

"Thank you," squeaked the fortune-teller, and he made another hasty exit through the foliage.

"Well?" said Cortado. "Now can you do it?"

"You are an impatient man, Cortado."

"Very," said the ringmaster.

"I must study the key in more detail," said Nura, "and we will have to find the resting place of the Egg's maker. I hope your talk of money was not an idle boast."

"The maker's *resting* place?" said Cortado, an edge of anger in his voice. "I want to use the thing, not give thanks to some Voodoo Vinnie for making it."

Nura's face remained impassive. "The Tiger's Egg

is not a toy," she said. "The shaman who created this Egg put his soul into its making. Only by evicting his soul can you make space in the Egg for your own, and that can be done only at the place where he is buried."

"Evicting him?" said Cortado, barely above a whisper.

"He has gained immortality in the Tiger's Egg. Now he will die," said Nura, "and you will drink the sun in his place."

The Great Cortado struck a match and put it to his cigar. He puffed slowly for a while. "That explains why the tiger can talk," he said at last.

Behind the screen Miles stared open-mouthed from Cortado to Nura. He saw her hesitate for just a fraction before answering, but still her dark eyes gave nothing away. "That's why the tiger can talk," she said.

CHPTER TWENTY-SIX
A PACK OF LIES

Doctor Tau-Tau, flake-skinned and sweat-salted, sat on a pallet of straw and scratched himself furiously. His sunburn had become unbearably itchy, the clothes he had bought in the last village appeared to be infested with lice, and he was sure he had picked up food poisoning from that terrible breakfast. His guts still churned at the thought of it, making a sound like a trombone player sinking in a swamp. He looked at the torn curtain that served as a door to their hostel room and belched in disgust. If Cortado had all that stolen money, how come they always had to stay in the most rancid flea pit in town? It was hardly fit accommodation for a clairvoyant of his status.

And that was another thing. They had been sent to this dump by that rude sister of Celeste's, after she and Cortado had left him standing like a door-to-door salesman while they talked business. He had tried to draw attention to this oversight, but the sister's striking resemblance to his dead mentor had unnerved him, and instead he had found himself babbling something inane about Celeste's face, as though an idiot had taken over his tongue. He was unaware even now that he was muttering his grievances aloud, much to the annoyance of the Great Cortado. It seemed the idiot was still in charge.

The Great Cortado, meanwhile, sat on his own straw bed, his back against the lumpy wall and whip-thin lizards darting now and then across his feet. There was not even a chair in this hovel that he could occupy in order to lord it over his accomplice. He mulled over Nura's words. The news was not good. It seemed he would have to find the grave of the Egg's maker and evict his soul from the Egg in order to occupy it himself. It was not what he wanted to hear, but Nura's reading of this so-called key seemed to make as much sense as any of this mumbo jumbo did.

He glared at Tau-Tau, hopping and twitching on

the other bed. If it turned out that they had made this expensive trip in vain because the fez-topped fool had failed to understand a little ditty he had carried in his head all along, there would be hell to pay.

He wondered if the blind man and the brats had turned up yet at Nura's door. They were in for a surprise when they did, he told himself with a snigger. Celeste had been fiery enough, but that Nura was a flinty-hard version of her dead sister, and he had no doubt she would have them put to the sword without hesitation. He rubbed his hands together and giggled with glee. Soon he might have the boy's head on a pole after all, and he wouldn't even have to get his hands dirty.

Miles Wednesday, thirst-quenched and Egg-restored, sat at the table with his explorer friend, his adopted sister and his newly found aunt, having emerged from the stuffy laundry with some relief. As they sat at the table Miles took every opportunity he could to examine Nura's face without appearing to stare. She did not look quite so formidable as she spooned a variety of aromatic foods onto their plates, and she smiled at him as she placed his meal in front of him. "You have never seen a picture of your mother, have you?"

Miles shook his head. "Cameras didn't agree with her," he said.

Nura laughed. "We were very alike," she said.

"You must miss her," said Little.

Nura looked at her in mild surprise. It evidently seemed strange to her that a spirit could feel concern for anyone. "I am still waiting for her to come home," she said, the sadness returning to her dark eyes. "I was not with her when she died, though I knew at once that something terrible had happened to her. Sometimes I still feel that she's across the ocean waiting for my visit, or that someday she will walk through this door when she is least expected."

"What Cortado said was all lies, wasn't it?" said Miles. "I mean about my father?"

"A truthful word would choke that man like a fish bone," said Nura. "It was he who told me that Celeste's baby had died when I visited the circus shortly after her death. He sounded almost happy about it, but he was twisted and feverish from the tiger attack and I could not detect any lie in what he said. It must have been the grief that clouded my eye."

"I don't think so," said Miles. "Cortado himself believed that I was dead. The Bolsillo brothers told him so for my protection."

"Those three little clowns?" said Nura.

Miles nodded. "They brought me to the orphanage, and they hid the Tiger's Egg in my stuffed bear. They were afraid Cortado would find that too."

Nura poured sweet mint tea into small glasses and handed them to her guests. "Then they did you a great service," she said.

"They did," agreed Miles, "but I often wonder ..." He hesitated with sudden shyness.

". . . why they didn't send me to find you?" finished Nura. Miles nodded.

"They were away when I visited the circus, as far as I know," said Nura. "I came as soon as I realized that something had happened to Celeste. When I arrived she was already buried, Barty had disappeared without a trace and you were apparently dead. It seemed to me that fate had covered Celeste's life like blown sand, and after taking the few keepsakes I could find there was no reason for me to stay, and I returned home."

Miles thought about Nura's lonely journey back to her home village, a handful of Celeste's trinkets packed in her case, while unbeknownst to her the orphanage closed around her sister's child like a gray cloud of cruelty and graft.

"Barty didn't exactly disappear," he said.

"You have traced him?" asked Nura.

"Sort of," said Miles. "Doctor Tau-Tau tried to cure him of his grief after Celeste died, but he messed it up. He made the potion far too strong, and it turned my father into a sort of hollow shell. All that's left is a hairy giant of a thing that people call The Null. It lives with us now at Partridge Manor."

"A hollow shell?" said Nura.

Miles nodded. "I've looked into its eyes from closer than I wanted to, and I can see only emptiness inside. I only know it was once my father because Tau-Tau admitted what he'd done. I thought that if I could learn to use the Tiger's Egg I might be able to bring him back."

"I'm afraid that might be impossible," said Nura. "A Tiger's Egg is hard enough to master, but if it's true that the tiger can talk then there's something even stranger going on. I've never heard of such a thing."

"I've spoken with him often," said Miles. "At least, I did until Tau-Tau and Cortado stole the Egg from me. That's when I fell out with the tiger."

"You said the Egg that Cortado has is a fake," said Nura, pouring more tea.

"That's right. We managed to swap a fake Egg for the real one yesterday," said Miles. He pictured

Temzi handing the Tiger's Egg to him with a secretive smile. He remembered the feel of her warm fingers brushing his hand and for a moment he forgot what he was saying.

"The fake Egg is mine," said Baltinglass through a mouthful of food. "A little curiosity that I bought in the Far East. Not a spark of life in it, of course."

"You told Cortado that the tiger can speak because the creator of the Egg put his own soul into it," said Miles. "Wasn't that the truth?"

"Not at all," said Nura. "I told Cortado a pack of lies. You asked me to send him back to his own country, so I told him he would have to find the shaman's grave. It seemed as good an excuse as any, and it's up to us where we say the grave lies. I can tell him it's in the middle of a pig farm if you like."

"Or in the gardens of the asylum he escaped from," said Miles.

Nura laughed aloud, and Miles could see a light of happiness break through her melancholy. "If only that would work!" she said. Her bracelets jangled as she wiped the tears from her eyes; then she sighed deeply. "Perhaps you'd better let me take a look at the real Tiger's Egg," she said.

Miles took Tangerine from his pocket and placed him on the table. The bear keeled slowly over.

Nura looked at Tangerine in surprise. "It's still inside the toy?" she said.

"Little stitched it back inside for me," said Miles. "I've talked to Tangerine all my life, and I think that's how I got the hang of the Egg without realizing it."

Nura picked Tangerine up and examined him closely. Suddenly she twitched as though an electrical current had passed through her, and she put Tangerine down quickly. "There is more than just a tiger's soul in there," she said. She sucked her finger thoughtfully, as though she had just burned it. "I think," she said, "that it's time you met your grandmother."

She stood up abruptly and handed Tangerine to Miles. "It's better that we go alone," she said. She took his hand and they swept from the room and along a cool corridor, Miles taking long strides so that he didn't have to run to keep up.

"Will she . . . will my grandmother know more about the Tiger's Egg?" he asked.

"It was your grandmother who first told us stories of the Tiger's Egg," said Nura in a loud whisper. "Celeste and I would sit at her knee when we were children, and she would tell us how it could build cities of power and beauty, or bring terrible destruction on entire peoples. Of all the stories she told us, those were the ones that captivated us most."

"Is that why...," began Miles, but they had arrived at a tall arched door, and Nura put her finger to her lips. They stepped inside and found themselves in a cool, dim room with a large four-poster bed taking up most of the floor. The old lady who had passed them earlier in the courtyard sat upright in the bed, supported by pillows and apparently fully dressed. She had her eyes closed, and her hands were clasped loosely in her lap.

Nura motioned Miles to stay at the door. "Mother," she said, approaching the bed. The old lady's papery eyelids snapped open. "I've brought a guest to meet you," said Nura.

The old lady beckoned for Miles to come closer. She struggled to a more upright position, reached out and grasped Miles's chin. She turned his head from side to side and pulled downward on his cheek to get a better look at the whites of his eyes. "Can't see much wrong with him," she croaked. "Bad teeth, might have worms. Nothing out of the ordinary."

"He's not here for a cure. He has something to show you," said Nura.

Miles looked at her uncertainly, the feel of his grandmother's hard fingertips still printed on his cheeks. He reached into his pocket and produced

Tangerine, holding him out for the old lady to see.

"What's this?" said his grandmother, her fierce eyes flicking from Tangerine to Miles and back again.

"Take it, Mother," said Nura. She watched the old lady take the bear in her age-knotted hands with an expression that Miles could not even begin to read.

The old lady held Tangerine for a while; then suddenly she took in a deep breath, and she looked at her daughter with wide eyes. "A Tiger's Egg!" she said. "So rare! Where did it come from?"

"It belongs to the boy," said Nura.

The old lady clutched the bear tightly, as though she could draw from it enough strength for another eighty years. A look of puzzlement grew on her face. "This is not pure," she said. "What is in there with the tiger?" She looked at Miles accusingly.

"I think it's more of a 'who' than a 'what,'" said Miles.

The old woman held Tangerine to her nose and closed her eyes. She put him up to her ear and shook him, and she held him against her skinny rib cage to measure him with her heartbeat.

"It's no one I know," she said, handing Tangerine back to Miles. He took the bear with a sigh of relief, and an involuntary smile spread across his face. The old lady was watching him closely. "It's someone very close to you, though," she said. "Who have you lost, boy?"

Miles opened his mouth to answer, but found he was unable to speak. Tangerine had been his lifelong companion, and he had never looked for any other explanation for the closeness he felt to the bear. Now he realized that what his grandmother said made perfect sense. He had lost two people in his life, and if it was not someone the old lady knew, then it must be . . . His knees felt suddenly weak and he sat down quickly on the end of the bed.

"My father," he said when his voice returned to him. "It must be my father."

CHAPTER TWENTY-SEVEN

A GHOST IN A STONE

Miles's grandmother, knife-eyed and pillow-throned, looked at the young stranger who sat shakily on the end of her bed. It was not like Nura to interrupt her siesta, and it troubled her. She turned to her daughter and raised a bony finger in warning. "Don't get mixed up in this," she said. "That Egg will bring nothing but trouble and heartache."

Nura's dark eyes flashed. "It was you who told us stories of the Tiger's Egg when we were children, Mother," she reminded her.

"The stories of your childhood do not make a path for your life," said the old woman.

"Is that what you think?" said Nura. "What of Celeste?"

The old woman seemed to shrink visibly. "Celeste always went her own way," she said. "She was as restless as you are stubborn, and look where it brought her."

Nura folded her arms and frowned darkly. "The boy needs help to cure his father," she said.

"There are plenty of healers," said her mother.

"Look at the boy's face, Mother," said Nura. "Look beyond his teeth and his eyelids."

The old lady stared at Miles for a moment, then she closed her eyes and sank back into the pillows.

"This is Celeste's son," said Nura gently. "Your grandson. His name is Miles, and he did not die in the orphanage after all. The Egg in the bear is the one he inherited from Celeste, and he needs our help."

The old woman said nothing. She lay among the pillows, breathing slowly as though she had fallen asleep. Eventually she opened her eyes again. "There's nothing we can do for him," she said. "His father is a ghost in a stone. How can that be cured?"

"What used to be my father is still alive," said Miles. "It's just a part of him that's trapped in the Tiger's Egg, along with the tiger."

"Impossible. Even the greatest shaman could not do what you describe."

"Maybe not," said Miles. "This was achieved by an idiot. He was trying to cure my father of a broken heart. He told me that he made his potion too strong, but I think now that he tried to use the Tiger's Egg in the cure. I know this man well, and if there's a way to get something completely wrong he'll find it."

"You can't fix this with further meddling," said the old woman. "My advice is to return the Tiger's Egg to its original owner. Where was your father when you needed him? You owe him nothing."

"I can't do that," said Miles, fighting back the tears. "I don't know what my father went through, but I'm all he has. Besides," he said, "I can't return it to the Fir Bolg without fulfilling Celeste's bargain."

The old woman sat up sharply in the bed as though she had just swallowed a mouthful of strong mustard. "The Fir Bolg?" she choked, and Miles saw Nura wince as her mother turned to her with a furious look. "You told me she bought the Tiger's Egg from a one-legged antique dealer in Calcutta."

"I didn't think there was any point in upsetting you," said Nura.

"Well, I'm upset now!" said Miles's grandmother.

"No wonder Celeste came to a bad end. The Fir Bolg are shiftless little troglodytes, and no good ever comes of dealing with them." She turned to Miles, and her face was like thunder. "What was the bargain? Speak up!"

"They wanted to be freed of their fear of the light," said Miles. "Celeste promised to find a cure for them in exchange for the loan of the Egg."

"That would be lunacy! What was the term?" asked the old lady.

"Twenty-one years. It expired when I turned eleven."

The old woman clicked her tongue disapprovingly. "They will consider that binding on you, boy."

"I know," said Miles. "I've already met them. They only let me go in order to find the Egg and bring it back."

"My advice is not to return the Egg to its original owners under any circumstances," said the old lady. "Pay no attention to any bargain they may claim to have made. The Fir Bolg would break their word at the drop of a hat. Take the thing and throw it in the sea."

"He can't throw his father in the sea," said Nura with an exasperated gasp.

"It's not his father," said the old woman. "It's a pebble."

"You always told us that a Tiger's Egg was the most precious thing known to man," said Nura.

"A pure one would be a great treasure," said her mother. "This one is flawed, and no use for anything."

Miles stood up and put Tangerine back in his pocket. "It was nice to meet you," he said, more politely than truthfully. "My father is more than a flaw in a stone to me, and I'll do everything I can to find a way to bring him back."

He turned and left the room, and heard his grandmother's voice echoing along the stone passage as he went. "I forbid you to get mixed up in this, Nura. Do you hear me?"

Miles Wednesday, clean-eyed and sharp-clawed, lay under cool cotton sheets beneath a high ceiling in the house where his mother was born. His mind was racing and sleep seemed far away. The possibility that he had found the way to restore his father at last seemed very real, but big answers have a habit of bringing new questions trailing after them, and this one was no exception. Would Barty Fumble's soul survive being returned from the Tiger's Egg to The Null? And even if it could be done, would that turn The Null back into Barty Fumble after all this time, or would it just become a giant hairy monster that could actually speak to you as it tore you limb from limb? What if he was wrong and the extra soul in the Tiger's Egg was not Barty Fumble at all, but a retired postman or a fugitive nun from Casablanca? There was one final question too that for some reason he found it hardest of all to face. Supposing he did succeed against the odds in freeing his father from the Tiger's Egg—what would happen to the tiger himself?

There was one thing he knew for certain: Blue-hart would not stop searching for him, and sooner or later Miles would run out of tricks. He had been lucky so far, but the thought that he might regain his father only to lose his own life made a mock-ery of all his plans. He would have to find a way to tackle Bluehart head-on. He looked across at Little, lying in the other bed. The starlit glow on her skin was so faint now that he could barely see it.

"Are you awake?" he said.

"I am now," said Little.

"I'm going back to the Realm," said Miles.

Little propped herself up on one elbow. "I don't think that's a good idea," she said.

"You don't need to come," said Miles.

"Going on your own would be an even worse idea, Miles."

"I know what to expect now," said Miles. "I'll be able to take care of myself."

"You'll only alert Bluehart," said Little. "You've cheated him so many times he's going to make it really bad for you."

"What can he do that's worse than killing me?" asked Miles.

"A Sleep Angel doesn't kill you," said Little. "A rock slide or a snakebite or double pneumonia kills you. It's a Sleep Angel's job to conduct you to your next life, and there's lots of ways Bluehart could make that much worse for you, believe me."

"All the more reason for me to go back," said Miles. "Bluehart tricked me out of the chance to make my own defense the last time. Why would he have dragged me away from the Council if there's no chance I could change their minds?"

Little sighed. "What would you say to them?"

"I've got the Tiger's Egg," said Miles. "They've been searching for it for years without success, and

I could agree to hand it over as soon as I've used it to restore my father, if they agree to let us live in return."

"All right, Miles, but I'm coming with you. Let's just make sure we don't lose sight of each other for a second this time."

Miles smiled in the dark. "Okay," he said. He lay still and tried to relax, but if you have ever tried to make sleep come quickly so that you can defend yourself before a tribunal of shape-shifting angels on a charge of stealing a tiger's soul, you will know that the more you try, the less likely you are to sleep. That's just how it was with Miles. He could hear Little's slow, even breathing, and he could imagine her waiting impatiently for him to find her. He hoped she didn't head for the Council thinking that he'd gone ahead of her, and he wondered . . .

"Are you just going to float around like a blob hoping and wondering things, or can we get going?" said Little's voice.

Miles opened his eyes in surprise. "Where are we?" he asked. He seemed to be in the middle of a gray cloud.

"Instead of 'Where are we?' try 'Where do we want to be?'" suggested Little.

"At the Council, I guess," said Miles. The cloud

around him at once began to condense into figures of all shapes and sizes, milling restlessly about. There was a great deal of shouting going on, and somewhere in the distance the Storm Angels were rolling thunderballs through the flickering sky.

"Blend in," whispered Little at his ear, "quickly!"

Miles looked around him and let himself flow into what looked like an average shape. "How will we know each other?" he said, turning to look at Little. She looked like herself, but less so, he thought, but she gave him a mischievous look and stuck out a bright green tongue for an instant. He pictured his own tongue in electric blue, and stuck it out experimentally.

Little laughed. "That'll do," she whispered.

The angels seemed to spend most of their time in a vague or changeable form, taking on sharper definition only when they wanted to be seen or heard, and Miles noticed that he could follow the discussion as it passed through the assembly like ripples of clarity. Most of the time there were several ripples on the go, spreading and jumping in a bewildering jumble of argument. He could not tell how any of the discussions actually got started, so after listening for a while he decided to throw the dragon into the henhouse, as the Chaos Angel had put it.

"What about the Tiger's Egg?" he said in a loud voice, when he felt nobody was looking directly at him.

"What about it?" asked an angel in the center of the melee.

A figure on the far side replied immediately, "It hasn't been found yet, has it?" and to his surprise Miles caught a momentary flash of emerald green in the speaker's mouth. He couldn't see the angel clearly, but Little was not by his side where she had been a moment ago. The crowd was too dense to force his way through, so he shut his eyes briefly and imagined himself standing beside the other angel. When he opened them again he was on the other side of the crowd.

"Well done," whispered Little in his ear.

Miles turned around in time to hear a cold voice from a tall, smoky angel in the center of the assembly. "Bluehart has been charged with the recovery of the Egg."

"Well, he's not doing a very good job, is he?" said Miles. He knew that he would become more visible as the other angels turned to look at him, and without giving it a second's thought he made himself slate gray and smoke-edged like the Sleep Angel he had answered. The effect was dramatic. The other angels seemed farther away without actually having changed position. Even Little seemed to shrink somehow. He felt a surge of strength spread through him, and he spoke again. "The boy who hides the Egg has given Bluehart the runaround for months. How hard can it be to track down one boy?"

He was beginning to enjoy himself now, and did not see the alarmed look on Little's face. "Miles," she hissed, but before she could say anything further a quiet voice came from just behind him.

"That's a dangerous game you're playing, meat-made." Miles glanced over his shoulder to see Fish-fly, the Chaos Angel, looking at him with a glint of amusement. He felt a heady confidence at his new-found ability to change himself at will. "I know what I'm doing," he said.

"Is that so?" Fish-fly chuckled. "Do you know you're wearing Bluehart's face while you're bad-mouthing him to the Council?"

Miles turned around with a sinking feeling. Several angels stood in front of him, their stone-dark eyes peering at him closely. "What's the game, Blue-hart?" said one of them, and in a flash he remembered how closely Bluehart's features had resembled his own. His mouth felt dry and he licked his lips nervously. The Sleep Angels recoiled at the sight of his electric blue tongue. In the distance the rumble of thunder grew louder.

"He's not himself at the moment," said Little, a slight tremor in her voice.

"That's right," said Miles. "I think I need some time off."

"Time . . . *off?*" said a Sleep Angel.

"Time off." Miles nodded. "The boy . . . that is . . . I have a feeling he'll surrender the Egg when he's finished with it. Then I can, you know . . ."

". . . reexamine the case," finished Little.

"That's a bit soft for you, *Blue*hart," mocked the Chaos Angel from behind him. "What happened to your plan to send the boy back as a tapeworm inside a swamp buffalo?"

"Well?" said the assembled Sleep Angels with one voice.

Miles glanced at Little in the hope that she would be ready for what was coming. He took a deep breath that seemed to leak out between his ribs before he could get the benefit. "I'd send the lot of you back as tapeworms if I could," he began.

A ripple of shock ran through the assembly, and the Sleep Angels' stony faces became even stonier. "That would teach you some humility," Miles went on. He looked again at Little, who was starting to dissolve around the edges. He was not entirely sure he would be able to disappear at will himself, especially with the attention of a hundred stunned angels fixing him in place, but it was too late to change course now. "Then with you pebble-heads out of the way I could start running this place properly" he said.

There was an enormous crash of thunder as he spoke. The cloud lit up inside, giving a brief glimpse of a fabulous network of galleries and domes that opened out from one another like an endless hall of mirrors, and it seemed to Miles that every eye in the entire Realm was turned on him. He closed his eyes, which seemed to him a necessary part of disappearing. A hand gripped his shoulder and began to shake him. He pulled himself free and opened his eyes to see Nura leaning over him.

"It's all right," she said. "You were having a bad dream."

Miles nodded, struggling into a sitting postion. He looked across the room and saw to his relief that Little was sitting on the edge of her own bed, rubbing sleep from her eyes. "What time is it?" he asked.

"It's early," said Nura, "but you must get up." She opened the shutter on the arched window, letting in the pearly dawn light. She turned to him and smiled. "I've spent the night thinking about yesterday's events," she said, "and I've decided I will have to honor the Great Cortado's request and have you all beheaded."

CHAPTER TWENTY-EIGHT

HEADS IN THE SAND

Nura Mahnoosh Elham, night-wrapped and rose-fingered, ushered the Great Cortado and Doctor Tau-Tau into the courtyard and invited them to sit. A jug of iced water and a pot of mint tea sat on the mosaic table. She poured two cups of tea, spilling some on the tiles. "I'm sorry," she said, "it's a little dark in here." She crossed to the lamp that hung on the opposite wall and turned up the light. Doctor Tau-Tau raised his glass to his lips, but no sooner had he taken a mouthful than he gave a choking gasp and sprayed himself, the table and the Great Cortado with tea.

The turbaned Great Cortado leaped up with a

gasp of anger; then he stopped as he saw what had so startled his accomplice. Even Cortado himself seemed momentarily shaken, but he collected himself and forced a smile. In a corner of the room the severed heads of Miles, Little and Baltinglass of Araby sat carelessly on a carpet of sand, dark red stains blooming around each of them.

Doctor Tau-Tau's face changed like a traffic light from red to green. He stood up abruptly, sending his chair crashing to the floor, and stumbled wordlessly out of the courtyard, a pudgy hand clasped across his mouth.

"I'm sure he knows where the bathroom is by now," said Nura coolly. She righted the wrought-iron chair and sat herself at the table. "You must forgive me for not fully trusting you yesterday," she said. "Your visit was a little unexpected after all these years. However, when these bandits turned up I realized you were a man of your word, and I had them dealt with appropriately." She poured herself a tea and took a sip. "I have given your proposal some thought, and have decided to go with you to find the grave of the Egg's maker. I don't think Doctor Tau-Tau will be able to effect your transformation on his own. He doesn't even know about your plan, does he?"

"He knows only what he needs to know," said the Great Cortado.

"I will require full payment up front," said Nura.

"I don't think so," said the Great Cortado with an unconvincing smile. "I'll pay half your fee now, and the rest when the process is complete."

Nura shrugged. "Very well," she said. "We will leave at sunset and travel in the cooler hours. In the meantime I would caution against using the Tiger's Egg unless absolutely necessary. The transformation you want to achieve is an ambitious one, and if the power of the Egg is depleted from overuse your chances of success will be far slimmer."

She stood up. "Now I have much to do. We will meet at sunset by the well at the bottom of the steps. You may collect your squeamish associate on your way out."

The Great Cortado paused in the archway and took a last look at the severed heads. "One other thing," he said. "I would like the boy's head boxed to bring with me."

Nura raised her eyebrows. "It won't smell that sweet after a few days in your saddlebag," she said.

"Tau-Tau doesn't smell too good either, but he has his uses," said Cortado with a strained giggle. "You can pack it in ice, can't you?"

"It will cost you extra," said Nura.

The Great Cortado sniggered. "It will be worth every sou," he said, and he went in search of the distressed fortune-teller.

Now, picture if you will the grim scene in that leafy courtyard. Beneath the well-tended plants sit three human heads on a bed of sand. The heads belong to people we know well—a grizzled old man who has crossed every continent and whose fire has been rekindled by the spark of his young companions, a small girl who has learned that love is the heart of friendship and loyalty only its skin, and a boy full of courage and hope whose dream of weaving a family from the scattered threads he has inherited seems so close to completion. There they sit, their eyes closed and their lips sand-coated, as the echo of a door slamming far below them seems to put a final end to their story.

It will probably not surprise you to find that it is no such thing. One of the boy's eyes opens a fraction, and he attempts to spit out a mouthful of sand, which merely dribbles down his chin. Little laughs. "Even I can spit better than that, Miles," she says. The three heads squirm and wriggle in a manner that's quite unsettling to look at, and that only makes them more uncomfortable than they already are.

"If this is being dead," grumbled Baltinglass of Araby, "I'd rather go back to being a living fossil."

"Patience." Nura laughed as she swept back into the room. "It will take a little time to extract you from there."

It did indeed take some time, as the trapdoor through which their heads poked had to be carefully dismantled again before they could be released. They were stiff and cramped from crouching on the stone staircase that led down from the trapdoor into the storeroom below. Miles, who had toured with the Circus Bolsillo as a magician's assistant, was more accustomed than the others to being confined in awkward spaces. It was he who had spotted the trapdoor in the corner of the room and had given shape to that part of Nura's plan. They had cut three circular holes in the trapdoor and separated the wooden boards so that they could be assembled around their necks once they were in position. He knew that it would be no easy task to fool the Great Cortado with a circus trick, but as the rest of the floor was tiled in stone he reasoned that hiding the trapdoor with sand would make it look all the more convincing, and it seemed he had been right. A liberal sprinkling of berry juice had been enough to complete the illusion.

"There's a small snag," said Baltinglass of Araby, knocking his pipe on the table to dislodge sand that had found its way into it. "As things stand we'll have to make the return journey without the boy's head, which has proved fairly useful in the past."

"Can't we just give Cortado a box of ice and nail it shut?" said Little.

"We'd have to put a rock in or something," said Miles. "Once the ice has melted and the water has run out the box will be too light. If he gets suspicious and tries to open it, it will be a disaster."

"You're right," said Nura. "But we can do better than that. I'll have a sheep's head packed instead. When the ice runs out it will begin to smell, as I warned him. It will quickly become unbearable and I will persuade him to throw it away unopened. No ship will take him on board with it anyhow."

Miles nodded his agreement. It was a little unsettling to be discussing the fate of what might easily have been his own head, but on the other hand he was pleased to discover that his aunt seemed to see the world from a perspective that was familiar to him. He thought of the plans he could have made with his mother had she lived, and the fun they could have had together; then he reluctantly put the thought out of his head.

They spent the morning preparing for the return journey of Miles, Little and Baltinglass, who would make a head start in order to get to Al Bab as quickly as possible. The air was unusually humid, and thunder-clouds rumbled over the distant mountains. Miles helped Nura pack the saddlebags with fresh provi-sions and clean clothing, and they buckled them onto the camels in silence while a couple of the local children kept watch for any sign of Tau-Tau and Cortado. When they were finished Nura smiled at Miles and said, "You should say good-bye to your grandmother."

"I think I got off on the wrong foot with her," said Miles as they climbed the stone stairs into the cool-ness of the house. "And I don't think she was all that pleased to see me in the first place."

"It would be a mistake to believe that," said Nura. "My mother hardened herself when Celeste died, but inside her heart beats the same as before." They reached the old lady's door and Nura knocked softly. Miles's grandmother sat in her accustomed place, propped up on her pillows with her hands crossed in her lap.

"Miles will be leaving soon," said Nura, and she pushed him gently inside.

The old lady patted the edge of the bed without a word, and Miles sat down.

"I am a little too old for surprises," said his grandmother, "and on the rare occasions I meet one I usually just want it to disappear. You are obviously a boy of great courage and determination and I should not have dismissed you as I did."

Miles shifted uncomfortably. "That's all right," he said.

"You plan to try to release your father from this stone," said his grandmother, "and to restore him to himself?"

Miles nodded. "Do you think it can be done?" he said.

"If it were anyone else asking I would say absolutely not. In your case, Miles, I think it is unlikely, but not impossible."

"Because I'm his son?"

"Because you are Celeste's son," said the old lady. "I never met your father. By all accounts he was a kind man and good with animals, but those talents would be of no use in what you are trying to do. It is the gifts that you inherited from your mother that turn the odds just slightly in your favor. Nura tells me you have both the far eyes and the bright hands." She looked at Miles with her piercing eyes. "Do you know how unusual that is?"

"I'm not sure if I really have," said Miles. He could not remember discussing anything of the kind with Nura.

"You can see things that have not yet happened?" said the old lady. Miles nodded. "And you have healed injuries that looked beyond curing?"

"I suppose so," said Miles.

The old lady clucked disapprovingly. "'I think,' 'I suppose,'" she said. "I never heard of anyone besides Celeste who possessed both gifts. You've grown up without anyone to teach you how to use them, though you are not to blame for that."

She leaned forward and grabbed Miles's chin as she had when examining his teeth the night before, but this time she looked into his eyes. "You have much to learn," she said, "and a short time to do it in. To restore your father you will need the far eyes to see all parts of the puzzle at once, and the bright hands to steal the energy to do what's necessary. The Tiger's Egg is just a tool to help you focus your powers. You have learned the key?"

Miles nodded. "I don't know what it means, though," he said.

"You might never know until the moment comes to use it," said his grandmother. She sat back against the pillow. "In this case the tiger's power is entangled twice over. It is tied up with the soul of the very person you wish to save, and it is also bound by the promise your mother made. You will have to keep her promise to the Fir Bolg."

Miles looked at her in surprise. "Yesterday you advised me to ignore it," he said.

"Yesterday I told you to throw the stone in the sea. If you did that you'd have no reason to keep the promise. You did not make it yourself, after all." She sat back and crossed her hands in her lap. "But you cannot undo the Tiger's Egg without discharging any promise that binds it."

Miles looked at his grandmother as he tried to take in everything she had told him. His strange abilities to ease pain and to predict what was about to happen had seemed up to now to be random accidents that were largely outside his control. Now that he had the Tiger's Egg back and was about to set off for Partridge Manor he realized he could no longer afford to view them in this way.

"Can I ask you something?" he said to his grandmother.

"What is it?" she said.

"If I do manage to restore my father, what will happen to the tiger?"

His grandmother smiled sadly. "The tiger has had a long life," she said. "Longer than most."

Miles was surprised to see tears glistening in her red-rimmed eyes, and it made him embarrassed at the question he had asked. He waited to see if there was more to her answer, but the old lady just sighed. "Always the tigers," she said, shaking her head. "You are just like your mother."

CHAPTER TWENTY-NINE
THE HICCUP MAN

The Great Cortado and Doctor Tau-Tau, villain-in-chief and fool-in-a-fez, sweated and snored in their no-star lodgings, sleeping away the afternoon heat. They had given the smallest coin they could find to a boy whom they found loitering in the street outside, and asked him to wake them before sundown. The boy had reported straight back to Baltinglass of Araby, who had given him twenty times as much to make sure that he woke them as late as possible. Now as they slumbered in their itchy beds three camels padded quietly past their window, bearing on their backs a Song Angel, a blind adventurer and the boy whose head Cortado believed would be boxed and safely packed in his saddlebag.

Miles had agreed with Nura upon a story that would bring the Great Cortado and Doctor Tau-Tau to Larde in search of the grave of the Egg's creator, where they could be arrested by none other than Sergeant Bramley. Miles had explained to Nura that the sergeant was familiar with both men and was sure to oblige without the need for explanations and evidence, two things in which he was not a great believer in the first place.

Now Miles and his companions were headed for Wa'il, where their camels could be watered and they could have a short rest before resuming their journey well before Cortado and Tau-Tau had even set out from Kagu. The prospect of a long camel ride had lost much of its appeal, but Miles had not forgotten that he was leader of the expedition, and he made it his business to keep up his spirits and those of his companions.

They reached Wa'il as the sun began to sink behind the bluffs. They had no difficulty finding Captain Tripoli's house. Their camels remembered the cool stables and the fine feed they had been given on their previous visit, and almost broke into a trot as they made their way unerringly through the narrow lanes.

They were greeted warmly by Dassin, who told them that the captain had left the day before to repay his debt to Kadin al Arfam. He had taken Temzi and two of his sons with him, and to Miles's disappointment they were not expected back until the following day. A supper was quickly laid out in the courtyard, and they sat down to eat while their camels were being tended. Miles was impatient to get back on the road, and he had to make an effort to be polite. As they finished their meal one of Captain Tripoli's younger daughters came into the courtyard, giving Baltinglass a nervous sidelong glance as she approached her mother.

"The Hiccup Man is outside," she told Dassin. "He says he knew Mr. Baltinglass before he was dead."

Baltinglass paused, a mouthful of food halfway to his mouth. "Am I dead?" he said.

"The dead do not have such an appetite, Baltinglass effendi," said Dassin. She seemed mildly irritated at the news of their uninvited guest.

"Didn't think so," said Baltinglass, "but when you get to my age it's as well to check now and then."

"Who is the Hiccup Man?" asked Little.

"He lives in a cave on the edge of town," said Dassin. "He calls himself an inventor. He is always busy with some new contraption. There are sometimes explosions, but he is harmless enough."

"Harmless in-hic-deed," said the Hiccup Man, letting himself in without waiting for further introduction. He was a gangly man with bird's-nest hair, and he peered about the yard through a pair of wire-framed spectacles. He spotted Baltinglass at once and marched over toward him, hand extended, like a clockwork stork. "Baltin-hic-glass!" he said. "I heard a rumor you had passed through here, but I didn't hic-believe it! I've taken you for dead these many years." He showed his buff-colored teeth in a crooked smile. "You won't re-hic-member me, Baltinglass. I joined an ill-fated expedition of yours many years ago, when I was just a boy of six-hic-teen, working for the local paper."

Baltinglass sat upright, and his jaw dropped slightly. "Tenniel?" he croaked. "Of course I remember, but I lost you to a sandstorm. I've had your death on my conscience all these years."

"I was lost for a long time, but I survived," said the Hiccup Man. "The people here took me in and they were good to me. When the time came to hic-leave I got half a day's ride along the track; then I turned and came back. There was noth-hic I wanted that I didn't already have, and I've lived here ever since."

Dassin brought a clean cup for Tenniel and

poured him a coffee. "Sit," she said.

"It's good to hear your voice again, boy," said Baltinglass. "I don't mind telling you that you drove me up the wall on that journey, but that's nothing to the sleepless nights you've given me since you've been dead."

The Hiccup Man hic-laughed. His hair, his clothes, even his skin were a uniformly sandy color, as though he were gradually turning into the stuff of his adopted home. "I'm no more dead-hic than you are, Baltinglass, but I'm hardly a boy either."

"Do you have hiccups all the time?" asked Little.

"I've had hic-hiccups ever since the afore-hic-mentioned sandstorm. Xaali the healer says a bad spirit entered me while I was lost in the storm, but it's hic-lodged so deep she can't flush it out." He leaned forward and spoke in a loud whisper. "You've arrived at the perfect time, Baltinglass. I've been working on a fabulous contraption—a machine that can fly! I'd be delighted to give you a demonstration after supper."

"No time, I'm afraid," said Baltinglass. "We'll be leaving as soon as our camels have been plumped up and dusted. This young adventurer, Miles Wednesday, is on an urgent mission and we need to get going as soon as possible."

The Hiccup Man turned to Miles, his eyes glinting. "Then perhaps I can shorten your journey!" he said. "My fly-hic-ing machine will go faster than any camel, with the right following wind and a high-hic-hoctane fuel and a little luck."

"You can save your breath, Tenniel," said Baltinglass. "We came down from our last sky jaunt in flames. I'm lucky to be talking to you without barbecue sauce on, boy."

"Well, of course, a camel-hic ride is far *safer*—," began Tenniel, but Miles interrupted him.

"How much faster?"

"Oh . . ." The Hiccup Man grinned, scratching his sandy hair. "Three times?"

"And it could carry all of us?" asked Little, her eyes shining.

"Without a doubt," said Tenniel, looking like his doubts were being quietly smothered. "The design is based on the drawings of Leonardo da Vinci, with some modifications of my own. It's pure hic-genius. I'll just need to add a couple of extra seats."

"How long would that take?" asked Miles.

"I can have her fueled and refitted in an hour, at hic-most," said Tenniel.

Miles looked at his companions. He could see Little's thoughts were already headed skyward, but

Baltinglass was muttering darkly to himself from inside a plume of hookah smoke. "We'll take a look," said Miles, "and see what we think."

"By all hic-means, do!" said Tenniel. "You won't be disappointed."

They thanked Dassin for their supper and said their good-byes, and Dassin promised that Temzi would look after the camels if they did not come back for them. They set off on foot for the Hiccup Man's cave, keeping a sharp lookout for any sign of Cortado, Tau-Tau and Nura on the road, although they did not expect to see them for some time yet. Tenniel stalked ahead enthusiastically, jerking with each hiccup as if one of his cogs were missing a tooth. Miles carried the singed duffel bag over his shoulder. Something sharp poked into his back, but he did not want to spend time rearranging the contents, so he shifted the bag to a more comfortable position. The heat had left the evening air and a cool breeze blew, bringing the scent of distant rain and the sound of cicadas, chirping their washboard songs to the evening stars.

CHAPTER THIRTY
THE *RUNAWAY CLOUD*

Baltinglass of Araby, once-bitten and fly-shy, stumped along beside Miles, his cane measuring out his temper on the dusty road. "You sure you're not making a big mistake, Master Miles?" he said quietly. "It doesn't sound like Tenniel has a reputation for mechanical genius. We'll be lucky to get off the ground, never mind flying three times faster than a camel ride."

"It's not the speed I'm thinking of," said Miles. "It's the sea crossing. We can't take the same ship as Cortado and Tau-Tau, and we certainly can't wait a week for the next one."

"Stowing away was good enough for me when I

was a boy," grumbled Baltinglass.

"We can't risk it," said Miles. "If Cortado were to see any of us alive there's no knowing what he'd do to Nura." Thunder rolled on the horizon, and Miles saw an unaccustomed anxiety in the old man's face. "I'm sure it'll be all right," said Miles. "The design is Leonardo da Vinci's, remember?"

They took a narrow path that wound up from the main track toward the Hiccup Man's cave. The entrance was a natural arch in the rock face, and inside the cave it was surprisingly cool and airy. Tenniel lit an assortment of lamps that were suspended from the ceiling, and the cave was bathed in a warm yellow light.

Standing in the center of the floor, surrounded by a jumble of wood, wire and metal, stood Tenniel's contraption. It was indeed a sight to behold. There was a pyramid-shaped wooden frame like the skeleton of a tepee, topped by an enormous conical screw, while mounted on the spars of the frame were four canvas bat wings attached to a series of pulleys and cables that issued from a squat engine inside the frame. The whole structure was built on a concave circular platform like a giant saucer, onto which a pair of rickety wooden chairs had been bolted. Miles let out his breath in a whoosh at the sight of the machine.

"Describe the thing to me, boy," said Baltinglass.

"How long have you got?" said Miles.

The Hiccup Man produced a large book with yellowed pages and held it out for Miles to examine. The pages were covered in diagrams and spidery brown writing that Miles recognized from the entry on Leonardo da Vinci in Lady Partridge's encyclopedias. There was a machine with many pulleys and four narrow wings sticking out at an angle, and another that featured the large conical screw that stood on top of Tenniel's frame. In both drawings men were sketched inside the frame, where the engine stood in the Hiccup Man's contraption. The men in the sketches were hard at work pedaling or cranking to provide power for their machines.

"Of course, I have combined-hic a couple of the original designs, and introduced the modern adaptation of an engine," said Tenniel, "but essentially she is da Vinci's ornithopter brought to hic-life. Isn't she a beauty?"

"Will she fit through the door?" asked Miles.

"Certainly," said Tenniel. "She's measured to the millimeter."

"Never mind that," said Baltinglass. "Does it look like it will fly?"

Miles glanced at Tenniel, who was looking at him expectantly. "Well . . . ," he said, "it doesn't look like it was made to do anything else."

"I've hic-tested two smaller models with only a fifty percent crash rate," said Tenniel proudly.

"Where's the one that didn't crash?" asked Miles, wondering if there would be time for a brief demonstration.

"Ah," said Tenniel, "I'm afraid that one blew up before-hic it left the ground, but I've made a modification that should prevent that from happening again." He smiled at Baltinglass. "Don't worry, old friend. In an hour or so we'll all be soaring through the air."

"That's what I'm afraid of," muttered Baltinglass. He commandeered Tenniel's hammock and settled himself for a nap while the inventor set to work fitting an extra pair of seats. Miles and Little sat at the mouth of the cave, watching the faint shine of stars between the stars, and keeping an eye on the road. From the cave behind them came a muffled metallic ringing, like a saucepan hitting a kneecap, followed by an interval of frantic sawing, all punctuated by a steady stream of hiccups. Around midnight they saw three camels approaching, and they warned Tenniel to douse the lights and keep silent as the Great Cortado and his traveling companions passed by. Miles was sure he saw Nura glance over in his direction, as though she knew he was there in the darkness of the cave mouth.

"What happens when we go back, Miles?" asked Little quietly, when they had passed out of sight among the houses.

"Nura will bring the Great Cortado and Tau-Tau to Larde, where she can tip off Sergeant Bramley to arrest them," said Miles. "The Great Cortado will be sent straight back to the secure hospital. As for Tau-Tau, I suppose he'll end up in prison for a while."

"And your father?" asked Little.

"Nura promised she would help me to restore him if she could."

Little looked at Miles, and he smiled back. He did not tell her how slim his grandmother had thought his chances of success. "We'll have to stop off at Hell's Teeth on the way to Larde," he said.

"Where the Fir Bolg live?" asked Little. "Why?"

"My grandmother says the Tiger's Egg can't be unlocked until the promise my mother made is kept."

"Did she tell you how that could be done?"

Miles shook his head. "I'll just have to try to work it out as I go along. I don't have any choice if I'm to bring my father back."

"Will Nura help you with that too?"

Miles shook his head again. "Nura has to bring Cortado and Tau-Tau to Larde. There's no way she could stop at Hell's Teeth without arousing their suspicion. This is one we'll have to figure out on our own."

Little was silent for a while as she drew spirals in the sand with a stick; then she said, "I'm worried about Silverpoint. He was nowhere to be seen at the Council. He wasn't with Bluehart either the last couple of times he came for you."

"That's a good thing, isn't it?" said Miles.

"Not if he's supposed to be with him."

A rumble of distant thunder came faintly on the breeze. "Maybe he's just busy," said Miles.

There was a grinding cough from the cave as the engine burst into life. Baltinglass woke with a start.

"Hic!" said Tenniel in delight. "The sound of genius! Help me hic-wheel her out onto the launch-pad."

They paved the soft sand with an assortment of planks and wheeled the flying machine out under the stars, her folded wings just scraping the arch of the cave mouth. The engine ran smoothly except for the occasional hiccup, which made Tenniel beam at it with fatherly affection. He wound a winch here and hauled on a cable there, and the four enormous bat wings unfolded slowly against the sky.

"Now all she needs is a name," said Tenniel. He produced a dusty long-necked bottle of beer from a nook at the back of the cave. "I have a short list," he said. He straightened out a piece of crumpled paper and perched a monocle in one eye. Miles looked at the ungainly machine, at the laboring pistons, the tangle of cables and the creaking frame. He cleared his throat loudly and said, "I think Little should choose a name."

"You do?" said Tenniel. He looked momentarily disappointed; then he smiled broadly and handed Little the beer bottle. "Of course-hic. I am forgetting my manners. As the youngest person and the only lady-hic present, would you care to do the honors?"

Little thought for a moment. "I have a name for her, but you'd better get aboard first," she said.

"Why do you say that?" asked Tenniel.

"Because it's a cloud name, and once I've named her she will want to fly," said Little. She looked at the brown bottle and wrinkled her nose. "Do I have to drink this stuff?"

The Hiccup Man laughed. "I can see you haven't

made a hic-habit of launching vessels," he said. "It's supposed to be champagne, but that's rather hard to come by. You smash the bottle on the bow, which would be"—he pointed to a spot on the rim of the machine's circular base—"there, I suppose."

The rest of the crew climbed aboard, and Little raised the bottle. She opened her mouth and sang a name for the flying machine. It was a name that billowed and glowed like the ivory clouds of summer, and made everyone who heard it feel lighter than air. No one aboard could hope to repeat it, but it gave such a lift to the crossbred contraption that Little barely had time to smash the beer bottle and clamber aboard herself before the great wings had begun to beat the air and the enormous spinning screw had lifted the machine from the ground, creating a circular sandstorm on the launchpad beneath.

"What kind of a hic-name is that?" asked Tenniel, beside himself with delight to be airborne and still in one piece.

"It means . . . 'runaway cloud,'" said Little, "more or less."

As they rose slowly and noisily into the night Miles looked down to see the slim figure of Temzi running toward them on the sandy road. She came to a standstill at the sight of them, her mouth open in surprise as she watched the ascent of Tenniel's fabulous contraption. Miles leaned out and waved at her, wondering if she had returned early in the hope of seeing him. He watched her as she waved back, her eyes shining in the darkness of her face, until she was swallowed by the distance and the pale desert sands.

CHAPTER THIRTY-ONE

A NEW SECOND

The *Runaway Cloud*, canvas-winged and piston-hearted, flapped through the night sky like a ragged mirage, brought to life by the stubbornness of its creator and the musical charm of a four-hundred-year-old girl. It was a triumph of optimism over gravity, but its flight was far from the stately glide of the *Sunfish*. The whole craft bucked and plunged with the complex rhythm of her four wings, and the roar of the engine rose and fell as it fought to master the currents of the desert air. Above their heads the rapidly spinning screw created a constant downdraft that blew the exhaust fumes out through a circular hole in the floor before they could suffocate the passengers.

Miles gripped the sides of the wooden chair in which he sat, and wondered what kind of passing madness had made him volunteer them for this outlandish experiment. He watched Tenniel wrestle manfully with the levers and pedals that controlled the pitch of the wings. He felt the little swoop caused by the pilot's every hiccup, and tried to calculate just how much fuel was held in the assortment of containers that was strapped around the rim of the machine. The machine tilted forward slightly, as though eager to get to its unknown destination. "How far will she fly?" he called.

"Not-hic sure," said Tenniel. "She may even make it to Al Bab at a pinch."

"We're heading for Fuera," shouted Miles into the wind. "We left Baltinglass's car there."

Tenniel laughed. "For a hic-moment I thought you said Fuera," he said.

"I did," said Miles, "but I suppose we'll have to refuel at Al Bab."

Tenniel did not answer. He looked at Baltinglass, who smiled benignly in his seat; then he shrugged and fell silent except for his frequent hiccups, bending himself with grim determination to the task of keeping the *Runaway Cloud* airborne. Between his feet was an ingenious compass housing in which several glowworms lived, lighting the compass with a soft glow, and the inventor consulted it now and then to maintain his course.

Miles watched the stark landscape that passed below them. He had flown only over the sea before, but now he could see an ocean of sand with lines of dunes marching like waves to the distant horizon. Here and there an outcrop of rock sheltered an oasis, where the tiny sparks of cooking fires glimmered among the little model tents and the toy palm trees. Once they flew over a herd of migrating oryx, whose hooves trampled a broad trail in the sand. They passed by the finger of rock that rose out of the wadi, where Captain Tripoli had put Cortado and Tau-Tau to flight, and Miles in desperation had kicked the royal backside of the king of beasts.

For a while the *Runaway Cloud* took the meandering course of the wadi before leaving it to follow the ridge. Three camels walked sedately below them. They were too far away to see the faces of their riders, but from their shapes Miles was almost certain they were Cortado, Tau-Tau and Nura. The camel riders looked up at the sound of the flying machine, and the largest of them pointed skyward. He could see them for some time before they dwindled into the distance.

Baltinglass dozed against all the odds, and Little watched the sky anxiously through flapping wings and creaking cables. Ahead of them violet flashes of lightning played among storm clouds bulging with thunder, and now and then an escaping peal could be heard above the engine's din.

The *Runaway Cloud*'s flight became more erratic as they approached the troubled air around the storm's edge. A sudden blast of thunder woke Baltinglass from his sleep. "Not yet! Too soon!" he shouted, and would have leaped from his rickety seat if Miles had not grabbed his sleeve and held on tight.

The clouds loomed over them now, blocking out the stars. Dampness condensed on their faces. "Will she still fly in the rain?" shouted Miles.

"I hope so," yelled Tenniel. "She's designed for desert flight. Rain didn't enter my calculations."

"Maybe we should fly around the storm," said Little.

Tenniel shook his head. "Too far. We'd use-hic too much fuel. She'll be fine!" he shouted. "They had thunder-hic-storms in da Vinci's day."

The approaching storm clouds seemed to rush forward to meet them. The air crackled with electricity and the flying contraption plunged and bucked like a cork in a flood. Rain flew at them from all directions at once, and before long they were all soaked to the skin.

There was no way of telling how long they flew through the storm, their engine coughing and catching, the cables creaking and the wood straining under the increased weight of the sodden wings. It seemed to go on forever, as though they were traveling with the storm wherever it was headed. Little clung onto Baltinglass and Tenniel clung onto the levers, but Miles stood and faced the storm, his hair standing out like a startled cat's tail, feeling an exhilaration unlike anything he had ever known. He was the leader of the expedition, the unappointed captain of this mongrel ship. He was deep in the territory of the Storm Angels, yet he felt it was the last place Bluehart could find him, and what could happen to him if he was hidden from the Sleep Angels?

He felt a hum of electricity running from his right hand, which gripped the *Runaway Cloud's* frame, along his arm and into his shoulder. He turned to see a figure standing beside him. For an instant he feared he might be wrong about being hidden from Bluehart, but then he saw that the visitor was Silverpoint. The Storm Angel was staring straight ahead as though concentrating on keeping the storm on its course.

"What are you doing here?" Miles shouted over the wind.

"Where else would I be?" asked Silverpoint.

Little looked up at the sound of Silverpoint's voice. She opened her mouth to shout his name, but the Storm Angel put his finger to his lips. He indicated Tenniel, hunched over the controls and staring straight ahead. "Best not to startle the pilot, softwing," he said. His voice cut through the din of the storm without his having to shout, but Tenniel seemed unaware of it, and Baltinglass was once again snoring through the danger. Little jumped up and embraced Silverpoint, and he smiled briefly.

"Bluehart's not with you?" said Miles.

"Bluehart has disappeared," said Silverpoint. "Apparently he appeared at a Council meeting behaving very strangely, and nobody has seen him since."

Little laughed, and the wind softened for a moment. "That wasn't Bluehart; it was Miles! He pretended to be . . ." Her voice trailed off as she saw the icy look on Silverpoint's face.

"It wasn't deliberate," said Miles, "but I think it may have bought us more time."

"I wouldn't be so sure," said Silverpoint. "The Sleep Angels no longer trust Bluehart to do the job properly, so they've made Stillbone his second. I've never heard of two Sleep Angels being put on one case before, but it looks more like your chances have been halved."

"Then we need your help," said Little.

"What do you think *this* is?" said Silverpoint. He waved his arm at the storm that surrounded them, and a searing bolt of lightning flew from his outstretched fingers and lit up the cloud like a Chinese lantern. "I can hide you in here for a time, but I don't know how long this . . ." He struggled for the word.

"Contraption?" said Miles.

Silverpoint nodded. ". . . will last," he said. "If you fall out of the sky you can guess who'll be waiting for you."

"Have you any idea where Bluehart might be?" asked Miles.

"It's a safe bet he's looking for you," said Silverpoint, "and so is Stillbone, now. You'll be vulnerable again once you leave this storm. I presume from your direction that you're headed home to Larde?"

"Eventually," said Miles. He was beginning to wish fervently that his mother had never made any promise to the Fir Bolg, but if she hadn't she would never have acquired the Tiger's Egg, and he would never have known Varippuli, and his father. . . . His entire life began to unravel in his mind, and he shook his head to clear it.

"I have to get to The Null before the Sleep Angels can reach me," he said. "But I have to stop at Hell's Teeth on the way."

Silverpoint looked at him incredulously. "Do you think the Sleep Angels are going to wait while you make rest stops?"

"It's not a—," began Miles, but he was interrupted by Little.

"I have a plan!" she said, with a look of surprise on her face. Miles and Silverpoint turned to look at her. "Silverpoint," she said, "you can go and tell Lady Partridge to meet us at Hell's Teeth, and to bring The Null with her. She'll get the sergeant to drive them in his van. He always does what she tells him!"

"I'm not a messenger boy, softwing," said Silverpoint with a scowl.

"You're the fastest flier I know!" said Little. "If you can do this for us there's a chance that Miles will be done with the Tiger's Egg before Bluehart and Stillbone find him. Then maybe the Sleep Angels will reconsider, you know...."

Silverpoint looked at Little for what seemed like an age; then he shook his head slowly. "Always trying to bend the rules, little softwing," he said.

Little smiled. "Rules are there for bending, Silverpoint. It's how we know we're alive."

Silverpoint smiled suddenly and turned to Miles. "You will reach Al Bab in a couple of hours," he said. "The storm is blowing you in the right direction, but it will run out of steam soon after I've gone." He stepped onto the edge of the flying machine's base. "Good luck," he said. He did a backflip into the wild night, and in an instant he was gone.

They flew on through the crashing storm, and Miles began to wonder if it would ever fizzle out as Silverpoint had promised. His earlier exhilaration had vanished, leaving him at the mercy of the sky's fury, clinging to the fragile machine like an ant to a matchstick. Eventually the stinging rain subsided and the wind began to ease. A pale yellow light filtered through the thinning clouds, and all at once they emerged into the dawn. The great wings scattered sprays of water droplets that sparkled in the sun's first rays, and below them bloomed desert flowers that showed their faces only every hundred years.

Ahead and to the west they could see the domes and minarets of the port of Al Bab. Tenniel banked left to correct their course. The engine coughed, and the Hiccup Man tapped a fuel container with the toe of his sandal to coax the last few drops from it.

"Is that the end of the fuel?" asked Miles.

"Just about," said Tenniel, without taking his eyes from their destination. "Be prepared for an abrupt hic-landing."

They came in low and fast, and half a mile from the outskirts of the port the engine began to stall. Tenniel throttled back and the *Runaway Cloud* tilted backward and made a hasty descent, narrowly missing a stand of palm trees that stood a little way from the road. She landed with a bone-shaking thump, almost tipping over before righting herself, and her great bat wings came to rest with a loud creak of relief.

"My hic-pologies for the landing," said Tenniel, leaping down into the sand and beaming proudly at his creation. He looked anything but sorry.

"I take my hat off to you, boy," said Baltinglass of Araby. "I thought we'd be fried, drowned or squashed like beetles. Are we all present and correct?"

"We're all here," said Miles. He stepped down from the *Runaway Cloud* and walked around to the other side of the palm trees. He shaded his eyes with his hand and looked back along the road, but there was no sign of anyone coming. The machine was well enough hidden by the trees, but after taking a critical look from various angles he collected some fallen palm fronds and attached them to the frame, making a shady place to shelter and ensuring that the flying machine was completely invisible from the road.

"We can't all go to Al Bab," said Miles. "We don't want the Great Cortado to hear of anyone matching our description when he passes through later. Tenniel and I will go, and the two of you can mind the contraption and get a bit of sleep." He took out his indigo head cloth and made a turban of it as Baltinglass had taught him, wrapping the long end around his face and neck until only his eyes could be seen. Baltinglass gave him a handful of coins from his seemingly bottomless purse, and the boy and the inventor set out for Al Bab at a brisk pace, their clothes steaming in the gathering heat.

They had already dried out by the time they entered the outskirts of the town. Down at the quayside the port was coming to life, but here on the fringes of town the sleepy silence was disturbed only by the husky scrape of a crowing cock. "How can we carry enough fuel to cross the sea?" asked Miles. "It took two days by airship, so we'll need twice as much fuel as it took to get here."

"Not necessarily," said Tenniel. "You were probably flying into a headwind coming down to Al

Bab, and with luck you could make it back in half the time. As for the fuel itself, the quality is more important than the quantity. It's hard to come by good fuel in Wa'il, and most of what we had was homemade. We flew the last couple of hours on fermented prune juice."

"Really?" said Miles. "I never realized prunes had so many uses."

They found a small shop with assorted containers of benzine piled outside it. They woke the proprietor with some difficulty, and Tenniel hic-haggled with him until he arrived at a price for the entire stock of fuel and some dates and cheese from inside the store. The proprietor loaded his camel cart with the goods, along with several water skins, and they set off back along the road.

They reached the palm trees where the *Runaway Cloud* lay hidden, and Miles and Tenniel disappeared behind the trees, emerging a minute later with the empty containers they had detached from the rim of the contraption. The shopkeeper, whose curiosity fortunately never woke up until after midday, exchanged his full containers for the empties without question, and turned his cart back to Al Bab and his waiting hammock.

As he carried the last of the benzine from the

road to the trees Miles looked back along the road toward Wa'il, but there was no sign of anyone in the shimmering haze. He took out the food, wondering if Nura and her companions had passed by while he and Tenniel were buying fuel, and they breakfasted on cheese and dates and satisfied their thirst with lukewarm water. He roped the full containers into place while Tenniel connected the complicated system of pipes and tubes that would feed the benzine to the engine; then they lay down in the shade of the palm fronds to catch up on some rest before the heat made sleep impossible.

In the cool of Miles's pocket Tangerine lay still and quiet. No dreams entered his simple sleep, but nestled in his sawdust-filled head the Tiger's Egg hummed inaudibly, and somewhere between the light the tiger himself paced, restless and disturbed and aching to scratch a deep itch that he could not understand.

CHAPTER THIRTY-TWO

SOME EXPLAINING

The Great Cortado, road-dusted and turban-heavy, made his way down to the port to arrange passage back to Fuera, leaving his companions outside a small café. It was the kind of task he would normally give to his grumbling accomplice, but when the saddlebags were unpacked and they were met with the foul smell from the wooden box he decided that he would go himself after all. He took off hurriedly, leaving the fool and the mystic in charge of his reeking luggage. When he got back he would have to leave the boy's head somewhere near an anthill while they waited to sail, and be satisfied with a skull on a pole instead. Not quite the same impact, perhaps, but it would have to do.

He hoped to find the *Albatross* still in port. He had business with its captain, an enterprising man named Savage, who had agreed to pay them a wad of money for sabotaging the *Sunfish* in the race from Fuera to Al Bab. The Great Cortado felt he had achieved that end in spectacular fashion. Setting fire to the airship had been his idea, not Savage's, but by his reckoning the captain owed them at least the price of a return trip, and he intended to hold him to his promise.

In the shaded café garden Nura sat in a corner and lit her clay pipe. Doctor Tau-Tau sweated and muttered beside her, trying in vain to wipe the grime from his forehead with his tea-towel veil, and wrinkling his nose at the smell from Cortado's grim souvenir. He looked enviously at Nura's pipe, which was producing a fragrant smoke that at least partially masked the smell. They had ridden all night and on through the morning, not stopping even when a freak thunderstorm soaked them to the skin, and he felt as though he had not slept for a week. Sweat trickled down his back, mixing with the sand that seemed to get everywhere, and he squirmed in discomfort and cursed under his breath.

"You are anxious," said Nura. "Are you afraid of the sea?"

Doctor Tau-Tau gave a bitter laugh. "The sea is the least of my worries," he said.

"Then you are afraid of Cortado?" she said.

"Aren't you?" asked Tau-Tau. "The man is deranged. He's carrying a boy's head in a box."

Nura exhaled slowly. "You're forgetting where he got it from," she said. "A true clairvoyant fears nothing, especially if he carries a Tiger's Egg."

Tau-Tau grunted. "To tell you the truth I don't have the faintest idea how to use the thing," he said. He was too weary for pretense, and, forbidding as she was, something about this dark-eyed woman made him want to unburden himself.

"That is why I agreed to come with you," said Nura.

"That's what I'm worried about," said Doctor Tau-Tau. "With you here I become expendable. How long before he's carrying *my* head around in a box?"

"I see what you mean," said Nura. "Why don't you take out the Tiger's Egg and I will teach you some simple principles."

Doctor Tau-Tau eyed her suspiciously, but he reached into his sleeve nonetheless and produced the bogus stone from its hiding place. Nura held out her hand and he placed the stone on her palm, where it was lit to a soft gold by a shaft of sunlight that broke through the vines above them.

"What would you like to learn?" she asked.

"Cortado wants to effect some kind of transformation," said Tau-Tau. "I don't know what it is exactly, but I overheard him talking about it."

"All right," said Nura. "The Tiger's Egg magnifies your desires and helps you to achieve them. What would you most like to transform at the moment?"

The fortune-teller looked about him. "I'd like to make that . . . thing . . . a bit less smelly, for a start," he said, pointing at the wooden box.

Nura handed the bogus Egg back to him. "Hold it tightly in your left hand," she said, "and put your right hand on the box. Do you feel the Tiger's Egg beginning to get warmer?"

Now, it's a funny thing that a person under stress can often be persuaded of something just by having it suggested to him. Hypnotists use this trick all the time, and indeed Doctor Tau-Tau himself had used it for years in his dubious sideshow act. At this moment, however, he was the one under stress, and no sooner had Nura mentioned it than the stone felt several degrees warmer. He nodded nervously.

"You will find it becomes extremely hot as the power surges through it," said Nura, looking him straight in the eye. "Now," she said, "repeat this incantation after me, and make sure you get every word right. Even the smallest mistake could have unforeseen consequences."

"Shouldn't we practice . . . ?" began Tau-Tau, but Nura had already started.

"*Eifantolim brussala bulomen brussala bulomen tromtata . . . ,*" she intoned rapidly, and Doctor Tau-Tau stumbled through the unfamiliar words behind her, clutching the small stone for all he was worth.

Nura finished and sat back in her seat, taking a long puff on her pipe. Doctor Tau-Tau dropped the stone into his lap and shook his burning hand. He stared nervously at the wooden box, trying to detect any easing in the smell without risking too deep a breath.

"I don't think you got that right," said Nura, without removing her pipe.

"What do you mean?" asked Tau-Tau. "I repeated every word."

"Did you say *bulomen brussala* or *bruloman bosala*?" she asked.

"I . . . I can't remember," said the flustered fortune-teller.

"We'd better take a look," said Nura.

She took a long knife from Cortado's saddlebag and used it to pry the lid from the box. A cloud of flies and an indescribable smell emerged. Doctor Tau-Tau covered his nose with his tea towel and glanced hesitantly inside. He did not have to look closely to see that something had gone badly wrong. Two curved horns rose from a tufted crown, and below them a clouded yellow eyeball stared sightlessly up at him.

"Oh, dear," said Nura, looking at him and shaking her head slowly. "*That's* going to take some explaining."

CHAPTER THIRTY-THREE
A SILENT HUM

Little softwing, pearly white and sky-shaken, hummed very quietly to herself as Tenniel's flying contraption pitched and plunged a thousand feet above the waves. If you want to know just how quietly she hummed, imagine the sound of jelly setting; then turn the volume up just a fraction. She hummed because she knew that without her song the *Runaway Cloud* would not stay aloft for long, and she kept her humming as quiet as she could because she was afraid it would attract the attention of the wrong sort of angels.

They had taken off in the late afternoon, after sleeping longer than they had intended in their improvised shelter beneath the palm trees. They detoured around the port of Al Bab and headed out across the cobalt sea. The engine ran better on the superior fuel they had bought, and they gained altitude steadily so that they could hide among the clouds. As the light faded they saw far below them the *Albatross*, running under full sail toward Fuera.

Miles had pestered Tenniel into letting him take a turn at the controls, pointing out that he had recently learned to drive a car without mishap (he didn't mention crashing into an anchor). Besides, he said, a copilot was needed so that Tenniel could get some rest. In truth the Hiccup Man's shoulders ached from the previous night's flight, and he was more than happy to sit in the passenger seat and give the boy a flying lesson. From time to time Little distributed food from the small stores they had, and she helped Tenniel with the complicated business of switching the fuel lines as each container emptied. Before darkness fell Tenniel made a last round of the fuel tanks, counting those they hadn't used and making calculations with a stub of pencil on the wooden frame.

"Do you think we'll make it to Fuera?" asked Miles.

"Make-hic it?" said Tenniel gleefully. "My boy, the *Runaway Cloud* has excelled herself. She seems to get a hic-little farther on every tank."

"That's because she's lighter with each tank we empty," said Miles.

The Hiccup Man slapped his forehead and scribbled some more figures on the wood. "You're a hic-genius, boy," he said. "That's exactly what's happening. At this rate we could get far beyond Fuera before we'd need to refuel."

"We have to land in Fuera," said Miles. "That's where we left Baltinglass's car."

"Never mind Morrigan," said Baltinglass. "That young boy will look after her like she was his own mother. The question is, will this bone shaker get us all the way to Larde?"

"We're not going straight to Larde," said Miles. "There's been a change of plan. We're going to Hell's Teeth." He could not think beyond the daunting task of restoring his father and undoing the Tiger's Egg. If he survived that, he thought, he would happily crawl onward to Larde on his hands and knees.

"First I heard of it," said Baltinglass, sounding slightly miffed, "but I'm sure you know what you're doing."

"How hic-far is that from Fuera?" asked Tenniel, sucking his pencil.

"About half a day by road," said Baltinglass.

The Hiccup Man calculated some more, squinting at his figures in the gathering twilight. "Then we might just make it," he said. "We're starting-hic on our second-to-last tank now."

"Full steam ahead, then, if Master Miles is in agreement."

"Full speed ahead it is," said Miles.

"We can always refuel when we make our stop," said Tenniel.

"I don't think so," said Miles, picturing the jagged teeth of stone beneath which the Fir Bolg lived their stark lives. "Not unless she can run on stewed rabbit." He sat at the controls of the *Runaway Cloud* with knots forming in his stomach, his mind racing as if to outrun the engine. Soon they would reach Hell's Teeth, and his makeshift plan felt as precarious as the contraption that carried them through the darkening sky. He was sure their change of plan left something out of kilter, but he could not put his finger on it.

He tried to lay all the elements out clearly in his mind while his hands were busy with the levers. Silverpoint would have reached Larde sometime that morning, and Miles knew that Lady Partridge would set off with The Null as soon as the Storm Angel had delivered his message. The Fir Bolg would be lurking beneath the standing stones of Hell's Teeth, where Little could find them and tell them that Miles had come to settle his mother's debt. The Tiger's Egg was safe in his pocket and its cryptic key in his memory.

All he needed was Nura's help to interpret the key, but she was still on the road to Larde, and there, Miles realized, lay the snag. He nursed a glimmer of hope that he might be able to help the Fir Bolg on his own, having cured Dulac Zipplethorpe and Baltinglass of Araby more or less by accident, but the task of unlocking the Tiger's Egg and transferring his father's soul was an altogether more daunting one, and he had been relying on Nura to help him when the moment arrived.

He wished he had asked more questions of his aunt and his grandmother in the short time he had spent with them. The things they had told him about the Tiger's Egg now seemed frustratingly vague. "You will need the far eyes to see all parts of the puzzle at once, and the bright hands to steal the energy," his grandmother had said. She had told him he needed to master his gifts to have any chance of success, but how was he to do that now? There was not much opportunity to practice healing while flying through the night sky, but he supposed he could try to find a way to practice using the far eyes.

It was hard to know where to start. He imagined it would be a bit like entering the Realm, except that he would have to do it without falling asleep. Once again he wished he could ask Nura's advice, and then it struck him. Nura had said that she knew at once of Celeste's death, even from hundreds of miles away. It was true that they had been twins, but Miles at least was family. What better way for him to practice the far eyes than to try and contact her now? Not only was she the person he needed to talk to, she was the one who was most likely to hear him.

He checked their heading on the compass, then stared into the blackness ahead of him and deliberately let his eyes slip out of focus. He pictured Nura as he had first met her, holding his eye with her penetrating stare. The uncomfortable feeling of being unpacked for inspection came back to him, and suddenly he felt lost, a tiny speck in the vast, expanding night sky. He was tumbling or flying; it all seemed the same thing, and still he could see his aunt's piercing eyes as though they were right before him.

"Nura?" he said, without actually speaking.

He heard his aunt's reply much as you can hear the silence when you enter an abandoned house. It was there and yet not there. "I'm here, Miles. Are you all right?" she said.

"We're okay," he said. "Can you really hear me?"

"Of course," said Nura. "How else would I be answering you?"

Miles felt a sort of giddiness rise up from his stomach, and he almost laughed out loud. "I've changed our plan," he said. "Can you meet us at a place called Hell's Teeth?"

"You plan to visit the Fir Bolg?" said Nura.

"I don't think I have a choice," said Miles. "I have to fulfill my mother's promise, but time is short. I've arranged for . . . for my father to be brought there too, but I'll need your help. How soon can you get there?"

"We are making good speed in Cortado's van," said Nura. "I'll try to think of a way to get away from them for a while, Miles, but I can't promise anything. You may have to rely on your own wits."

"Okay," said Miles. The rising giddiness threatened to overwhelm him. He could not believe he was speaking to someone far away, using nothing but his own thoughts.

"We're flying!" was the only thing he could say that seemed to fit.

"I know," said Nura. "Be careful, Miles." A moment later she was gone.

It felt as though she had left without closing the door. Miles was vaguely aware of his hands on the levers of the *Runaway Cloud*, as though they belonged to someone else, but his gaze was still settled on the middle distance. Tufts of cloud rushed toward him like dark pillars on a dark background. They reminded him of the standing stones at Hell's Teeth, but he knew that they had not come that far, or descended so low. A flood of images came suddenly into his mind. He imagined he saw tiny figures fanning out ahead of him. He saw the tiger, no longer fierce but trailing a mist of sadness, and he saw Baltinglass standing on a rock, lit up like a Christmas tree and roaring at the sky.

He saw himself too, standing face to face with Bluehart, who stood with his back to a tall rock. Bluehart was watching as another Sleep Angel, who looked like Stillbone, approached Miles from behind. Stillbone reached out to touch his shoulder, and Miles saw himself fall at the angel's touch. A chill ran through him and he wondered if the things he saw were just warnings, or images of an unchangeable future. He closed his eyes to escape them, and the *Runaway Cloud* gave a lurch and began to tilt dangerously.

"My hic-turn, I think," said Tenniel, taking the levers from Miles. "It's time you had a break, boy. You were hic-falling asleep there."

"Thanks," said Miles. He felt groggy as he vacated the pilot's seat, and his legs almost buckled beneath him. He had never felt so exhausted in his life, and within moments of strapping himself into the co-pilot's chair he sank into a confused, roller-coaster sleep.

CHAPTER THIRTY-FOUR
STARS AND SNOWFLAKES

Miles Wednesday, far-eyed and fog-brained, was jerked from his sleep by a shout. "Man the controls, Mr. Wednesday," yelled Tenniel. Behind him Miles heard the engine coughing like a sick patient. He struggled from his chair and his dreams, and grabbed the levers while the Hiccup Man darted across the lurching platform to the final fuel tank. "Just a hic-switchover," he called. "Caught me napping. Normal service will-hic resume in a moment."

The *Runaway Cloud* was losing height rapidly. A sliver of moon cast a feeble light, but it was hard to make out what lay below. "Where are we?" shouted Miles into the rushing wind.

"Approaching our target, I hope," said Tenniel, twisting open the valve on the fuel tank. The engine shuddered back to life and the screw began to spin again. The Hiccup Man sat back and wiped his brow with his sleeve. "That was a close one!" He turned to Miles. "We've been keeping just east of the mountains, and we've descended to about three hundred feet. Baltinglass said we'd be able to see Hell's Teeth, but it's pretty dark, and I think—"

He was interrupted by a loud bang from the motor. It stopped dead, leaving a silence that was more frightening than any noise you can imagine. The contraption began to fall again. Baltinglass woke with a start, and Little's humming became distinctly audible. Tenniel flicked on a torch and shone it at the fuel container.

"What's happening?" shouted Miles. The levers had gone dead in his hands, and the great canvas wings angled upward as they fell. He reached into his pocket and grasped Tangerine tightly.

Tenniel's torch picked out a glistening slick on the underside of the fuel tank. "I think I see the problem," he shouted. "This hic-tank has sprung a leak. There's nothing in it after all."

"That's it for us, then," shouted Baltinglass. "I knew I should have packed those parachutes."

"Switch to manual!" called Tenniel, ignoring him. He yanked out a pair of foldaway cranks from inside the contraption's frame and began to turn one of them frantically. Miles grabbed the other and hauled on it for all he was worth. With the engine dead, the handle bore the entire weight of two of the wings, and it took all his strength to turn it once, twice, his feet lifting off the platform with the effort. The wings began to beat ponderously, and the rate of their fall slowed. The dark mass of the ground was still rising to meet them, but it was hard to tell how soon they would land, or on what kind of terrain.

"Brace yourselves," panted Tenniel. The ground was suddenly near, a clutter of black shapes rushing up at them. Miles clenched his teeth and cranked harder. He had a blurred impression of slanting in toward trees or rocks; then everything was confusion. A tall shape loomed, a scatter of tiny figures fanned out in the blackness, something whipped past his face; then the world somersaulted with a splintering crash and a jolt of pain, and for a while there was . . .

. . . nothing. Stars and snowflakes mingled at the corners of his vision, and Miles came to his senses slowly. His ribs ached and he felt like he had been worked over with a steak mallet.

"Miles?" said Little. She was kneeling beside him in the long grass.

"Are you okay?" said Miles.

Little nodded. "I'm used to landing," she said. She leaned forward. "Miles, Baltinglass needs your help."

Miles got gingerly to his feet. By the faint light of the moon he could just make out the explorer lying in the twisted wreckage of the flying machine. Tenniel was bending over him, hiccuping and fluttering his hands in a nervous way. He was more used to repairing machines than human bodies, and he moved aside with relief when Miles and Little approached.

"That you, Master Miles?" said the old man.

"It's me," said Miles. "Are you hurt?"

"My leg," said Baltinglass. "Not the one you fixed a few months back—I could kick my way through"—he paused to gather his breath—"through a barn door with that one, but the other one has snapped like a twig. Needs a splint, boy. Do you know how to make a splint?"

Miles forced himself to look down at Baltinglass's leg. It was stretched out straight enough, but his foot was at a strange angle, and it made Miles giddy just to look at it. He reached out toward the old man's leg, but he was still dazed from the crash and he felt as though he would faint before he could achieve anything.

"I don't know if I can do this," he muttered to Little.

"Use the Egg," she whispered. "Your grandmother said it helps to focus your power."

Miles looked at her, glad to distract himself from the broken leg for a moment. "She told *me* that. Were you listening at the door?"

"Of course," said Little. "That's what doors are for, isn't it? So people can't see you listening."

Miles took Tangerine from his pocket. The small bear had survived the crash intact, having nothing much to break. Miles held him to his chest and reached out for Baltinglass's leg. "This might hurt," he said. He gripped the old man's foot, feeling as if he were in a country without maps and wondering what exactly had triggered his healing powers when he had used them before. He closed his eyes and pictured the Tiger's Egg that nestled inside Tangerine's head. Now that he knew what it looked like he could see the deep amber stripes and the way they seemed to glow softly with a light of their own. He could hear a wordless echo of the tiger's deep voice as though it lived in the Egg all the time, just waiting for someone to listen for it. The closer he listened, the more distant his surroundings became. The sound of the wind faded into the distance, and he felt light and cold to the very tips of . . .

"Well done," said Little, and the feeling dissipated in an instant, just as he felt it was gathering strength. He opened his eyes, feeling slightly irritated. A rumble of thunder sounded in the distance, and in the back of his mind he wondered if Silverpoint was on his way back with another storm to cover them.

Baltinglass was sitting up, rubbing his leg and looking a great deal happier. "By the trunkless legs of Ozymandias, you've done it again, Master Miles," he said. "That's some party trick you've—"

He was interrupted by another panicked shout from Tenniel. "*Tiger!*" yelled the inventor, who was undoubtedly seeing more excitement in a few short days than he had in the previous forty years. Miles looked around to see the tiger standing close beside him, his pelt dull and his ribs heaving with labored breathing. He was looking at Miles with a weary expression. "Here we are, then," he said.

"Hold him off, Master Miles," called Baltinglass of Araby. "I'll get me pistol, soon as I can find the blasted thing."

"No, you won't," said Miles with an effort. "It's all right."

"Because you say so?" rumbled the tiger. "How do you know I wouldn't prefer the bullet?"

"It's all right," said Miles again. He tried to find a way to explain what he wanted to say. "You're with me now. There'll be no more of—"

"With you, with them," said the tiger, settling himself down in the grass with slow, painful movements. "Somewhere, nowhere. There are things going on that I don't understand, but I know it's no kind of life for a tiger."

"I won't be asking for your help again," said Miles, a lump forming in his throat.

"I seem to remember you saying that before," said the tiger.

"I can stand on my own two feet now," said Miles. "You've taught me to do that."

"You have had the benefit of my wisdom on many occasions," agreed the tiger, and some of the old spirit came back into his voice. "We've had some entertaining jaunts."

"I wouldn't be here at all if it weren't for you," said Miles with feeling. He was not sure if the tiger would know what he meant. He wasn't sure he knew himself.

The tiger held his eye for a long time. "What now?" he said. "Now that you can stand on your own two feet?"

"I have to bring my father back."

"You mean that beast you keep at the orphanage?" said the tiger.

"I think I may be able to cure him," said Miles. He could not meet Varippuli's eye as he said this, knowing that it might cost the magnificent tiger his life.

"You are a stubborn boy, Miles," said the tiger, "but a good heart and a quick mind make a virtue out of stubbornness. Your father never took the easy path, and I suspect you will do what is necessary, however hard it might seem."

Miles turned the tiger's words over in his head. It seemed as though Varippuli understood on some level that Barty Fumble's life was inextricably tied with his own, and it was almost as if he were excusing Miles for what was to come. A match flared nearby as Baltinglass lit his pipe. There was a growing murmur beyond him in the darkness too, a sort of agitated sound that Miles could not identify, but his head was already overflowing with confused thoughts, and he paid it no attention.

He concentrated with difficulty on what he had to do. He could do nothing to make Lady Partridge or Nura arrive any sooner, nor to delay the Sleep Angels in their search, but at least he could try to free the Tiger's Egg from the bounds of his mother's promise, while he waited to see which of them reached him first. "Little," he said, "I need you to fetch the Fir Bolg. See if you can find Fuat, daughter of Anust, and tell her I've come to fulfill Celeste's promise."

CHAPTER THIRTY-FIVE

THE LIGHTNING KEY

The Fir Bolg, night-dwelling and cave-pelted, crept slowly inward through the long grass, closing a circle that had pinged outward from the falling sky machine like grease from a drop of detergent. They had planned to take advantage of a dark and cloudy night for a major rabbit hunt to stock their winter larder, but they had hardly emerged from their caves when they were rudely interrupted by a bat-winged monster crashing right into their midst.

The Fir Bolg were angry, and they bristled with spears. Their keen eyes could see four people among the wreckage. Two of them sat in the grass, one plainly hurt. The Fir Bolg were pleased about that. Two others stumbled about collecting the machine's broken bones. They probably planned to make spears of them, and that would have to be prevented.

The Fir Bolg crept closer, waiting for a decision to make itself. They had no leaders, but their number included many agile minds, and when those minds sparked together it was a sure thing that something would happen. What that something would be was never easy to predict, but it was those little surprises that put meat on the bones of life.

A surprise came soon enough, but it was not one of the Fir Bolg's making. A tiger appeared, bold as the moon, and sat himself down to discourse with the people who had tumbled from the machine. He did not behave as tigers were supposed to. There was no roaring, and none of the people present disappeared down his throat.

"The Pookahs are abroad tonight," whispered Fuat, daughter of Anust, daughter of Etar, to all those who could hear. "I feel them in my waters, but they have brought with them trickier tricks than usual. A bat made of wood and iron, and a tiger with no appetite are strange things whatever way you toast them."

"It's likely that we'll never have a hunt without this vexation," whispered a small man whose hair was festooned with brass beads that rattled as he moved.

"It's true," said Fuat, "but you can aim a spear at a tiger and not at a Pookah, and that may be the weakness in their plan."

The other man took this as an invitation to display his skills with a spear, and he drew back his arm to take aim at the tiger. Before he could throw his spear, however, a light flared in the small circle of wreckage, causing him to drop the weapon and screw his eyes shut. The other Fir Bolg flinched too, and covered their eyes. The light was still a curse to them, and this had been the main topic under discussion before the interruption had fallen out of the sky. Where was the boy who bore the promise? Where was the son of Celeste, who had escaped them without returning the Tiger's Egg or lifting from them the burden of the darkness?

Fuat, daughter of Anust, tilted her head to one side and regarded the tiger as the painful burst of light faded. There was a lesson in the animal's strange behavior, and she would shake it out like a dog shaking a rat. If the tiger was not eating the people, then the people had power over the tiger, and that could mean only one thing. She stood up from her crouched position and raised above her head the switch that she always carried. *"Tawn tUv Reevoch onsho,"* she cried. "The Tiger's Egg is here!"

Baltinglass of Araby, dread-cold and ground-rattled, sat in the long grass and held a match to his pipe. It might be the last smoke he would ever have, and his hand shook as he lit the tobacco. He had always been a great believer in looking on the bright side, but for the first time since his blindness he was finding it hard to remember what a bright side looked like. The boy would be all right, he told himself, and with luck that banana-smelling beast would somehow turn back into his father. The girl had charm enough to open any door she chose, and Tenniel no longer stalked accusingly through his nightmares. All in all things seemed poised to work out for the best, at least for everyone else.

"And for me?" he muttered under his breath. "'Power grows from two to three.' Better to go out in a blaze of fire, Baltinglass. Fading away in a hospital cot is not for the likes of you."

"Did you say something?" said Miles, but before Baltinglass could answer, a shout like a crow's call pierced the darkness. The shadows erupted and a

host of small, hairy figures surrounded them, jab-
bering loudly and pointing sharp sticks in their
direction. The tiger leaped to his feet with a roar
and swung to face their ambushers. Miles slipped
Tangerine into his pocket and shouted, "Down!" at
Varippuli. It was hardly the most dignified command you could give a tiger, but he was too flustered to think of anything better, and it worked
nonetheless.

The nearest Fir Bolg shrank back quickly, but
the tiger did not attack, merely gave another loud
roar as a warning to any of the little men who might
feel inclined to try their luck. Baltinglass of Araby,
meanwhile, had leaped to his feet and was brandish-
ing his swordstick in the other direction, although
Miles was relieved to see that he did not seem to
have located his pistol.

"It's all right; I know them," said Miles. He was
not at all sure it was all right, but it seemed that one
of his principal jobs as expedition leader was to try
to stop fights from breaking out at every available
opportunity.

A tiny tattooed woman stepped forward and
peered closely at him. "You are Celeste's boy," she
said. "Fuat remembers you, and the promise your
mother made . . . and your own tricky escape, which

impressed us greatly but angered us too."

"That's what I wanted to talk to you about," said Miles, feeling slightly flustered now that he was faced with Fuat herself. A fat raindrop landed smack in the middle of his forehead, and another on his arm.

"Did you bring the answer your mother was seeking?" asked Fuat. "Can you fulfill her promise to the Fir Bolg?"

"I hope so," said Miles. Some of the Fir Bolg had begun to chant in the surrounding darkness, banging their spear butts on the turf. Distant lightning flickered, and the prospect that the storm might move closer only made them more agitated.

"Someone's coming!" said Little, just as Miles reached into his pocket for Tangerine. He turned to see a pair of dim yellow headlights bouncing across the field toward them. Miles could see the dark outline of a van behind the headlights, but to his surprise it looked far larger than the old police van he had been expecting to see. It turned slightly as it skidded to a halt, and the Fir Bolg broke into an angry clamor as the headlights raked across them. With a jolt of fear Miles caught a glimpse of curling circus decorations painted on the side of the van. It must be the Great Cortado's van, but was Nura in it, and was she alone? He forgot all about the Fir Bolg, and held his breath as he waited to see who would emerge from the van.

The Fir Bolg's chanting grew louder and the rain began to pelt down, lit up in slanted circles by the dim headlights. The van doors opened and slammed, and three figures ran toward them. Miles frowned in puzzlement. They looked too sprightly for Tau-Tau, too small to be Nura, and too curly for the Great Cortado. With a wave of relief Miles recognized them as the Bolsillo brothers, though they were the last people he had been expecting to see.

"What are you doing here?" he shouted over the rain and the chanting.

"We heard you were having a spot of trouble," said Fabio, as though he were a roadside mechanic.

"We were just sitting down to breakfast when Silverpoint showed up," said Gila.

"We had to eat it in the van," said Umor.

"I lost half of mine out of the window when we went over a bump," said Gila.

"Anyway, we've brought The Null," said Fabio.

"And Lady Partridge," said Umor.

"You owe me two rashers," said Gila.

Fuat gave Fabio's wrist a flick with her switch. "You have brought light with you, *lah-far*," she said sharply, her head turned away from the feeble head-lights.

"Sorry!" said Fabio. "Gila, turn off the lights."

Gila ran back to switch off the van lights, and Fabio smiled broadly at the assembled Fir Bolg, who had stopped chanting for a moment but were not looking any happier.

"Nobody going to say *Fawlche*, then?"

"What welcome do you expect?" asked the brass-bead man, "when you arrive without invitation, and the strangers who fell on our heads are your friends?"

"Pure coincidence," said Fabio.

"We know everyone," said Umor.

Gila opened his mouth to speak, but to Miles's delight Fuat reached out, quick as blinking, and tweaked his nose hard. "*Ommadawn!*" she said.

Fabio sidled up to Miles and Little, eyeing Varip-puli cautiously. "Do you have the you-know-what with you?"

Miles nodded.

"You haven't told them," whispered Fabio, "how you came to have it in the first place?"

"No," said Miles.

"I hope you know what you're doing," said Fabio.

"Not really," said Miles. "But I know what needs

to be done, and I suppose that's a start." He realized that he was out of time. The Null was here, the Fir Bolg were waiting, and there was no sign of Nura after all. He would have to interpret the key by himself. He began to run it over in his mind:

What time has stolen, let it be.

That part didn't sound too hopeful. It must refer to his mother, he told himself.

A flash of lightning spread across the sky, closer now and brighter. The Fir Bolg clashed their spears and howled as one, covering their eyes with their hairy arms. They were answered by a cackling laugh from the circus van, and Miles looked apprehensively at Varippuli. The tiger, however, seemed to have no energy left to react. Behind him Miles could see the hunched figure of Baltinglass, rummaging through the wreckage of the flying machine as though searching for something. He wondered vaguely what it might be.

Power grows from two to three, thought Miles.

This was the most puzzling bit. What could it mean? Was it his power, or that of the Tiger's Egg? If it was both, then who were the "three" to whom the power would grow? The Null, Barty Fumble, Varippuli? Did The Null and his father, or for that matter his father and the tiger, count as one or two? The whole thing seemed frustratingly obscure.

"What do you want us to do, Master Miles?" said Umor.

"The boy is here to fulfill his mother's promise," said Fuat, daughter of Anust.

"What promise?" said Gila, glancing nervously at Miles.

"His mother swore to lift from us the burden of living underground," said Brass Beads.

Embrace the fear and set soul free, thought Miles.

That was simple enough. He remembered the crushing embrace in which The Null had held him at the Palace of Laughter. It was true that it would have killed him if Little hadn't come to his rescue, but as he had learned more about The Null's bleak history he understood that embrace as the desperate echo of a father's love for his lost son. This time he would return it, and hope that the Tiger's Egg could work its magic quickly.

Varippuli was getting agitated now, and he answered the thunder with a rumbling growl that made the nearest Fir Bolg gnash their teeth. Little rested her hand on the tiger's shoulder and whispered softly in his ear.

Miles racked his brain for the last two lines.

To drink the sun in place of me.

That was it. He didn't want to think too hard about this one, and it was almost a relief when his thoughts were interrupted by a shout of triumph from Baltinglass of Araby.

"Found it!" yelled the old man. He stood up clutching in his hand a domed copper hat with a tall spike rising from its center. "You there, Master Miles?" he shouted over the rain.

"I'm here," said Miles distractedly. All his concentration was on the key. Another flash of lightning split the sky, and the Fir Bolg roared and clashed their spears for a second time. "A second time," thought Miles. Who knew what a third strike would do to the already enraged Fir Bolg? *Power grows from two to three.* The answer to the puzzle came to him in a sudden flash that seemed every bit as bright as the lightning itself. Baltinglass was weaving toward him, clutching the strange copper hat in which he had been struck twice by lightning. He had told them in the airship that the energy from those two lightning strikes still popped and fizzed in his body. Maybe the energy needed to unlock the Tiger's Egg could come only from someone who was struck a third time. . . .

"The Tiger's Egg," Baltinglass shouted in his general direction. "You have to give it to me."

"Why?" said Miles. "How do you know?"

"The key," panted Baltinglass. "It's just a riddle. Every sailor knows how to unpick a riddle. There's not much else to do on a long voyage. You need someone who's been struck by lightning twice, Master Miles, and folks like that aren't two a penny."

"But it says, 'from two to *three*,'" said Miles.

"That's right, boy; I need a third strike to do the job. Maybe with that I'll use up the whole charge in one go and finally get some peace. It's worth a try." Baltinglass reached out his hand, palm upward, and with the other hand he placed the unicrown firmly on his head.

Miles took Tangerine from his pocket and handed him numbly to the blind explorer. He hoped that Tangerine could feel no pain, but there was no time now to try to extract the Egg. "Are you sure?" he said.

"Sure as thirst, Master Miles. Let's get on with it."

Miles turned to Fabio. "Can you get Silverpoint and Lady Partridge, and bring The Null too?" he said. "I don't think it will give you any trouble."

"What makes you so sure?" said Gila.

"We're bite-sized individuals, remember," said Umor.

"Do what the boy says," shouted Baltinglass, "or I'll bite you myself." He had found his way to one of the tall teeth of rock and was climbing it like a copper-hatted gecko, Tangerine tucked firmly into the waistband of his trousers.

Fabio disappeared in the direction of the circus truck, and Miles tried to prepare himself for the appearance of The Null. His head was spinning and he thought he might faint. The chaotic events of the night had left him no time to prepare for what he had to do, but Miles had inherited from his father an unshakable determination, and from his mother a mind that worked best on the fly. A plan was rapidly forming in that mind, a plan in which even fainting might have a part to play.

A howling cackle rang out through the storm, and Miles stared into the night until his eyes stung. The rain pelted down and the thunder rumbled, and suddenly there was the terrible shape of The Null shambling between the stone teeth, darker than the darkness itself, while the Fir Bolg scrambled over one another to let the monster through.

"I think," said Varippuli wearily, "that this is no place for a tiger."

"Too noisy," agreed Umor.

"Not sufficiently jungly," added Gila.

Umor turned to Varippuli and looked him up and down with a professional eye. Miles could tell he was concerned at the tiger's dejected condition. He placed his hand on Varippuli's neck, and to Miles's surprise the tiger made no objection.

"The wagon we brought has a bed of dry straw in the back," said Umor to the tiger.

"You could get some rest," said Gila.

"We can leave the door open," said Umor, who knew Varippuli would not willingly be caged.

The tiger turned to Miles. "That sounds like just what I need. A long journey calls for a sound rest." He looked Miles in the eye and smiled, but though his smile was full of warmth it made Miles feel sadder than he could ever have imagined. "Just remember, Miles," said the tiger, "keep your eyes clear and your claws sharp."

Miles could think of nothing to say in reply. Even if the words had come he could not have said them for the painful lump in his throat. He nodded at the tiger, and managed a watery smile.

"I'll go with him," said Little to Miles, "just to check that he's comfortable." The tiger and the Song Angel turned toward the van, giving the approaching Null a wide berth. Miles felt a hollowness that threatened to overwhelm him. As he watched the tiger retreating and The Null getting closer, that emptiness grew to be an unbearable ache, and for the first time he wondered if he was really doing the right thing.

CHAPTER THIRTY-SIX
A NEON SCARECROW

Miles Wednesday, bright-handed and crash-landed, stood in the bleak jumble of Hell's Teeth waiting for The Null, that terrifying hairy emptiness into which he hoped to pour the lost soul of his father. The creature's red-rimmed eyes spotted him and its mouth opened in a soundless howl. It broke into a lumbering trot and met him with such force that it knocked him clean off his feet. Its massive arms enveloped him and began to squeeze, and Miles reached around The Null's barrel chest and squeezed back for all he was worth. The air whooshed out of him in the monster's deadly embrace and the pain of his already bruised ribs made him dizzy. "I'm here," he said. "It's me. It's Miles."

Over The Null's shoulder he could see Baltinglass straighten himself up on top of the slippery rock, the unicrown clamped onto his head like a second skin. "Where's that electric vandal?" the old man roared through the storm. "Silverpoint!"

"I'm here," said Silverpoint. He emerged from the darkness and stood at the base of the rock, for once looking a bit lost.

"Light me up, Spark Boy," roared Baltinglass, holding Tangerine in his clenched fist. "Let's see what I'm made of!"

Silverpoint hesitated for a moment, then raised his face to the rumbling sky. The Fir Bolg chanted louder, and Miles felt himself sliding into a faint. He was ready to slip sideways into the Realm as soon as he lost consciousness, and almost before he knew it he was standing beside himself, looking at his own limp body clamped in The Null's hairy embrace. There was no time to lose. He had to guide his father's soul from the unlocked Tiger's Egg to the empty Null just as soon as Silverpoint called down the lightning. He wondered what was taking the Storm Angel so long, and he suddenly remembered that he had not yet fulfilled the promise to the Fir Bolg. He turned to speak to Silverpoint, but what he saw made his heart plummet, and drove all thoughts of the Fir Bolg from his mind.

Silverpoint was no longer standing with his face raised to the sky. He lay in a crumpled heap at the feet of a dark figure, whose smoky edges made him immediately recognizable. It was Bluehart, standing over the lifeless Storm Angel like an unwanted guest come to spoil the party. The Sleep Angel moved in a sudden blur and appeared right in front of Miles, who stood outside his own body in the dark and the rain, feeling like something peeled for the pot.

A cold rage shimmered around Bluehart, which was visible to Miles as a faint bluish light. "You've thwarted me for the last time," hissed the angel.

"I'm about to empty the Tiger's Egg," said Miles desperately. "That's what you want, isn't it?"

Bluehart laughed. "The last thing I want is to damage the Egg. It's not yet ready."

The chanting of the Fir Bolg seemed to be tuning in and out like an old radio, and Miles could see Baltinglass swaying slightly on top of his rock, his mouth open wide. It was as though time had hit a sticky patch, and only his conversation with Bluehart was entirely real.

"Ready?" he said, desperately trying to think of a way to distract Bluehart. "What do you mean?"

The Sleep Angel waved dismissively. "It's customary to get a swift rerun of your life in the seconds before your death, sort of like a goody bag at the end of a party," he said. He glanced across at Miles's inert body, counting down his last breaths, and sighed. "Stubborn little fellow, aren't you? Frankly I can't be bothered with the rerun, so I'll answer your question instead. This Tiger's Egg was created on my orders many centuries ago, and I left it with the Fir Bolg to mature. There are six other Eggs, one on each continent, all in the charge of hidden peoples. At least they were until these witless wonders lent one to a fortune-teller and started all this trouble. You have eight breaths left, by the way. Make that seven. Can't that . . . *thing* squeeze any harder?"

"Why did you have them made?" asked Miles. He was looking around for something he remembered from the jumbled visions that had come to him on the *Runaway Cloud*. He had seen his own death, but that was not supposed to be possible, and in any case something didn't match. In the vision he had seen Stillbone reaching out from behind him to touch his shoulder, but behind him now there was only a tall column of rock.

"I created them to gain power," said Bluehart. "Why else?"

"You already have power," said Miles, stalling for time. He thought he could see Stillbone now, smoking toward them through the rain. Something was falling into place at the back of his mind, but he could not quite see it yet. Something to do with what Baltinglass had taught him, about putting himself in his opponent's shoes.

"Angels are made of pure thought," said Bluehart. "We control the elements, but we exist only because enough people believe we do. Whoever controls what people think down here ultimately controls the Realm. It's a sort of chicken-and-egg thing, and I've never been happy about owing my existence to something as fickle as the human imagination. Once these Eggs have matured I will be able to use them to control the beliefs of millions of people, and that," he said with a humorless smile, "will make me the poultry farmer."

Miles gave a deliberate yawn. "I think I would have preferred the goody bag," he said. His comment had the desired effect—the Sleep Angel glowed blue with renewed anger. Miles could see Stillbone coming up fast behind Bluehart, and suddenly he knew exactly what to do.

"Power is no good without courage," he said, allowing his features to become just a little smoky, like those of the Sleep Angel he faced.

"You have two breaths left," said Bluehart. "You think I lack courage?"

"Of course," said Miles. "You take people's souls, but you don't know how that feels yourself. I bet if you took on the form of your victim properly you wouldn't be able to do it. It would be like staring your own death in the face."

"Watch me," said Bluehart coldly. He solidified rapidly into the shape of Miles, becoming a perfect replica of the unconscious boy hidden in The Null's embrace. Stillbone arrived behind him at that moment, and in an instant Miles transformed himself into the smoky image of Bluehart. The image of Miles stared at him in puzzlement. "What . . . ?" he began, but Miles glanced past his shoulder at Stillbone.

"He's all yours," said Miles, copying Bluehart's dismissive wave. "I'm knocking off for the night."

He looked away as the Sleep Angel reached out to touch Bluehart's shoulder. He didn't need to see that again. There was a sudden rushing sensation, like the wind at the end of the world, bringing with it a horrible sucking sound that seemed to pull at his very core. When he looked again Bluehart had vanished completely, and he knew that he would never be bothered by the Sleep Angel again. Stillbone was looking at his own hand in surprise. "Funny," he said, "they don't usually do that."

"That one was rotten," said Miles, keeping the likeness of the vanished Bluehart with difficulty. "You can go now," he said. Stillbone nodded distractedly, and, still staring at his fingers, he turned slowly to smoke and drifted away on the breeze.

All at once it seemed as if time were freed from its jam. Silverpoint got shakily to his feet, and there was a shout from the top of the pillar. "What's the holdup? Get the finger out, Sparky!" Silverpoint looked up at Baltinglass, and his serious expression gave way to a flash of annoyance. He nodded sharply in the old man's direction, and the sky was instantly split by a twisted rope of lightning. The Fir Bolg flung themselves, howling, on their faces as the lightning found the tall spike in the unicrown's center. Baltinglass's entire body lit up with a crackling blue-white glow, and he flung his arms out like a neon scarecrow. His grizzled fist clasped the small bear, and he let out an incoherent roar. Miles thought he heard an answering roar from somewhere in the darkness, drowned out an instant later by the loudest blast of thunder he had ever heard.

The crackling energy from the lightning snaked

down the old man's outstretched arm and his fist glowed with a dazzling light that even Miles could not face.

Miles turned away and found himself buried in coarse hair, his ribs on fire. He had not meant to look away for fear of missing Barty Fumble's soul as the Tiger's Egg was unlocked, but somehow he was back in his own body and he was being held too tight to turn around. There was nothing he could do but say, "I'm here, it's me. It's Miles," over and over again into the darkness.

The howling seemed to recede, and the downpour eased. The hairy arms that held him relaxed a little, and he found he could breathe once more. He heard a voice that was at once familiar and strange. "Miles," said the voice thickly. "Now, why does that ring a bell?"

Fuat, daughter of Anust, daughter of Etar, tugged sharply on Miles's sleeve and said in her crowlike voice, "That was a fine cure you devised for us, Miles, son of Celeste, and it will be remembered well in stories."

Miles looked at the little tattooed woman in surprise. He sat on a fallen stone beside the hairy hulk of his father, nursing his aching ribs. The chanting had stopped and the Fir Bolg seemed to have melted away before he had even had time to think of how he might have fulfilled his mother's promise to them. "It was?" he said.

"*Cyart go lore,*" said Fuat. "Your mother promised to lift from us the burden of living underground, but I did not understand until now the true meaning of her promise."

"You didn't?" said Miles. He was still completely at sea.

"It took your sharp wit to whittle the truth from it," said Fuat, "and you made it so plain that even we simple folk could understand. You have cured us of the foolish notion that we might live happily on the skin of the earth."

"So you've changed your minds," said Miles.

"You changed them for us," said Fuat. "It's true that our lives can seem as gristly as an old rabbit's ear, but the life of aboveground folk is strong meat indeed. Giant bat-trees falling from the sky, blind men drinking fire from the clouds and boys death-wrestling with monsters are not the easy life that we had pictured in the long nights underground. Our ancestors wisely chose the bosom of the earth as a refuge, and that wisdom has returned to us with alacrity. We will stay where we are truly happy, and look on our home with more fondness from now on. It seems you have undone the power of the *Uv Reevoch*, but we have no further need of it, and we deem your mother's debt satisfied nonetheless. *Ah mor-ort!* Good luck be with you, Miles, son of Celeste."

"Miles!" boomed the voice of Lady Partridge, and as the monumental lady swept toward him Fuat was gone, leaving only a rustle in the long grass.

"Hello, Lady Partridge," said Miles, grinning weakly.

"Thank goodness you're all right!" said Lady Partridge. "The whole world seems to have gone mad."

"You're not the first person to say that," said Miles. "Is Baltinglass okay?"

"As well as can be expected for a foolish old man," said Lady Partridge. "He's being looked after by a foreign lady. She says she doesn't have the bright hands, whatever that means, and that you will be needed as soon as you can be spared."

"Nura?" said Miles. "But if she's here, then so is Cortado."

"You don't need to worry about him," said Fabio, appearing out of the darkness.

"He's had a meeting with the tiger," said Gila.

"And it didn't go his way," said Umor.

"Varippuli!" said Miles, struggling to his feet.

"Varippuli?" echoed a voice behind him.

Lady Partridge looked at the hairy figure of Barty Fumble in astonishment. "Well, blow me down!" she said. "It spoke!"

"He's not The Null anymore," said Miles. "This is my father, Barty Fumble."

"I'm delighted to meet you, Mr. Fumble," said Lady Partridge, her politeness getting the better of her astonishment, "though I'm sure I have no idea what's going on."

"That makes two of us," said Barty. He scratched himself vigorously. "I seem to have been asleep for a long time, and now I wake up as a carpet."

"It's very complicated," said Miles.

"There'll be plenty of time to explain later, I'm sure," said Lady Partridge. She helped Miles steady himself, and they followed the Bolsillo brothers slowly toward the circus wagon. A lamp had been hung over the back door, and Little stood there alone in a pool of light. She smiled sadly at Miles, her face wet with tears.

Miles took a deep breath and looked into the back of the wagon. He knew what he would see, but no amount of forewarning could soften the blow. The tiger lay stretched out on the clean straw, his eyes closed and his striped flanks still. He looked old and at peace, a magnificent beast who had lived his span of years and more, but the terrible stillness that filled him was hard to grasp. Miles fought back the tears, a lump expanding in his throat, and he stared hard at the tiger's body as though he could will him back to life. He could not believe that he would never again see the welcome sight of shifting stripes in the grass, or feel the fire from those amber eyes filling him with confidence and strength.

He felt Little's hand slip into his, but he kept his gaze on Varippuli until the tears flooded his eyes and he could no longer see clearly. He was about to turn away when he noticed something strange. Sticking out from underneath the tiger was a knee-length boot. The boot was as still as the tiger himself, and it belonged unmistakably to the once Great Cortado. It was clear the ringmaster too was dead, a hungry soul who had reached the end of a crooked path. Miles understood now the echoing roar he had heard from the darkness. It was Varippuli's last stand, and the end of the villain who had tried so many times to kill him, and who had finally perished trying to steal the tiger's very soul.

He felt a hand on his shoulder. "The tiger was a friend of mine too, a long time ago," said Barty

Fumble, "but all things must come to an end."

Miles swallowed with difficulty. "I didn't know him for long enough," he said.

"Maybe not," said his father, "but a friendship should be judged by its depth, not by its length."

Miles looked up at Barty's face. There was something in his sad, quizzical smile—and perhaps the faintest echo of a roar in his voice—that made Miles wonder if the tiger had truly left them after all.

CHAPTER THIRTY-SEVEN

A POSSIBLE FUTURE

Barty Fumble, Egg-restored and bushy-bearded, sat against the outside wall of the gazebo that had once held The Null, drinking in the winter sunlight and scratching himself from time to time. Miles and Little sat on either side of him in comfortable silence, she with her new silvered wings tucked discreetly away, he with his floppy orange bear sleeping soundly in the inside pocket of his old overcoat.

"Tell me again," said Barty Fumble in his deep, rumbling voice, "about the Palace of Laughter."

Miles began the story of how he had first met Little at the Circus Oscuro, and how they had traveled to the Palace of Laughter in search of Silverpoint and Tangerine. It was not the first time Miles had told this tale, but his father's memory was slow to return and he seemed to enjoy hearing it over again, especially the parts about the tiger.

"I remember all those conversations, you know," he said. "In all the time I was lost in the blackness my tiger dreams were what I lived for." He chuckled deeply. "Remember that nasty little boy you brought to lunch in the olive grove? The one who tricked you into picking apples?"

Miles laughed. In the days since he had restored his father to himself he had come to realize why Barty's voice had seemed so familiar to him. The tiger he had befriended had been half Barty Fumble, a tiger and a man rolled into one, though mercifully unaware of his own strange nature. When Miles thought back over his adventures with Varippuli he could not separate the two in his mind, and he had ceased to try. There had been enough of Barty Fumble in the tiger for him to get to know his missing father, and there was enough of the tiger still in his father to ease the pain of losing Varippuli. All in all, he felt, it could have turned out worse.

"So this is where you're hiding out," said Nura, sweeping around the corner of the gazebo in her midnight robes.

"I thought you had the far eyes," said Miles with a smile.

Nura looked at him sternly. "You of all people should know how draining it is to use such a gift," she said. "Do you think I'd waste my energy searching my mind for three lazy goats such as you?"

"Celeste always seemed to know exactly what you were doing, even when you were thousands of miles apart," said Barty.

"That was easy," said Nura, sitting down beside Miles. "We were twins, and all twins have the far eyes for each other."

"You never told us exactly what happened to the Great Cortado," said Miles.

Nura shrugged. "Cortado wanted to be joined with the tiger," she said. "He got his wish, but not in the way he imagined."

"How did you make him enter the cage?" asked Miles.

"I didn't," said Nura. "I would not want that on my conscience. I brought him and Tau-Tau to Hell's Teeth because there was no other way I could get there to help you. I left them sitting in the van, parked about half a mile away, and told them to await my return. As it turned out I was too late to help you, but Cortado's suspicion had gotten the better of him, as I suspected it might, and he and Tau-Tau had been following at my heels. While I was occupied with Baltinglass of Araby they found the tiger resting in the back of the van, and the Great Cortado saw his opportunity."

"But why did he get in with the tiger?" asked Little. "He was terrified of Varippuli."

"Doctor Tau-Tau interpreted the key for him," said Nura. "He told him that he must enter the tiger's cage."

"That explains a lot," said Miles. "He can always be relied on to get things wrong."

"He didn't get it wrong," said Nura. "The key turns differently for everyone who uses it. That is what a well-made key does, and this one was exceptionally good."

"You mean it has more than one meaning?" said Miles.

"Of course," said Nura. "The key makes happen what is meant to happen. You embraced your father and returned him to himself. Baltinglass found the power to unlock the Tiger's Egg in his third lightning strike. All this was in the key, and more."

"Then what was Tau-Tau's interpretation?" asked Little.

"He told Cortado to embrace the tiger he feared,

while Tau-Tau uttered an incantation over the fake Egg. He knew that the Great Cortado and the tiger had clashed twice already, and the key told him that the third time would be decisive."

"Decisive for who?" said Miles. "Varippuli or Cortado?"

Nura looked at him with a glint in her dark eyes. "Whom do *you* think he had his money on?" she said.

Miles leaned back against the gazebo wall. He could feel Tangerine stirring awake in his pocket, and the thought of the small bear brought a broad smile to his face. His aunt returned his smile. "You are thinking of the bear?" she said.

Miles nodded. "I'm just glad the life has come back to him, though I still don't understand how it happened."

"The world is not here to be understood," said Nura. "A small bear who had been home to two souls, and who had been sung to life once before, was struck by lightning. There are no recipes for such strange ingredients. It has probably never happened before, and will almost certainly never happen again. Some people attract odd happenings like a magnet attracts nails, and you are such a person, Miles. Just be grateful that he wasn't burned to a crisp."

"I am!" said Miles with feeling, and he reached inside his pocket to give Tangerine a squeeze.

His father scratched at the last remains of the shaggy pelt that had fallen out in tufts as he returned to his former self. He seemed to have lost the drift of the conversation. "What happened to the blind gent?" he said after a while.

"Baltinglass is still a bit shaky, but he's better than he was. Constable Flap has taken him back to Cnoc to help sell his house," said Miles. "He's agreed to come and live at Partridge Manor, as long as he can plant an orchard here."

"And the fellow who made that fabulous flying machine—what was his name?"

"Tenniel," said Miles. "I heard he's set up an aviation company with Captain Tripoli. I don't think either of them is truly happy unless he's flying."

"Speaking of which, I have to go," said Little. "There's chaos to be spun, and I can't sit around here all day." She jumped up from her seat and looked around to make sure there were no strangers watching before she unfurled her wings. They were brand-new ones, silvered with liquid chrome yet still as fine as the ones she had lost, and she was immensely proud of them. As far as anyone knew she was the only Song Angel ever to have been invited to join the Rascals, and those few angels who had protested had been argued down by the entire Council. It was well-known that she had traveled to the hard world and befriended the boy who had brought Bluehart's treachery to light. Stories of her heroic exploits spread in the Realm much as the adventures of Miles himself did in the town of Larde, and to most of the Realm's citizens she could do no wrong. She and Miles had been officially pardoned by the Council, and Little had even managed—in the face of some resistance—to have that pardon extended to everyone who had encountered the tainted Egg.

"Do you have to go right away?" said Miles.

"They're calling me," said Little, "but I'll be back. I can come back whenever I want."

"Are the Sleep Angels okay with that?" said Miles.

Little nodded. "It's not like when I was a Song Angel," she said. "The Sleep Angels don't have much control over the Chaos Angels. And besides, since we exposed Bluehart's plan I'm back in their good books."

"As much as anyone can be," said Miles with a shiver.

"Exactly. Some of them are still suspicious of me, but it's never been known for a Sleep Angel to go to the bad, and I think it shook them up a bit. I still keep out of their way as much as possible, but I always did that."

Miles nodded. "I'll see you soon, then." He gave her a hug, wondering if she would always come back often to see him, or if her absences would grow longer and her visits fewer. Only time would tell, and he made himself smile as she launched herself effortlessly up into the sky and out of sight.

"Soon it will be time for me to leave too," said Nura. "Your grandmother will be wondering how we fared. You must come to visit us again, now that you know the way."

"I'd like that," said Miles. "Maybe when my father is fully recovered we could both come." He felt the desert might have gotten into his veins too, as it had with Baltinglass of Araby. He had only to close his eyes to feel the rolling gait of the camel, and to see in his mind's eye the welcoming oases and the ancient towns that seemed carved out of the desert itself. A picture of Temzi came into his mind, and he remembered with a smile that he had some camels to discuss with her.

"Of course," said Nura. "You would both be welcome. Now I must go and prepare for my return journey." She kissed Miles on the cheek and walked back toward the manor, humming quietly as she went.

If you've ever felt that everything has worked out remarkably well against all the odds, you will have some idea of the satisfied feeling that came over Miles as he sat by his father in the last of the evening sun. The Great Cortado's own hubris had finally caught up with him and finished his schemes for good. Doctor Tau-Tau was serving time in prison, pleased to be free of Cortado's bitter clutches and touchingly relieved to find that Miles, Little and Baltinglass had not been cruelly murdered after all. He was not allowed any luxuries in his cell, but he kept the bogus Tiger's Egg carefully hidden, still believing that it held powers he might someday learn to use in a daring escape.

Silverpoint had returned to storm duties. He was viewed with some suspicion by others of his caste, but with great respect by the Chaos Angels for blasting an old man in a copper hat, which was just the sort of thing they found entertaining. After his experiences with Miles and Little, Silverpoint secretly preferred the admiration of the Rascals to the confidence of his peers, and though his aim with lightning had always been exceptional he had taken to sending the odd bolt astray, just to liven things up a little.

The Bolsillo brothers were wintering still in

Partridge Manor's extensive stables, preparing their incomparable show for another season. Miles and Barty visited them often to reminisce about their respective days on the road, and there were many evenings around the campfire that were long on music and laughter and the occasional show of impromptu acrobatics. Barty vowed that he would return to the circus life once he was back to normal, though Gila commented that they would have much more use for him while he still looked like a molting yeti.

So here they are at last, barrel-chested Barty Fumble and his courageous son, Miles, sitting quietly together in the last of the evening sun. "What was the worst thing of all?" Miles asks of his father, as he watches Tangerine push through the weeds like a miniature jungle explorer.

Barty Fumble chuckles. "The worst thing?" he says. "Probably shedding all this hair. You have no *idea* how itchy it's been! Sometimes I thought I'd go out of my mind."

He looks at Miles out of the corner of his eye and bursts into a great, booming laugh that makes the gazebo windows rattle. "I thought I'd go out of my mind!" he says.

They talk on in the gathering twilight, Barty telling

stories of Celeste that make her come more alive than any photograph could, and Miles slowly filling in the things that Barty Fumble has missed. He tells his father how he outwitted the Stinkers at Pigball, about his heart-stopping flights in the Realm, and how the key to the Tiger's Egg was revealed to him in a flash of lightning, and Barty listens to his son's adventures with pride and delight. They speak too of the future that stretches out before them, and as the last sliver of sun winks out on the horizon they are talking there still, making plans for a life that once seemed impossible, where their adventures will be shared and their stories linked like the twin trunks of the great beech tree in Lady Partridge's garden.

The Julie Andrews Collection
encompasses quality books for young readers of
all ages that nurture the imagination and celebrate
a sense of wonder.

For more information about
the Julie Andrews Collection, visit
www.julieandrewscollection.com.

Words. Wisdom. Wonder.

Did you like this book? Julie Andrews would love to read your review of THE LIGHTNING KEY, or any of the books in the Julie Andrews Collection. Write to her at:

JULIE ANDREWS
THE JULIE ANDREWS COLLECTION
HARPERCOLLINS CHILDREN'S BOOKS
10 EAST 53RD STREET
NEW YORK, NY 10022
or
INFO@JULIEANDREWSCOLLECTION.COM

From time to time we will post reader reviews on the Julie Andrews Collection website. Please include permission to quote your review and include your name and location when you submit it.

Other books you might enjoy in the Julie Andrews Collection:

BLUE WOLF by Catherine Creedon

DRAGON: *Hound of Honor* by Julie Andrews Edwards and Emma Walton Hamilton

DUMPY AND THE FIREFIGHTERS by Julie Andrews
Edwards and Emma Walton Hamilton,
illustrated by Tony Walton

DUMPY'S APPLE SHOP by Julie Andrews Edwards and
Emma Walton Hamilton,
illustrated by Tony Walton

DUMPY'S EXTRA-BUSY DAY by Julie Andrews Edwards
and Emma Walton Hamilton,
illustrated by Tony Walton

DUMPY'S HAPPY HOLIDAY by Julie Andrews Edwards and
Emma Walton Hamilton,
illustrated by Tony Walton

DUMPY'S VALENTINE by Julie Andrews Edwards and
Emma Walton Hamilton,
illustrated by Tony Walton

DUMPY TO THE RESCUE! by Julie Andrews Edwards and
Emma Walton Hamilton,
illustrated by Tony Walton

GRATEFUL: *A Song of Giving Thanks* by John Bucchino,
illustrated by Anna-Liisa Hakkarainen

THE GREAT AMERICAN MOUSICAL by Julie Andrews
Edwards and Emma Walton Hamilton,
illustrated by Tony Walton

HOLLY CLAUS: THE CHRISTMAS PRINCESS
by Brittney Ryan, illustrated by Laurel Long
with Jeffrey K. Bedrick

THE LAST OF THE REALLY GREAT WHANGDOODLES
by Julie Andrews Edwards

THE LEGEND OF HOLLY CLAUS by Brittney Ryan

THE LITTLE GREY MEN by BB,
illustrated by Denys Watkins-Pitchford

LITTLE KISSES by Jolie Jones,
illustrated by Julie Downing

MANDY by Julie Andrews Edwards

THE PALACE OF LAUGHTER by Jon Berkeley

PEBBLE by Susan Milord

SIMEON'S GIFT by Julie Andrews Edwards and
Emma Walton Hamilton,
illustrated by Gennady Spirin

THANKS TO YOU by Julie Andrews Edwards and
Emma Walton Hamilton

THE TIGER'S EGG by Jon Berkeley

EXTRAS

THE WEDNESDAY TALES ~ NO. 3

THE LIGHTNING KEY

featuring:

Pages from
The Diary of Celeste Mahnoosh Elham

Pages from
The Diary of Celeste Mahnoosh Elham

Diary of Celeste Mahnoosh Elham

November 1920

Packed my belongings and left home in search of the Tiger's Egg. Mother says at 17 I am too young to leave, but here in dusty Kagu time stands still, while beyond the horizon the whole world awaits me. It was she who told us stories of the wondrous power of the Tiger's Egg, tales that set my soul on fire. Now she tells me it is just a myth, but she knows I can read the truth in her eyes.

Last night I dreamed again of the tiger, of the strange traveling show and of the small men who live like jerboas beneath the ground. I can make little sense of these dreams, but I have no doubt they are shadows of what is to come.

Mother refused to leave her bed and bid me farewell. Nura also tried to make me stay, but I know she wished she too had the courage to leave. She walked with me as far as Wa'il, then we said our good-byes. I will miss her so, yet my feet can hardly wait to start on the long road to the future.

4

August 1921

I have traveled far to the north, following the clues in the tales that live in my memory, and oh, such things I have seen as I never would have imagined. Using the skills of healing that Mother taught me, I have worked my way across the sea, and learned much of use.

It's said there were once five Tiger's Eggs, but one only is known to survive, and that is in the keeping of the Fir Bolg. I heard a description of these hairy little people from a sea captain whose grandfather had once had the misfortune to meet them. The captain might have been describing the little men of whom I have often dreamed! I drew them for him, and he was amazed.

The Fir Bolg are believed to live in a place called Hell's Teeth, yet the captain warned me to have nothing to do with them. His own grandfather had been cursed by them after a bargain went sour. His teeth at once fell out and ever after he smelled of strong cheese.

5

April 1922

After many months of searching and countless
cold nights waiting and watching among the eerie
standing stones of Hell's Teeth, I have finally met
the Fir Bolg.

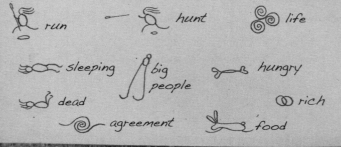

They are everything I had
been warned
about, and more.
They fight
continually,
they steal even
from their own
brothers and uncles.
(They would not dare steal from their aunts or
sisters, who are like hairy sand vipers). They smell
like damp washcloths and scream with fear at the
sight of a comb, yet they are quick-witted and
loyal in a fight, and when their bellies are full they
sing like a deep echo of the days before time began.
They write in simple pictures on their cave walls.
Here are some words I have learned:

run   hunt   life

sleeping   big people   hungry

dead   rich

agreement   food

October 1922

An AGREEMENT made this month of the first frost between the Shriveled Fella, son of Etar of the Fir Bolg, and Celeste, daughter of Asiya of the big people, sworn on heart and bone and binding on the blood and kin of both parties for twenty-one winters, or else good luck desert them and ill fortune take its seat.

CELESTE, daughter of Asiya, does agree to return to the skin of the earth and hunt down with all her wits and wiles the solution to the burden of the excellent people of the Fir Bolg, namely that they must pass their days in condition of damp and hunger in the guts of the earth in fear of the bright day and the breeze of noon where once their fathers' fathers walked without blindness nor bewilderment if there's any truth in their stories.

THE FIR BOLG do agree to lend to CELESTE for twenty-one winters the Tiger's Egg, which gives to its master a powerful blast of good luck, a long life and the loyalty of the tiger whose soul sleeps inside it, unless it's on falsehood we were nurtured. The Egg will be kept secret and especially hidden from people of a smoky appearance or excessive curiosity.

7

September 1930

The insufferable Mr. Dank has forgotten to feed the horses again. I found him trying to wrap one of my scarves into some kind of turban. He's a fool, but I feel sorry for him.

I do not have the time or energy to train him properly. The birth of our son approaches, yet when I should be happiest I dream of dark clouds, and I see a boy facing the world alone and forgotten.

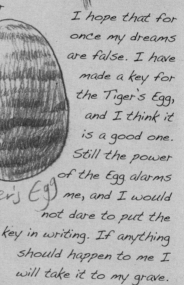

The Tiger's Egg

I hope that for once my dreams are false. I have made a key for the Tiger's Egg, and I think it is a good one. Still the power of the Egg alarms me, and I would not dare to put the key in writing. If anything should happen to me I will take it to my grave.

Varippuli has been restless of late and Barty is busier than ever. The performers mistrust Cortado and bring their troubles to Barty, and he can turn nobody away.

Varippuli

Celeste Mahnoosh Elham

What time has stolen
Let it be
Power grows
From two to three
Embrace the fear
And set soul free
To drink the sun
In place of me

EXTRAS

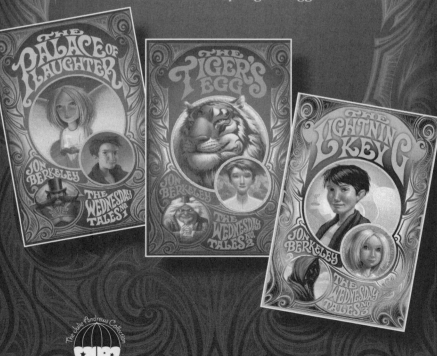